THE HUNTED:
SINS OF THE FATHER

THE HUNTED:
SINS OF THE FATHER

A Psychological Thriller

BY SARA ENNIS

Dedicated to:
Alicia Rideout, Brandee Jenkins, and always, Framily

CHAPTER ONE

Wednesday, September 9, 2009, Time Unknown

HARPER

"We should've just had the threesome with Oakley," I say to no one in particular.

It's dark in the cages now, but the overhead lights were on when the woman called Vero dragged Emily back to the cage by her ankles, kicking and shoving until she got Emily inside. Emily didn't move. For a minute I thought Emily might be dead. Then I heard a soft whimper. Only a Nine, then. A Nine is terrible, but it isn't a Ten.

I have started rating the 'sessions' as I think of them. A One is being left alone. A Two is when the woman named Vero delivers our nightly meal of wet dog food. A Three is having your clothes taken and a dog's shock collar fitted around your neck. Five is your basic old-fashioned man-on-woman rape. The scary thing is, that would have been a Ten in my previous life. I had no idea there were so many things that could be added to make it worse. A Seven, that's when the S&M contraptions come out. A Nine involves tools— dental tools, construction tools, surgical tools. And Ten, well, we haven't got to Ten yet, and I pray we don't.

Because at Ten, you're dead.

Personally, I think the Oakley comment is a little bit funny. Emily would, too, if she could think.

"How long do you think we've been here? A week? Two? More?" I ask. "I wonder if Oakley went looking for us. I wonder if he called the cops. Oh, shit. That really wouldn't do any good, would it." I laugh at the irony.

Emily doesn't answer. She hasn't answered in a while, now that I think of it.

"But if he did call the cops, they would've called our families. They'd be worried. Well, your dad would. Your dad would demand an investigation, right? Report us missing to police in Nashville? Right? But maybe he didn't tell my mom or your dad because then they'd know what a freaking ass he is. Oakley's not so big of an ass that he wouldn't call them, though, right? He's not, right?"

Still, Em doesn't respond. I don't care. Talking makes me feel better, even if I'm talking to myself. It's distracting, and I need distracting. Because if I think about reality, I will surely die. "If we'd stayed with Oakley, and we were in LA now, we'd be moving into our fabulous new apartment. Sure, it would be a tiny studio in some questionable part of town, on a bus line so we can get to interviews and auditions. There'd be a great bar—a great gay bar because gay guys are the best friends a girl can have in a new town—right around the corner. We'd be hanging out there, making plans, making friends, maybe making some connections. Doing stuff. Starting our lives. On our way."

The man's voice, low and slow, drifts in from somewhere, interrupting my conversation with myself. I'm a writer, so I collect characters. Until just recently, I've always favored villains. Jonny— that's what Vero calls him—is an excellent villain. He's handsome as hell, with pretty boy features and thick dark hair, and a great body... if middle-aged rapists are your type. I hear him say, "Getting tired of the dark-haired one. No more fight in her. 'Bout time to turn her loose."

My pulse quickens. Did he say, "Turn her loose?" Is he going to let us go?

Ha. You're a fool, Harpy! No way can he turn us loose. They can't leave us alive, not after everything they've done to us. For Harper White and Emily Bright, best friends with rhyming names and big dreams, this is the end of the road.

I feel wetness on my face and jerk. I remember now. Emily is gone. He "turned her loose" hours ago. I'm pretty sure I know exactly what that means.

CHAPTER TWO

ANGEL

I will never get used to the sound of air brakes, especially in the moment of panic that shoves me out of sleep into waking. I hate the way my hands clench, resent the feeling of clawing for clarity, even though I know I'm safe, even though it has been a couple of years since I've had any reason to jerk awake in fear.

The body does not easily forget.

Or, as CB would say, "It does not go gently into that good night."

CB is kind of a Dylan Thomas freak, even though he died ten years before she was born. If they were living at the same time, she'd be his Yoko Ono. "Not that the pretty Welshman could handle a hot Afro-Latina like me, but a girl can dream!"

I'm confident any man in his right mind would sacrifice part of his body for a chance to 'handle' CB. Not only is she beautiful in a JLo-meets-Dolly Parton sort of way, but she's wicked smart, hysterically funny, and kind. CB—short for Chickee Boom, she claims—drives a semi back and forth across the southern US, and I ride with her. We're not related, but she's become my best friend, my sister, my teacher and some days, my mother. I'm not exaggerating when I say I don't think I'd be here if she hadn't picked me up two years ago. I was a fifteen-year-old hitchhiker who had convinced myself I was strong and everything was great, and I didn't need anyone or anything. Boy, was I delusional.

4

In the here and now, CB moves around the cab of the truck we call *Casita*, collecting things she'll need. "Sorry, kid. Was hoping you'd sleep through, but we need to fuel up."

I shove myself into a sitting position on the lower bunk and rub my eyes. Beyond the expansive windshield, the blackest night is dotted with neon and halogens. It is very late, or very early. I yawn, stretch the stiffness out, and carefully move the European history textbook I was reading before falling asleep. I stash it in a small nook next to the microwave. The cabin of the big rig is a mess. We need to clean during our next rest period. "What time is it?"

"Almost eleven. We'll be back on the road in twenty and in Albuquerque for breakfast."

"Gonna stretch my legs, hit the head, grab a lil snackie. Sweet or salty?" I shimmy down the driver's side of the cab, and navigate around CB, who has dropped down onto the tarmac, and is now performing a series of complex stretches she developed to "unkink things that shouldn't be kinky."

"Red Vines, *por favor*." CB grunts, her 5'2" body twisted into what I call Drunk Frog Pose. "Take your phone."

I smack the butt of my jeans to show I already have it and head toward the truck stop. This one, just west of Oklahoma City, is small compared to some. It's one of my favorites because you can access the restrooms directly from the outside. During the day, the place is crawling with kids, moms, and drivers—perfect conditions for claustrophobia, or worse, a panic attack. It's nice to be able to avoid some of that human congestion.

I am not a people person, in any sense of the word. I would be content to spend the rest of my life alone, with few exceptions. One of those exceptions is back at *Casita*, contorting herself into a pretzel.

The women's restroom is blessedly quiet. I slip into the farthest clean stall, sit, and yawn again.

"You've got a racehorse bladder hidden in that skinny body," CB teased when we first met. It took a while for me to tell her why I can hold my bladder for so long. I'd rather walk barefoot on molten lava than give anyone a reason to feel sorry for me. CB says some people are onions, with lots of layers; I'm a nectarine, shiny and sweet on the outside, with all the important stuff kept safe inside my pit. There isn't a nosy bone in CB's body. She never pressed for information back then. That's why she knows most everything there is to know about me now.

I stand and tug up my jeans. My pocketknife and the cash I shoved into my front pocket fall to the floor, and I swear. Gross. I squat to grab the blade and the money, telling myself not to think about the filthy floor.

And that's when I see two bare, bloody, human feet—at least I'm pretty sure they're human feet—on the floor of the accessible stall next door.

I hear a breathy, hoarse intake of air.

My heart begins to thump, faster and faster, under my T-shirt. Fear can be a liquid thing pumping through your veins, and it's racing through my body, bringing with it a tidal wave of memory, both physical and emotional.

I know that sound. I've made that sound. *I hate that sound.*

Fight or flight tells me to run. No one will know. I can walk out, pretend I never saw the feet, never heard the desperate breaths. No one who knows my story would blame me. Well, that's not true. Bud would blame me. Olivia would definitely blame me. I'd blame myself.

I can't ignore that sound.

I step out of my stall and stare at the closed door of the next stall. *Now or never. Run, or stay.* "Do you need help?"

CHAPTER THREE

Wednesday, September 9, 2009, Late Night

ANGEL

A middle-aged woman in old-school gray sweats comes into the restroom, her discount store sneakers squeaking against the grimy tile. I fake-smile and lean against the accessible stall door like I'm waiting for someone inside. The woman does her business and leaves without washing her hands. God, I hate bathrooms.

"She's gone," I say softly. "Just us."

No response.

I suck in a breath, release it slowly. "I don't know what's happened to you, but I know what it feels like to be scared. Not sure which way to turn, who to trust, what to do next." I swallow and hook my fingers together to keep my hands from fidgeting. "I know what it's like to be badly hurt."

There's no response. What if the feet belong to a dead person? Maybe I imagined that soft breath.

Then I hear the faintest sniffle and a slight wheeze. Whoever it is, she is alive. Is she hiding from an abusive boyfriend? Or maybe she's a lot lizard who picked the wrong truck?

I could try to get CB, except that'd freak the mystery person all the way out. I'll have to get help at some point, but not yet.

"I don't tell this to many people, but I want you to know you can trust me, and trust comes from being vulnerable." I roll my eyes as the words leave my mouth. That sounds like something Dr. Phil would say, and I really, really hate Dr. Phil. "A few years ago, my brother and I were taken by bad people. They hurt us. I got away. It took a while, but now things are okay." Mostly.

There is rustling on the other side of the door. A shuffling sound. The little silver circle turns, unlocking the stall. I press it open with two fingers and slip inside. I lock the door behind me.

The woman slides down the wall until she's crumbled on the floor. "He still has Harper. We have to help Harper."

CHAPTER FOUR

ANGEL

I don't know exactly what I was expecting. It's nearly impossible to tell how old she is from her face. I think she has dark hair—maybe?—but it's hard to tell because the long strands are coated in dried blood. Her face and neck are rusty red, too, but the white T-shirt she is wearing—not her own, because it hangs on her like a dress—has not a single spot on it. The blood had time to dry before she put the shirt on. The front of the shirt says **Oklahoma Wind-farms**. Was she attacked by a wind farmer? That's not very crunchy.

I slide onto the floor, near her but not too close. Jesus. The bottoms of her feet look like raw steaks, and the tops are covered in cuts and scrapes. Her long legs are bare of clothes but not bare of marks. Diagonal slices, all too familiar to me, cover the tanned skin above her knees. There are so many bruises—some new, some older, but all recent—her body is a bizarre quilt of brutal color. It looks like her cheekbone is broken, and a gaping red gash on her brow bone emphasizes the blue of her irises. Not only is her hair bloody, but it is singed. I know that smell well. My fight-or-flight thing is back, and I take deep breaths to stay calm. When she opens her mouth, I see a glint of jagged white. She's got at least one broken tooth.

"Jesus, I'm sorry—Jesus," I say. I look her in the eye, or try to, but she refuses to meet my gaze, staring instead at her hands. They clench and unclench on her thighs. "We need to call the cops—"

9

The woman gasps and tries to push her way up the wall, obviously in agony, but fear driving harder than pain. "No! No! NO!" She whispers with the force of a scream.

"Okay! No cops! I'm sorry! It's okay!" I jump up and help support her slight weight as she gets into a standing position. I navigate her to the toilet seat and help her sit on the gaping O.

"My name is Angel. I promise I'm not going to hurt you. I won't call the cops. I won't call anyone—except I would like to get my friend CB. She helped me when I was hurt. She's just outside, putting gas in our truck." My physical wounds have healed now, but CB has done more for my mind than any of the shrinks the FBI and my legal guardian, Peter Baden, arranged for me. "She'll know what to do. How to get you safe. I swear on my life, she won't let anything happen to you. I won't either. I promise. Can I text her? Please? You can't stay here. Someone will find you. And it's filthy. With all those wounds..."

The woman stares at me for a long time. Finally, she nods once and says, again, "I have to save Harper."

CHAPTER FIVE

Wednesday, September 9, 2009, Late Night

ANGEL

The woman says her name is Emily, Em to her friends. She's twenty-three years old. Getting her out of the bathroom and into *Casita* without drawing attention is quite the adventure. CB doesn't ask questions when I text, "Need you in the loo, STAT." CB doesn't ask questions when I turn the knob on the stall door and let her in. She simply takes off her beloved vintage bomber jacket and gently drapes it over the strange woman's shoulders. Then CB takes one arm, and I take the other, and between the two of us, we half-walk, half-carry Emily out to *Casita.*

CB clambers up into the bright pink cab and tosses down a pair of thick pink fuzzy socks for Emily. We need to protect her feet as much as we can, or she'll end up with a raging infection, and she's already got a lot of entry points for bacteria. I sit her down on *Casita's* step and gently brush dirt and gravel from her feet. I navigate one foot, then the other, into the socks, flinching when Emily flinches. This is too close, too familiar.

I have to power through.

CB hands down a folding step-stool to give Emily a little bit of a boost climbing up and in. CB offers a hand to Emily, and I gently lift her butt, which is bare under the shirt. Awkward. But she needs my guidance so she doesn't fall backward.

Once she's in, I collapse the ladder and hand it back up, then follow, locking *Casita's* door behind me. I draw the cab shades closed for privacy. We have no idea who did this. We don't want the evil doer to see us if he's out there, although if he is out there, he probably saw us cross the tarmac and climb into the truck. It's hard to be subtle when you're driving a bright pink semi.

CB trades the bomber jacket for another of her favorites, her fluffy pink robe with the hood and deep pockets. She tucks Emily into the lower bunk, still messy from my earlier nap. I get a bottle of water from the fridge and hand it to Emily. I start to wet a washcloth at the kitchenette sink so I can wipe away some of the dried blood, but CB stops me.

"Emily, honey, before we clean you up, it's important we take pictures, so when the bad guy is caught—" the woman's blue eyes are enormous, because of, or in spite of, the black and purple bruises around it, and she seems to shrink into herself—"I know, sweetie, I know. But I'd like to take some pictures with my phone, so we have evidence if you ever need or want it. Okay? Then we can clean you up and see to some of these wounds. Is that all right?"

CB's low, accented voice has the same effect on Emily it had on me back in the day. If CB says it, it is good.

Emily doesn't argue, so CB takes a photographic inventory of the damage. It feels like it takes forever, and I have to turn away a couple of times because the wounds are too similar and the marks too familiar. Now that we're safe in the cab, and the adrenalin has slowed to an average pace, memories are trying to break through the barriers I've built. Now is not the time. CB can't manage two emotional messes.

Finally, CB collects everything she wants and touches my arm to let me know it's okay to proceed with clearing away the blood. I sit beside Emily on the bunk and gently wipe at the crusted red film all over her face, neck, and upper chest. Some of what looks like blood is dried mud, the color of a clay pot. And some of what is buried under the dried mud is worse than I could have imagined.

CB drops into the passenger seat and turns it to face us. She waits until I have cleared most of Emily's beautiful face, then asks quietly, "Do you know the person who did this to you? Is it someone you know, or someone you recently met, or a stranger?"

Emily takes a deep breath and seems to find a way back to herself, whoever she was before tonight. "He's a cop. A sheriff, I guess. He has a freaking crazy girlfriend who might be scarier than he is. And he's still got my best friend, Harper. I have to save Harper before he kills her."

CHAPTER SIX

Wednesday, September 9, 2009, Late Night

ANGEL

"A LEO? A deputy of the law? As in, a police officer?" CB confirms, her voice neutral, but I know how CB feels about law enforcement officers—aka LEOs. If there is a dirty cop around, it won't surprise CB or break her heart. I've had a very different experience, with lots of law enforcement folks fighting for me. It's one of very few agree-to-disagree situations between us. For now, anyway. If what Emily is saying is true, there may be less disagreement going forward.

Emily says, "A sheriff, yeah. I don't know if that's the same as a policeman. I never had a reason to think about it before."

"Is he local? Did you know him before he did this to you?" CB asks.

"We're not from here. Harper and I were driving to LA from Nashville. With my boyfriend, Oakley the asshole." Emily sucks in a sharp, angry breath. "Oakley somehow got it into his head that we were going to thank him for driving us with a threesome. When we told him to screw off, he pitched a fit. He pulled into the rest stop, set our bags on the curb, and told us to learn how to be grateful when someone does you a favor." Her hands clench. "Asshole! It was no favor. We paid for the gas and the food and were going to pay for the motel rooms."

Emily lifts the bottle of water and takes a slow, careful sip. That shard of broken tooth has to be sensitive. She flinches as the plastic mouth of the bottle skims against her raw, swollen lip. Every time she jumps, I cringe a little too. "After he dumped us, we figured we'd hitch a ride with a truck driver to the next big town and then find the bus station. We sat at one of the picnic tables and waited. It was the late at night, so not a lot of traffic. Finally, after we'd been there like an hour, the sheriff pulled up."

I wonder if Emily knows her eyes are leaking. They're tears, but she's not crying, exactly. "At first, he ignored us. Went inside, peed or whatever, then came back out. Went to his car and sat there for a bit. Finally, he came over and asked if we were all right. We said sure, told him our plan. He was really friendly, very nice. Not bad looking, either. He said it wasn't safe for us to be there alone, and insisted on giving us a ride into town where we could spend the night and get a bus in the morning. I mean, it sounded reasonable. Officer-like. Who doesn't trust a cop?"

CB sucks her cheeks and keeps silent. I smile encouragingly to keep Emily from noticing. "Did you happen to notice the car? Did it say what town or county or even state he was from?"

Emily shakes her head no, and continues. "He was kind of hurrying us along. We got in the back of his car, he put our suitcases in the trunk, and he headed to—wherever. He asked more questions. Harper was still pissed and she told him why Oakley ditched us, which made me feel kind of crappy since he is—was—my boyfriend. But whatever. The deputy asked if we'd called our families. We said no. I mean, it was the middle of the night." Emily's eyes glisten with actual tears now. She feels guilty, like she did or said something that caused what happened to happen. I know exactly what her brain is telling her right now. My brain and I have had that conversation. Brains are bitchy beasts.

"It was about twenty minutes before we reached anything that looked like a town. Average small town, not much to look at, especially in the middle of the night. Except he kept going right through the town. I thought maybe it was a different town than the one he was talking about. Harper had fallen asleep, and I didn't want to wake her, which was dumb, I guess. But he seemed fine. He was chatty and friendly when he picked us up. Once he got past the little town, though, he went quiet. No more talking. At all."

Emily takes another deep breath, replenishing herself. "I don't know when I realized we weren't going to this supposed town. We drove for a long time. Two hours? Three? Maybe more. And the bastard wouldn't say a goddamn thing. Finally, Harper woke up, and when he wouldn't answer us, she started hitting the panel between the front and the back seats. Didn't bother him at all. He just kept driving. Highway for a while, but then dark, country roads at the end. Then finally... "

Her voice hitches, but she gets control and continues, "Finally, he pulled up in front of these giant metal gates like they have at airports or prisons or wherever. There was a sign above it, one of those ranch signs, but I couldn't read it in the dark. He got out and unlocked the gate, drove through, and then locked it again. By now, we were freaking the hell out. Yelling. Hitting the panel. Threatening to report him. Anything we could think of."

"Did you have cell phones?" CB asks gently.

Emily shakes her head. "They were in our backpacks." She pauses again. "And anyway, who would we call? The cops?"

She clutches the robe tighter around herself, and her voice drops to a whisper. "He pulled up in front of this house. In the headlights, it looked kind of cute. Normal. One story, a small cottage with flowers in pots on the porch, curtains in the windows. A woman came out. Very pretty." Emily looks at CB. "Like you, actually. Small, but exotic-looking. She looked like she'd been asleep. When she came out, we thought we were safe; he just didn't communicate well. She'd tell us he'd brought us home to stay at his place for the night. It was going to be all right."

I know it isn't going to be all right. Not even a little. I would have known that without Emily's face and body telling her story.

"He unlocked Harper's side of the car and pulled her out by the hair. He grabbed her hair—she has long blond hair, and it was in a ponytail, and he grabbed it like it was a leash or something and dragged her out. He jerked her over to the woman, and the woman took the ponytail and pulled it so hard Harper was practically bent over backward, trying to walk and not trip, trying to fight and get away, screaming. No use. He came around and opened my door, and I scrambled across the back seat to get out the other side, but he caught my ankle and pulled me out in one long tug, so fast and hard I landed face-first on the dirt. I didn't have a minute to catch my breath or think before he hauled me up and dragged me after the woman and Harper..."

I slide my hand over until our hands are pinky to pinky on the sheet. The comfort of another human. She doesn't pull away.

"They took us into this big red barn. The front part was kind of a mess, like one of those hoarder TV shows. Old tools, tires and mowers just laying around. No animals, but it smelled—animally. Toward the back, there was a metal door, and he slid it open. There were three steel cages, like for dogs. Not the pet store kind, but the floor-to-ceiling kind they have at animal shelters with a door so people can walk inside and clean. The woman shoved Harper into one and me into another, with the empty one between us. I guess so we couldn't touch or whisper to each other."

She closes her eyes. "And the sheriff, he barely said a word. He'd look at us and smile, a jacked-up crazy-ass smile like I've never seen before and never want to see again."

I know that smile. Alfred had that smile. A smile that could rattle your innards and turn them into liquid fire.

"He said he had to get back. He told us the woman's name was Vero and she was there to take care of us. She smiled, and her smile was so demented, so terrifying, it was clear she's flat-out crazy. She took our clothes and said they were too nice for *putas*. She left us completely naked, then locked thick leather dog collars around our necks."

That explains the wide red rash around Emily's neck.

"She turned on a hose and used it to fill metal water bowls, like for dogs, and she didn't care that she got us wet. Then she left. She kept the lights on, though, so we could see where we were. Next to the cages there," she presses her eyes closed, "is an open area with what looks like a doctor's examining table. All sorts of gizmos and gadgets hang from pegs on the wall. At first, I thought they were farm implements, but then we started really looking. They're tools. Nail guns. Saws. And Harper pointed out there were medical tools, too, on trays on counters around the room..."

Emily takes two deep breaths. "I—I need to stop for a minute. Okay? I—I can't say the rest yet."

"Of course. Take as long as you need. Angel and I will stand guard and make sure no one comes near you." CB says in that CB voice that makes everything better.

Emily burrows into the covers and presses herself against the back wall of the cab, pillow clutched against her like a squishy shield. Her breathing becomes steady and shallow. I don't think she's asleep, but she's not fully awake, either. She's probably in shock.

I move over to the passenger seat. "What are we going to do?" I mouth to CB.

CB shakes her head slowly, and shrugs. "We have to do something. But I'm with her. No cops." She says in a very low voice, keeping an eye on Emily.

I nod. No cops. But seriously. What the hell are we going to do?

CHAPTER SEVEN

ANGEL

The story is crazy. The girl is beaten badly, but a cop? That is hard to comprehend.

CB is having the same thoughts. She says quietly, "Angel and I need to finish prepping the truck. We'll be right back."

Emily isn't asleep. A flash of fear crosses her face, and I don't blame her. For all she knows, she's jumped out of the proverbial frying pan into the fires of Hades. I smile as reassuringly as I can. "It's okay. We just have to finish getting the truck ready."

I follow CB out, and she shuts the door. She looks tense in the yellow haze cast from the tall pole lights scattered around the lot. Calm CB from a few minutes ago is gone.

"Do you believe her?" CB asks. She's pacing, hands on hips. I wonder if she's aware she avoids stepping in patches of oil and lubricant or if it's so ingrained it's automatic. The girl loves her shoes.

"Believe her?" I repeat. "She's a friggin' mess."

"I don't mean do you believe some *pandejo* beat her. Anyone can see she's been through hell." CB shakes her head and starts walking toward the trailer, checking each tire, even though we did that before we left North Carolina yesterday and don't need to do it again until we leave the load in San Diego and head back. She squats to check a cable, then rises and continues her path. "I mean, the who beat her up part."

19

THE HUNTED: SINS OF THE FATHER

"It seems like a crazy story. But I'm the wrong person to ask about crazy stories."

CB doesn't look at me but nods. "True that. I ain't no fan of the law. You know it. But this is way beyond, ya know? A sheriff that kidnaps women for fun? That's not even something that King dude would write."

Well, yeah, he probably would, but I don't say that.

"We know people are twisted. I'm living proof." I say. Saying those words confirms it for me: I believe Emily. I believe her as much as I believe anything, I guess. "Here's the thing. If she was beaten by her pimp, escaped a trafficker, or even ran away from her boyfriend, why make up a story like this? Why not just tell the truth? Or at least make up a slightly less nutso story. She has to know this is hard to believe. If you're in trouble and need help, you're going to go for the low-hanging fruit, right?"

CB is done with her inspection, and she leans against the back fender. "Yeah, I guess."

"Do you—do you not want to help her?" I ask, and it feels so weird even to be saying the words. Of course, CB wants to help her. That's who CB is, at her very core. She tries to present as a badass, and she is, but she's also a helper. The underdogs are her people.

"Did I say that? I did not hear words like that coming out of my mouth," CB snaps, and that, too, is out of character. I don't know what's going on with her. She has seemed off since we left yesterday. Everyone's allowed a bad day, so I wasn't going to pry, but now she's starting to worry me. "Are you okay?"

"I'm fine. I just wasn't expecting a battered woman with a crazy story to jump into my truck!" CB says sharply, then softens the words with a wan smile. "Caught me off guard is all."

"Me, too." I agree.

"Let's go back and hear the rest of this horror movie."

CHAPTER EIGHT

Wednesday, September 9, 2009, Late Night

ANGEL

Emily looks relieved to see us, and just us, when we climb back into *Casita*.

CB settles into the driver's seat, and I take the passenger seat.

Emily continues her terrible story.

The man returned after what felt like a day or two but might have been an hour or might have been a week. He stood in front of the cages, dressed in jeans and a denim shirt over a black T. Nothing left to identify him as a sheriff. He looked at Harper, then Emily, then Harper again, then Emily. He unlocked Harper's cage, and it didn't matter that she fought him with everything she had. He dragged her out as easily as if she were made of feathers. He threw her over his shoulder and carried her to the area next to the cages.

Where the table was.

Where the tools were.

"I didn't want to look," Emily admits, her voice soft and ragged. "I didn't want to see or hear what he was doing to Harper, but it felt like I would be abandoning her if I turned away." Emily sucks in a sob. There was a time when I felt the same enormous weight of obligation, so I understand. Oh, do I understand.

For her friend, Emily tried. As long as she could stand it, she tried. Emily screamed and yelled and begged him to stop and shouted to Harper, "I love you!" which made the woman named

Vero laugh and mimic her in a terrible high-pitched voice that Emily imitates now. Eventually, it all evolved into one awful sound as Harper's screams of pain blended with Emily's screams of terror.

When Vero dragged Harper back to the cages, Harper was barely conscious. She was bleeding from so many places. Emily couldn't see where one wound started and another began. Jonny stopped by the cages on his way out. He squatted down and smiled at Harper. "That was a good time! I can tell, you're going to be a fun one. All that spunk and spit are going to make the game extra exciting. Can't hardly wait!"

When he stood, he winked at Emily. "Rest up, buttercup! Next time I'm here, we'll see what you're made of! Sugar and spice and everything nice, I bet!" and made a show of licking his lips. Then he was gone.

In the safe space that is *Casita*, I am silent. CB is silent.

Eventually, Emily asks, "What's today's date?"

"September 9th," I answer.

Emily's eyes widen in their circle of bruises. "We were at the rest stop on August 14th."

My gut churns. So many days and nights of fear, of pain, of not knowing what was coming next, of not knowing if this day would be the last. "How did you escape?"

Emily shakes her head. "I didn't escape, exactly. He turned me loose."

CB cocks her head, confused. "He turned you loose?"

"Yes." Emily pulls the covers tighter around herself. "He showed up and pulled me out of the cage. I thought we were going to the table, but he shoved me through the barn, then to the outside. I was so confused, but also excited, I guess, even though that doesn't sound right. The excitement didn't last long. For one thing, I was naked. Why would he take me outside naked? There was no good reason. But I had no idea..."

She pauses and snakes a hand out from her blanket cocoon to grab the bottle of water. She takes a sip, calming herself. Small, regular movements are soothing when you're stressed. They also buy time. "He said he was bored of me, that I didn't fight hard enough. Now we'd both see if there was any fight in me at all."

Emily closes her eyes. "I didn't understand. He pointed toward the driveway and said, 'You have a one-hour head start. Then, I'm coming for you. You should probably start running.'"

A little mewing noise comes from her throat. "I still didn't understand. Stupid me, I still thought maybe he was letting me go. Vero was there, like she'd sneaked up behind us. She asked him, 'Do you want the bow and arrows? Or the knives?' and that's when I finally got it. He meant he was going to hunt me. Like an animal! I freaked out. Absolutely panicked. That made them both laugh. They went back into the barn, not a care in the world."

I shiver. I've been through some shit with Alfred. But nothing like this. *This is next-level crazy.*

"I slapped myself, really hard, to calm down. I was hurt, and naked, and so hungry, and terrified. How could I possibly win? I had to try. Not winning meant he'd shoot me with arrows or gut me with a knife. And Harper was still in there with them! I took a few stumbling steps toward the driveway, but then I stopped. Of course, that's where he wanted me to go, assumed I'd go, even had sort of suggested. My brain still worked, at least."

Emily looks angry. Good!

"I knew the driveway was absolutely the last way I should go. I could hear that crazy bitch's laugh from in the back, so they weren't spying on me. I looked around to see what was the other way, the opposite direction from the gate. There was the barn and the little house to the right. To the left of the barn was a small building like a chicken coop or something. I knew in my gut my only chance was to do the reverse of what he thought I'd do. By then, I was sure we weren't the first girls he'd done this to. I went to the left of the barn. That little building turned out to be the *actual* dog kennel. I didn't want the dogs to bark and tell them where I was! Somehow I got by without giving myself away. Behind the buildings is a mix of scrub woods and underbrush, with pockets of pasture in between. His ranch is big. I don't know how to judge the size, but lots and lots of acres, I think... "

She pauses again to calm herself. "An hour isn't very long, especially under those conditions."

I know better than anyone how true those words are. Lyrics to a Melissa Etheridge song play on repeat in the back of my brain because that's how I kept track of time when it was a matter of life-or-death.

"I thought, maybe I can find a neighbor, or a road. Maybe the whole property wasn't fenced, just the front where the gates were. Maybe, maybe, maybe. I went as far as I could, getting more scared by the minute. That clock was ticking. I was sure it had been more than an hour but hoped he'd gone the other way, toward the gate, and that would buy me time. I guess it did. When I eventually heard him calling out for me in that crazy sing-song voice, the sun was lower on the horizon."

CB has closed her eyes. Her head is tipped back against the tall seat. She looks calm, except her hands, folded in her lap, are clenched so tight the veins stand out, blue against her olive skin.

"His voice got me moving even faster, which is probably how I fell into the creek. I was trying to cross on a part that had some flat, wide stones. I could see a fence a few hundred feet away through a bunch of trees. I just had to get across the water. But I slipped and fell, and the water was very fast and rough, rapids, I guess. I was pulled downstream. I couldn't get my head up long enough to breathe, and I was pretty sure this was it, I was going to drown, but that was okay because it was better than being shot with arrows or gutted with a knife. So I sort of relaxed and accepted. Until I found myself being swept under a fence across the creek. Then I had to fight not to get caught on the barbed wire at the bottom of the fence, because being shredded by barbed wire, while at the same time drowning, seemed almost as awful as the knife or the bow and arrow. I got tangled up pretty good, but by some miracle, I came up, and then I was on the other side."

I told myself to check Emily's back. It would be another miracle if she didn't end up with sepsis.

"I crawled out of the water and laid there for a while, tucked into a mess of fallen logs. I was praying they would shield me from his view if he came back that way. The sun looked like it was getting ready to set, and I had to get out of there before dark. I refused to be a coyote's dinner after all that. As soon as I could muster up the energy, I started walking in the direction of the fence I had seen before I was washed through. Maybe there was a road there."

CB opens her eyes and stares at Emily. "Sweetheart, you are one badass bitch. I don't know if I could have done all that, especially with all those wounds. You are a *mujer fuerte*." Although she looks at Emily, her hand snakes across the space between our seats and grasps mine. Until that moment, I hadn't realized how much I needed her reassurance. CB always knows.

"Honestly, I don't know how I did it. I'm not usually brave. I guess it was fear, and adrenalin, and knowing Harper is still there. Maybe I was numb to the pain at that point. I don't know. But I found that truck and got to the truck stop and found you." Emily sucks in a tired breath. "Now I have to save Harper."

CHAPTER NINE

Thursday, September 10, 2009, Early Morning

ANGEL

Even though I'm not a driver, I know the rules by heart, because it's serious business, especially for truckers who cross state lines. They can't be on duty for more than 60 hours in seven days. They can be on duty for 14 hours; then they have 10 hours of off-duty time, and the rules even say drivers have to spend 8 hours of that in their beds. That's not all. They can only be driving for 11 hours of the 14. That means three of those 14 hours can be spent on paperwork, loading or unloading, etc. Oh, and they have to take a 30-minute break after 8 hours of being on duty. Being a truck driver is a lot more complicated than drivers of cars understand.

Most runs, we spend our off-duty time in *Casita*. It's not a big space, but we have everything we need. The bunk beds are comfy, and we have cabinets to store our clothes and necessities. The tiny kitchen isn't fancy, but we can make a damn good meal. We avoid particularly stinky foods—sautéed onions, salmon, anything with cumin—not because we don't like those flavors, but because we don't like them well enough to live with them for a week.

Our system works, now. It didn't always. At first, I felt claustrophobic in the small space. It reminded me too much of being locked up. But once I got comfortable with the idea that I could go outside anytime, I realized I enjoy being able to see everything I want or need without moving my head.

It works great for CB and me, but throw in a third person—not so much.

"We'll rent a motel room. More space, and that'll give me somewhere to really look at Emily's wounds." CB announces, starting up the rig.

I'm watching Emily, and I see another momentary flash of panic. We seem friendly, but what if we're just a different kind of bad? I've had those moments. I know how scary it can be to feel unsure coming off the heels of terror. I hope she trusts the supportive look I give her.

CB has a favorite motel at the outskirts of Oklahoma City. They're supportive of truckers, in particular, and travelers in general. We stayed here once before when a bad ice storm hit. I'm excited because their diner makes the best burger I've ever tasted. Not sure what's magic about it, but my mouth is watering just thinking about it. That makes me feel guilty.

It's just past midnight, so we haven't run out the clock on our driving time, but we can schedule a break and figure out what's next. CB pulls *Casita* into the lot and goes to the office to rent the room while I drop our go-bags down to the tarmac below.

Once I've got the stuff on the ground, I set about dealing with Emily. I can tell the adrenalin has worn off, and she's feeling her injuries much more intensely. Even if you're in great shape, it's awkward getting out of a semi. Still, Emily is a fighter. She gets down with barely a whimper.

CB grabs her bag, and I pick up my backpack, and we each grab one of Emily's arms the same way we did at the truck stop. We march-carry her to the room. Emily leans on me while CB unlocks the door.

The room is like any other old-school motel room. Paneled walls. Two queen beds on platform bases, headboards bolted to the wall. Ugly floral bedspreads. A low dresser with a box TV on top. Round table with two hard-as-a-rock wood captain's chairs in front of the window, where an air conditioner unit hums and occasionally belches. Everything is orange and teal. Always.

"You take the inside bed. CB and I will share this one." I dump our bags onto the bedspread. "Do you feel up to showering? I have a robe and some PJs." I put them on the bathroom counter.

"I haven't had a shower since the day I left Nashville." She tests her balance, puts a hand on the dresser for support as she takes one step, then the next, toward the bathroom. At the door, she stops and looks at me. "I don't know why y'all are doing this. I'm not sure I'd be eager to help a bloody stranger I found in a truck stop bathroom."

"Put it like that, you're right. Out with ya," I agree and point to the door. I drop onto the bed, testing the bounce. These beds are usually so old and overused they either bounce you high, or you sink into a hole. This one bounces, and I'm delighted. I'm seventeen. I'm still a kid in a lot of ways. "Remember I told you I'd been through something, too."

Emily nods.

"I remember everything about how I felt. If I can help someone else, I'm all in." I concentrate on my breathing because that lets me keep the memories and the emotions separated. Court appointed shrink trick #524.

"Well, thanks." Emily hobbles into the bathroom. She leaves the door open, just a crack. So she can hear what's happening in the room? To not feel alone? If it were me, I would've locked the door. But I spent months using a bathroom that didn't *have* a door. Or a mirror. Or a curtain on the shower. Only the bad places had doors.

Oh, crap, I'm spiraling. I'm shuffling through a slide deck of images, sounds, smells, and bursts of light, building a block of intense feeling so dark, so deep, I'm going to drown. *Oh no, oh no, oh no. Not now.*

I scream song lyrics in my head, choosing a song I don't have memorized, so I have to focus and redirect my mind to remembering the right words. Eventually, it works. Not as quickly as I would like, but quick enough. Emily comes out of the shower and I plaster a half-smile on my face. What have I gotten us into?

CHAPTER TEN

Thursday, September 10, 2009, Early Morning

ANGEL

Emily is asleep, which is good. She spent quite a lot of time tossing and turning and calling out in fear, or pain. Finally, she settled.

It's incredible to think it's been just a few hours since I found her in the bathroom. It feels like days.

The TV glows in the dim light, the volume is turned down. *Friends* is on, even though I don't particularly care for it. My other options are a 24 hour religious show, the weather channel, or some 1950s western. *Friends* it is. Ross and Rachel are arguing. This is the episode where they have different opinions of the definition of being 'on a break.'

CB's fingers are flying across the keys of her phone. She loves texting. According to CB, unless you're face to face, preferably with a tasty beverage in your hand, conversations are best had in short bursts. I wait for a pause in the barrage of typing, then ask, "What are we going to do about the run?"

CB chews on her lip. "In two hours, *Casita* and I have to be headed west on I-40."

I try not to whine, although that's precisely what I want to do. Even I recognize the pout in my voice when I say, "I guess Emily and I will figure out a plan while you're gone and be ready when you're back."

Emily catches us both by surprise when she asks, "How long will you be gone?"

"Two days," CB says. She's being optimistic. It's nearly twenty hours from here to San Diego, which means she's going to have to take a ten hour rest in the middle. That means it's thirty hours one way. If she ignores the rules on the way back, when she's empty, she could maybe make it to us in twenty-four hours with a short nap break.

"That's so long! It may already be too late." Emily yells, even though her voice comes out not much louder than a whisper. She grabs water from the nightstand and swallows large gulps to lubricate her vocal cords. When the mouth of the plastic bottle scratches at her torn lip, she gasps and winces. All of her looks worse now because she's clean, so each cut, tear, and bruise stands out.

"I know it's not ideal," CB says to Emily. "I have no choice. I have to get the load to San Diego, and there are laws about how long I can drive without stopping. I could lose my license and my income."

That's all true. But what's also true is that there are ways to deal with emergencies. We could ask a friend to finish the run, for example. I'd assumed that's what the flying fingers were about and start to ask, but CB has read my mind. She holds up a hand and shakes her head. "I have to do this run myself. One way or another, in two hours I head out. Let's not waste time."

I stare at her. She's avoiding eye contact. This is not at all like CB. All sorts of weird thoughts run through my head, none of them good. What the hell is going on?

Emily looks defeated and retreats deeper into her blanket fort, the whites of her eyes owlish in the purple and green bruises on her cheek and brow bones.

"Our first job is to figure out who this bastard cop is." I know better than to push CB. I'll wait until the time is right and ask my questions. Now, I pull my beloved notebook from my backpack and write, *#1 Bastard Cop.*

"Sheriff," CB corrects, and I cross out *Cop* and change it to *Sheriff*. I underline it twice, so emphatically the pen scratches a hole in the paper.

CB drags an old-school telephone book from under the bible in the nightstand. She flips through until she finds what she's after—the government services section. "Looks like that rest stop area is probably Waterford County, Texas Sheriff jurisdiction. That doesn't mean that's where he's from, though. He could be an Oklahoma sheriff, too. *Hostia puta!* I left my damn laptop in *Casita*."

"I grabbed it when I got the maps." I open my backpack again and lift out the computer.

CB makes a "You're a pain, but I love you" face and opens the laptop. As fast as she is on her phone, she is slow as molasses on a keyboard. She says it's because she had to take a typing class in high school, and they were very particular about which finger went where. Apparently they didn't like the way she used her middle fingers.

She rotates the laptop so I can see. A map shows the line between the Texas rest stop where Emily says they were picked up and the Oklahoma truck stop where we found her.

"Angel, give me the atlas," CB instructs.

I push my beloved Rand-McNally Road Atlas to her.

"There are at least a dozen counties around and between Oklahoma City and the Texas rest stop." CB grunts, annoyed. She flips back and forth between the Oklahoma and Texas pages, using her fingers to measure. "It's about an hour to drive from the rest stop in Texas to the Oklahoma City truck stop where we found you. How did you get from there to here?"

"Yeah, how did you get from the ranch to the truck stop?" I repeat. My cup is empty. I want more coffee but I'm not about to resort to the crap that comes from the tiny coffee maker on the bathroom counter.

Emily adjusts the covers so we can see her face. "Once I was on the other side of the fence, I started through the woods and found a road. A man was working on a windmill. I slipped into the back of his truck while he was distracted, and the truck stop is where he went."

I can't think about that barbed wire she described. The scars on my own back twitch when I do. Emily may look like a delicate flower, but she's a weed: tough and determined to live.

I have so many questions, but I only ask one for now. "How long do you think you were in his truck?"

"Maybe an hour. It felt like forever, but I don't think it was."

I get it. Time and I have a complex relationship.

I sketch out a simple map on a new page in my notebook and mark an X for the truck stop on the right side and another X on the left for the rest stop on the Texas side. I draw an imaginary circle around the truck stop with my finger. "Even if we limit the distance to a 60-mile radius around the truck stop, that's a lot of ground. Do you remember which way you drove? Was it a lot of turns? Were you driving fast, like a highway, or slower, like in-town or city traffic? Any idea which way you were headed?"

CB glares at me. "Give the woman some space, please."

"It's okay," Emily says. She smooths the blankets, hands needing to stay busy. "I'm pretty sure we only turned a few times. Left onto a dirt road just after I got into the truck, for sure. Then we got onto pavement, and we went straight at a good pace for quite a while. I got kind of cold from the air. That's why I felt around until I found the T-shirt. About half way, we made a," she closes her eyes, visualizing, "right. We made a right. And then we stayed on that for a while until we pulled into the truck stop parking lot. He parked on the side, and I waited a couple of minutes, then crept out. I ran for the bathroom when I saw it was right there. It wasn't totally dark yet."

"We can work with that. You don't happen to remember which

direction you were coming from, do you? North? South?"

Emily is embarrassed. "I never could figure those out. Only left and right."

"No worries. Until I started riding with CB, I didn't know either."

"I'm going to grab us some food. I'll be back." CB slips out of the room, phone in hand as if she's reading a text. I look at the map again, but now my mind is on CB. Who is she talking to? Why is she acting sketchy? Is she meeting someone in San Diego? Or are we carrying more than computer and car parts?

"Is CB your mom?" Emily asks, breaking into my worrying.

I snort. "There's no way this," I indicate all five-feet-eight inches of me, which is mostly legs, "could have come out of that tiny little thing. She's just a good friend. Sometime I'll tell you the story about how we came to be a team. Once we have Harper safe."

Emily's eyes get glossy. "I can't stop thinking about what he's doing to her, what that crazy woman is doing to her. What if she's not even alive anymore? What if I'm too late?"

I give it to her straight. "I'm not going to tell you it's going to be sunshine and puppies because it's not. All I can promise is that we will do our absolute best, the three of us, to find her and save her and stop that bastard from doing anything to anyone ever again. For Harper's sake, you have to stay strong and focused. You can feel sorry for yourself later. We'll schedule time for it. I promise."

Emily half-laughs at that. "Your meltdown has been scheduled for eight p.m. to ten p.m. If you're more than 15 minutes late, your reservation may be given to someone else..."

"Exactly."

CHAPTER ELEVEN

Thursday, September 10, 2009, Early Morning

C B

The motel door closes behind me with a bang I didn't intend. I'm trying to keep my cool, but this I do not need. I do not need another woman who needs to be saved. I love the one I got, but I am not, and never wanna be, CB's refuge for abused women.

I hot-foot it toward the Diner, the wood heels of my boots clicking on the blacktop as I weave between cars. The lot is packed, even though it's after midnight on a Wednesday. Technically, it's Thursday morning.

The timing of this could not be worse. I have two damn days to get this load to San Diego, or all hell will break lose. 'Cause, there's another *chica* who needs my help, and she don't even know it.

Mierda.

I need to keep on keepin' on down the road. That is absolutely positively what I gotta do tonight. I cannot up and change the plan. Nope. Absolutely cannot. Maybe I can convince the Emily woman to contact the police anyway. Then she'll be somebody else's problem.

Except I know calling the cops isn't an option. I'm an asshole sometimes, but not that much of an asshole.

I am no fan of officers of the law, but never did I think I'd hear a tale like this.

Who am I kidding? I can't walk away from this *chica*. Not a chance.

My phone buzzes in my hand as I get to the Diner door. I look down, expecting to see Angel's photo on the screen. Instead, "Unknown caller" stares back at me. *Bah!* My gut rolls. I spin around, eyes scanning the lot because the next words are, "Why the fuck are you at a motel?"

I feel the blood drain from my face, and lean against the newspaper rack outside the door to steady myself. They're watching! They're following me! I never considered this, but now I know, it's so freakin' obvious, and I feel freaking stupid. But, of course, they are. You don't send someone off with a stash of illegal something in their trailer and hope they'll just drive to the drop-off as instructed. How many people would pull over and have a quick look-see? Probably most. Some people might even take that load and see how they might use it for their own personal benefit. Of course, I've thought many times about pulling off somewhere and taking a peek since we left North Carolina. But how would I explain that to Angel? She has no idea we're hauling anything but computer and car parts, same as always.

I collect myself and type out, "Minor emergency. Heading out soon."

"What kind of emergency?" comes lightning fast.

"Partner is sick. Leaving her here." Not a total lie.

"Don't open the trailer. Get back on the road by 2 a.m. Do not be late."

I don't bother to respond. Jesus. What a hot damn mess.

It doesn't take long to collect the food. I hustle back across the lot and kick at the door with my foot. Angel opens it and takes the food. She gives me a look—she can read me like a comic book—but doesn't say anything.

The woman is huddled on the bed, buried in covers, shivering. *Shit.* Got so caught up in my own problems I forgot I have a broken bird to tend to.

"I'm getting my bag." I hurry to the truck and find my special floral gym bag in one of the upper compartments. I grab one more item from under the bed and shove it in the bag, and then I'm down and back in the room in less than two minutes. I hope that reassures whoever is watching I'm not up to anything nefarious.

Fuckers.

I lock the door behind me and casually nudge one of the chairs, so it's half-blocking the door. I work facing the window. The drapes are drawn closed, but I can see the parking light through them, and note the shadows. I leave my pretty little pistol in the side pocket where I stashed it, just in case.

CHAPTER TWELVE

Thursday, September 10, 2009, Early Morning

CB

I put the floral bag on the bed. Food first, then medical care.

"I heard something interesting." Angel is already into the bags, and she unloads them onto the table. Burgers and fries for us, soup for Emily. Two cups of coffee for the caffeine addict, a diet soda for me, and a hot tea for Emily.

"What's interesting?" Angel dips a fry into ketchup after settling Emily's food next to her on the nightstand.

I take a big mouthful of burger. This may be my last meal for a while and I intend to enjoy it. Screw the assholes outside. "I ran into a friend."

"That's not interesting. You always run into friends," Angel grunts.

"True. But this friend had an interesting story to tell." I stretch out on the bed with my food and take a long drink of Diet Dr. Pepper. "My friend heard tell of a woman who crossed the border from Mexico two or three years ago."

"We're in Texas. Again, not interesting."

I shoot her a warning look. I know she's not happy with me but she doesn't get to be a total smartass. "This woman left El Salvador. Rumor has it she killed her own father, her lover, and three members of their gang. Violently and intentionally. Not in self-defense."

Angel makes happy noises as she eats her burger, then looks at Emily, embarrassed to be enjoying her food. "She sounds charming, but what does this have to do with us?"

"Her name is Veronique." I say.

"That has to be the Crazy One!" Emily gasps. "She's from South America. I just wasn't sure where. I wouldn't doubt she'd kill people for fun."

I nod. "That's what I think, too. Apparently there were a couple of killings of wealthy men between the border and Oklahoma. The rumor mill said she's connected. But the murders never moved north of the Oklahoma/Texas border. The killings stopped. So either she was killed or captured, or she's busy doing other things."

"Like torturing me and Harper."

"Like that." I agree. "My friend said he met her once, before she disappeared. He was on mandatory break and was sick of his own company. He was at the bar minding his own, and suddenly a brawl broke out at one of the pool tables. This woman—apparently she's a stunner—had broken a pool stick in half and shish-kabobbed a man with it. Shoved it right through his belly. When a couple of men tried to stop her, she broke beer bottles and cut them up good, broke one man's jaw with a pool ball, was basically hell on wheels. She ran out before the law arrived."

Angel makes an 'ew' face and sets aside the rest of fries.

"But the thing that really stuck with Bo—my friend—was that she was laughing the whole damned time."

Emily nods. "That's her."

"Great. We're dealing with two psychos. But what do we do with that information?" Angel asks, frustrated.

"I'm not sure, yet. But at least we know something about who we're dealing with. They don't even know we're coming."

CHAPTER THIRTEEN

Thursday, September 10, 2009, Early Morning

C B

I move Styrofoam containers out of the way and start pulling items out of my bag. This isn't your mama's first aid kit. Next to the bandages and tweezers are tinctures and ointments and bottles and jars with labels that read like a spice cabinet but are used in many ways. A container of beeswax, a bottle of calendula infused oil, a jar of coconut oil, and a bottle of tea tree oil. Goldenseal. Thyme. Neem oil. Anise. Lavender oil. Honey. Turmeric paste.

My great grandmother on my mother's side was a healer in Cartagena, Colombia, the daughter of generations of healers. My mother had no interest in learning her skills, but I was obsessed. As a little girl I followed Lita around, absorbing everything she cared to share. It is one of the few things from my past I carry with me in my present.

"What's all that?" Emily asks Angel.

"Her medicine kit." Angel answers with a smile. She takes my potions dead serious. She's seen them work their magic on both of us at various times.

I'm working fast because the clock is ticking. The girls watch me mix, shake, grind, stir. Eventually, I'm ready. "I'm going to make a tea, which will help heal you from the inside. Drink it every four hours. Manuka honey for the open wounds. I've got a couple of different salves here that will work on the achy sore bits. Apply the honey and salve and change the bandages three times a day." I give it one last try. "I don't suppose you'd let us take you to the hospital?"

"No!" Emily nearly shouts, her voice ragged and hoarse.

I pull honey from the bag and put it next to the tea blend.

"You're really going to do the run?" Angel asks, her face scrunched in a frown.

"I have to get the load to San Diego," I tell her for the umpteenth time, and in my mind, beg her not to fight.

Angel frowns. "And tell me again why we can't call in a favor?"

"Not this time." The look on her face is killing me. By protecting one *chica* I love, I'm abandoning another *chica* I love. When it's all over, I'll tell Angel why, and she'll understand. But right now, this minute, she's as shocked as if I'd kicked a puppy.

Can't really blame her.

"Here's the plan." I point to Emily. "You are gonna take this time to rest up." I point to Angel. "You are going to try and figure out who this asshole is and who was dumb enough to hire his ass. See if you can get some idea where the ranch is. By the time I get back on Saturday—"

Emily gasps. "That's too long! Harper will be dead!"

I take a deep breath, trying to keep calm. "I don't think so. He's going to be looking for you for a while. He doesn't know you're not still on that ranch, hiding from his sorry ass. And he'll have to go to work, right? Pretend to be the great guy in the white hat? You said he was on the ranch for a few hours, then gone a couple of days. If he sticks with that schedule, we will be okay. This will work."

Angel starts to protest again, but I shake my head firmly. "I'm sorry. I can't. I have to make this run. Do not argue with me, *por favor.*"

Angel chews her lip, and her brows scrunch together. She's making me feel like I actually did kick a whole bunch of freaking puppies.

"Do not leave this room except to go to the Diner. Don't you open the door to anyone. Do not make phone calls," I glare at Angel and repeat, "to anyone." I was wrong about the last thing I need, because the last thing I really need is for her to call her buddy Nick Winston, FBI agent. He's her hero in shining armor. But for me, it's different. If he doesn't get me for kidnapping and taking a child across state lines, he'll lock me up for whatever the fuck is in the back of my truck, tucked between boxes of automotive parts and computer chips. No, *gracias*.

"No one, Angel," I repeat, and I pray that I've earned enough trust that she'll do what I ask.

"I don't understand." She looks so sad. I want to hug her, but she doesn't like to be touched. I'll grab her hand or touch her shoulder if she's having a meltdown, but that's it. I respect her boundaries, and she respects mine. That's why our friendship works.

"Please just have faith," I whisper. Then, louder, I add, "Keep your phone charged. Text me every few hours, so I know you're okay. I'm already gonna worry. Do not give me more reasons to worry."

I blow her a kiss, smile half-heartedly at Emily, and close the door behind me.

CHAPTER FOURTEEN

Thursday, September 10, 2009, Early Morning

ANGEL

CB thinks she's just going to bounce out of here without a conversation. She is wrong. I follow her out of the room. Neither of us says a word until we're inside *Casita*. CB goes about getting ready to leave as if it's an absolutely normal run. I stand in the center of the space we call our home and watch, momentarily speechless.

That doesn't last long. Words fly out of me like bullets. "How can you leave? Just abandon that woman? And me?"

CB doesn't say anything. That's completely out of character. She always has something to say. *Always.* Part of me realizes something is off, but the scared part of me overrules the logical part.

"Concetta Bonaventura," I hiss, pulling out the big guns, her real name, "this isn't you. You don't run when the going gets tough."

"I'm not running." She won't look at me, and her words are calm. She should be angry, insulted that I'd say such a thing.

This is not right. None of it is right.

"I'm doing my job. The job that pays the bills. The job that pays for the cute little house in North Carolina. The job that makes it possible for you to be the best-cared-for runaway that ever was."

Ouch. I want to say I earn my keep, but that's not entirely true. There's no extra pay because I ride along. I'm extra hands and extra eyes, but I don't bring in a single penny. Does she want me to leave? Is she tired of the permanent hitchhiker? I'm too afraid to ask.

Still, this isn't CB. This isn't us. "Please tell me what's going on? Please?"

"I will be back as fast as I can. But, Angel, you have to trust me. If I had another option, I would take it, but I don't. Please. Just do as I ask. Go back to the room. Figure out who the Big Bad is so we can take him down when I get back. Use that devious little brain of yours for good." There's no fire in any of this, just pleading. I wonder if she threw in a *Buffy the Vampire Slayer* reference on purpose. CB had no idea what a Big Bad was until she met me.

"Are you—are you angry with me? Tired of—" I have to drag the word out, "babysitting me?"

She spins, eyes flashing. "No! No, never! I just have to do this. I'll explain when I can. For now, you have to go, because I have to go. Trust me, Angel. Please."

I will not cry. I will not. I open the passenger door and hop down, slamming it behind me. My heart is threatening to break, but it's not yet broken. I believe. I'm terrified. But I believe.

CHAPTER FIFTEEN

Thursday, September 10, 2009, Early Morning

CB

When I was a kid, I worshiped my brother Alex. He was six years older than me, and in my opinion, he was the best human God ever designed. He knew everything. All the good things, I mean. Like, he could recite whole sections of books. Solve a math problem that had me nearly in tears. And sing—oh lord, could the boy sing! He was handsome and charming and funny and kind. He had our Mommy's glossy dark hair and strong bone structure, our Papa's height and swimmer's body, and his own green eyes. Our ancestors gave him strength and brilliance. I worshiped him.

I wasn't the only one. The girls at our Chicago private school fought for his attention, sometimes literally. But Alex wasn't the player type. He took different girls to dances and parties but never really dated. He said he had too many things he wanted to do, and for now, he was going to be selfish and keep his time for himself.

Our parents encouraged that thinking. Papa had big plans for Alex. First, Alex was going to Northwestern. Then he'd start work in Mommy's family's international transport business so Mommy and Papa, a civil rights attorney, could travel the world before they were too old and frail (Papa's words, not mine). Alex shared the vision and began taking college-level courses as soon as possible to give himself a head start when he arrived at the Northwestern campus.

Everything was going exactly to plan. And then, one day, he met a girl. She was a year older than him, a pretty white girl who loved poetry, art, and dance. And most of all, she loved my brother Alex.

She had a white girl name—Candace—and the whitest of parents. Those parents weren't thrilled she wanted to marry a half-Black, half-Colombian man, but at least Alex came from money. My parents weren't thrilled Alex wanted to marry a woman so white her family came over on the Mayflower, but they loved Candace because she was wonderful, even if her parents weren't.

After the wedding, Alex and Candace—never Candy—moved into an apartment at the edge of campus so Alex could finish his business degree. They got pregnant within a year, and Lexi, their daughter, was born two days after Alex graduated.

Alex immediately began working at the family business, starting on the warehouse floor, moving his way up through each department. They bought a nice house in a suburb with excellent schools and recreational opportunities. Candace was a great mom and wife, feathering their suburban nest, painting and writing poetry, and feeding her creative soul with Alex's blessing. Her art was noticed by some of the collectors around town. They were a success story by any definition.

One day when Lexi was four, new neighbors moved in across the street. Alex had a dinner meeting with clients and arrived home late. Most of the lights were off in the house. Lexi was asleep, and Candace was curled up in bed with a book, waiting for Alex. The garage door remote had been acting up, and this night it gave up entirely. Alex parked his car—a well-kept navy-blue sedan—in the driveway and went around the side of the house to enter through the kitchen door.

As he reached the door, three police cars pulled up, lights flashing. They didn't ask questions. They didn't wait more than 60 seconds before one of them shot Alex as he reached for the knob of his own kitchen door, keys in one hand, suit jacket and leather messenger bag in the other.

Candace flew out, screaming. The cops tried to keep her away from the man they said had been coming to rob, rape, and kill her. They didn't listen when she screamed he was her husband. When they finally understood, they stepped back and let her go to him, but it was too late. Alex was gone, barely having had time to live.

Candace never recovered. Within weeks, she disappeared into a haze of drugs and alcohol. Little Lexi tried to take care of her mommy, but eventually, the state said either Lexi had to live with family, or be placed in foster care, for her safety. The white grandparents whisked her off to their farm in rural Iowa in the middle of the night. My heartbroken parents didn't feel an ugly legal battle would be good for four-year-old Lexi. Candace died a few years later. I never saw Lexi after the funeral.

Alex's murder—because that's what it was, pure and simple—shook me to the core. I'd been planning to follow in his footsteps. College, join the family business, volunteer in the community, settle down with a family of my own.

But if a good man—the very best man, in my eyes—could be murdered just for being a different color, why bother? What was the point? My plans changed. I finished high school and hit the road in the cute little convertible my parents had given me for my sixteenth birthday.

I developed a routine: I'd land in a town I liked, rent a cheap apartment, take some classes at the community college, work at a diner, or a bar, once I was old enough. I'd find a man for a while, but no one I wanted to make permanent. When I felt I'd been in one place too long, I'd hit the road again.

I lived that life into my late twenties. Then I met a guy named Chad, who reminded me of Alex in so many ways. All the best ways. But instead of being an office guy, he drove a truck. I hopped in the passenger seat and never got out. I rode with him for ten years until he died of a heart attack just after my 39th birthday. He was 44. I decided God doesn't exist. Either that or he's a greedy asshole, because he took the two best people I've ever known away from me.

After Chad died, I realized I loved the traveling life. I got my license and was hired by his old company, and there you have it. Five years in, I inherited money from my great grandmother. I could've done anything I wanted at that point. What I wanted was to buy my truck, and become an owner-operator. So I did.

This isn't the story most people know about me. I tell them CB stands for Chickee Boom. They don't need to know anything about Concetta Bonaventure. Most of them think my life started with Chad. In a way, it did. I like my life. I like my friends. I love my truck and my sidekick Angel.

Life has been pretty great until last week when I got a text from Unknown Number. I ignored the first message—"Have you checked in with Lexi lately?"—because I didn't know who the hell they were talking about. Lexi who?

The next message was a photo. A beautiful young girl with soft brown curls, big blue eyes, and tawny skin she inherited from her father. That Lexi.

I'd heard through the grapevine she ran away from her grandparents in Iowa when she was fifteen. A Chicago friend heard she was stripping and doing private parties with the dual goals of offending the white grandparents, and making bank. Ten years ago, she reconnected with my parents. They persuaded her to move in with them, and she did. She got her GED, went to college, got married, and is currently running for secretary of state or some shit like.

The next text was another photo of the same girl, on her knees, servicing two men while a third watched. She couldn't be more than fifteen or sixteen.

I wanted to vomit.

Another text. "These will go public unless you do us a favor."

I was shaking, but I forced myself to stay calm. *Don't show your hand, CB.*

"We need something moved from NC to CA this coming week. After you pick up your load Tuesday, you'll give us access to your trailer. Not long, just fifteen minutes. We'll text the address. You'll stay in the cab. We'll do the packing and unpacking. You need to be in San Diego at 8:00 a.m. on September 11th."

I look at the clock in *Casita's* dashboard and press a little harder on the gas. It's after 2:00 a.m. on September 10th and, if I follow the rules, San Diego is almost 30 hours away.

CHAPTER SIXTEEN

Thursday, September 10, 2009, Midday

ANGEL

Emily is sleeping again, so I have time to obsess.

CB knows who I am and what happened to me. Once, when we were on a rest break, the national news threw my picture up on the screen along with Bud and Olivia, and Grace. It was during one of the early trials. Wyoming, maybe? I don't remember now. But the secret was out. I told her more than the news would ever be able to report. It was time.

I told her about being abducted by Jennifer, along with my twin brother Bud, from our house in Indiana. I told her about Alfred, and about being locked in a place called the Dollhouse with another girl, Olivia. I told her about the photo sessions where we were supposed to rewrite his terrible childhood. I told her about four-year-old Grace, the child Alfred kidnapped...and how she was the last straw. I told her about getting rescued. I told her how Peter Baden, Olivia's father, became my guardian, because my mother was dead, and my father was in prison. I told her about Nick Winston, the FBI agent that became my lifeline after the rescue. And I told her why I ran away, although I didn't, and still don't, think of it that way. I was giving myself a chance at a life that I chose, that I created, that I wanted. I had had more than enough of being controlled by other people.

It's only been a couple of years, but so far, I'm doing pretty okay.

And here's the thing about CB—well one of the things. She doesn't care about what happened. Everyone has something in their past that impacts who they are now. Bad things happen, and we can't always control them, but we sure as hell control what we do afterward.

Our deal is, if I need to talk, I can say or share whatever I need to. CB will never (okay, rarely) ask random questions, and if she does, it's completely up to me whether I want to answer. Most of it, she's figured out just because we live together. She's seen the scars that cover my body. She understands it's important to me to be able to move around where I sleep. I won't eat certain types of snack cakes or chips, and I despise chocolate milk. Once a year, on our birthday, I have a Bud sundae. And I have conversations with my (dead) twin brother.

Not long after I told her the story, we had a chance to drive a one-off load to Chicago. She said we could 'swing by' my old house, and I could see if I wanted to keep anything. The trailer, and land it sits on, were purchased and put in a trust for me. The sheriff there—a good one—kept an eye on things. But I'd never been back, never even for a minute thought of going back. CB said it was up to me if we were going to take the job, and if we did, if we would go by the house.

CB would've been fine turning down the job. But after a bit of thinking, I said yes. And one sunny summer day, CB and *Casita* and I pulled into the half-circle dirt drive, ignoring the Keep Out and Private Property signs. We'd stopped in town and got the key from the Sheriff, who offered to come, but I said no. I wasn't sure how I was going to feel—indifferent? Scared? Angry? Whatever, I didn't need an audience.

I asked CB to wait in *Casita*. She said she'd check on me in thirty if I didn't come out. That seemed silly. I figured I'd be long past done by then.

Someone was keeping the grass mowed. That same someone, probably, had painted over graffiti on the plastic picnic table on the concrete pad near the trailer door. It used to hurt that people found pleasure sticking their sharp fingers into the raw pain of people who've been through trauma. I was shocked to see some of the hateful notes. One of the most popular is, "You should've died!" I didn't realize people had enough passion to want to come here and spray paint nasty words.

People really can suck.

The screen door opened easily, but the front door stuck a bit, probably from lack of use. The Sheriff said Shine's best friend Lynn had cleaned up a bit to keep the bugs and rodents at bay, but mostly it was the same as when Shine died.

From what I've been told, my mother—Sunshine Evanston—overdosed on heroin and booze just a few weeks before we were rescued. Lynn said she had given up hope, and couldn't bear the accusations of the townspeople anymore. I repeat, people really suck.

When I got the trailer door open, the first thing that hit me was the smell. Instead of smelling musty or old, it smelled like Shine's favorite perfume. Brittney Spears Fantasy, in the bright pink bottle. Was the scent real, or my memory? I guess it didn't matter.

The place was clean. The kitchen counter seemed weird without half-empty bottles of tequila or generic bags of Captain Crunch cereal. A large stack of magazines sat on the coffee table, next to a piece of poster board. Shine was not the vision board type, but that's what it looked like. There were cut-out pictures glued to the poster board, but they didn't make sense. And then I saw words, not in cut-out magazine pieces, but in Shine's lousy printing in black marker: *Give my kids back to me.*

I felt gut-punched.

Once, when we were still at the Dollhouse, Bud and I talked about Shine and what she might be doing. Was she looking for us?

Did she feel bad for leaving us alone so we could be kidnapped? Now I had my answer.

If I let myself think too deeply, I'd fall apart. I kept moving. I went into her bedroom, and my fingers drifted over the items on the dresser. Her cheap jewelry was in the same chaotic pile as when she'd left on that trip years ago. The one suitcase we all shared was in the corner, open, the clothes I remember her packing for the trip still inside. She'd never unpacked. She'd come home and realized we were gone, and her life had stopped.

The only thing I wanted was a necklace our dad, Junior, gave her when Bud and I were born. Two silver dolphins were nose to tail, hanging from a cheap silver chain. Junior said it was the only thing the hospital gift shop had with two, and he wanted two because she was the mother of twins. Weird Junior logic. But it made total sense if you knew him.

Bud's room was just as he'd left it. Clothes everywhere. It was interesting to me that Lynn had cleaned up the living room, but not the bedrooms. I could smell Bud's sweat. That made me smile. His red-handled pocketknife was on the dresser. I slipped it into my pocket, then grabbed a T-shirt. An extra smelly one, so the scent would last a while. U2's *Joshua Tree* album cover graced the front.

That's when I began to shake. Small tremors started in my fingers and moved up my arms and into my jaw. Maybe I was having a seizure. I felt both highly aware of, and also separated from, my body. The tingling intensified, and I leaned against the door frame, afraid I was going to fall, but then I slid down, down, down, until I was on the ratty old carpet, my fingers kneading Bud's discarded clothes. His discarded life.

I was screaming, screaming so loud, screaming a scream I'd been holding back since the day Jennifer took us. It was the first and only time I have ever let the rage, anguish, pain, and fear loose. I was afraid if I let the genie out, I'd never be able to put it back. I'd be locked in an emotional hell worse than the physical hells I've survived. I still have that fear.

CB's arms were around me, and she was rocking me, and making soothing sounds, and eventually, the screams became sobs, and the tingling eased, and the shaking stopped.

I was stronger than the genie that day. I put it back in the bottle.

I got to my feet and clutched the T-shirt and the necklace.

"Do you want to check in here?" CB asked, unknowingly motioning to my bedroom.

"No. That person's gone. There's nothing there for me."

I slept in the back of *Casita* all the way to Chicago and back again to North Carolina. When we pulled into the driveway of CB's little house in Pittsboro, I was almost back to 'normal,' whatever that is for me.

Now, I am pretty sure CB arranged that trip. For the hundredth time, I realize I'd be dead if it weren't for CB.

I have to trust her. But damn, I'm scared.

CHAPTER SEVENTEEN

Thursday, September 10, 2009, Evening

ANGEL

Emily has been asleep for almost fourteen hours, waking only long enough to take more of CB's magic potions. She finally woke for real when I came back with dinner. That's given me plenty of time to think. I also poked around online, since CB left the laptop. Turns out that in the counties in our search area, there are at least fourteen damn officers named John or Johnny. There are probably more; those are the ones that came up with news stories.

"Don't yell," I say after Emily has been awake for a little bit and I've given her part of my magic burger. I swear her color changes with each bite. To my untrained eye, she definitely looks better. CB's witchcraft, burger magic, and rest are a prescription for health.

"Don't yell about what?" Em asks nervously.

"I have an idea," I say.

"Oh, no," Emily says, although she's half-smiling. "Am I going to like it? I'm not, am I?"

I shrug. "Well, it may get us a step closer to finding Harper."

"I like it already."

"We're going to hitch a ride to the rest stop where the LEO picked you up and try to find him." Of course, I present this suggestion as a done deal and sound upbeat about it. If I were a different kind of blond, I might have added a perky, "Easy peasy!"

Emily's face says everything she's thinking, which all comes down to the word that flies out of her mouth. "No!"

"Wait, hear me out. We get a ride with a nice trucker from the Diner. They drop us at the rest stop. We sit somewhere in the shadows and just watch. We don't contact him or let him see us. We wait and if he pulls up, we can figure out what agency he's with, and we'll have somewhere to start." It makes total sense. I mean, how the hell else are we going to figure out who this bastard is? As CB pointed out, there are almost a dozen agencies he could be associated with and a quick search of the 'nets told me there are a lot of law enforcement types down here named John or Johnny. We need to see him, and his official car, at the same time. The only place we know he goes is the rest stop.

Emily is silent for a long, long time. She picks at nubbies on the fake satin comforter covering her bed. She closes her eyes and has a long conversation with herself. Finally, she swings her legs over the side of the bed and carefully gets to her feet. Her balance is better but not great. Still silent, she walks slowly to the table where CB's floral gym bag still sits. She looks through it, careful not to make a mess of the contents. When she finds what she is looking for, she takes a deep breath and turns to me. She holds up a pair of sewing scissors. "We have to cut my hair off."

CHAPTER EIGHTEEN

Thursday, September 10, 2009, Late Night

ANGEL

Most truck drivers are very nice humans. We hitch a ride with a guy I met in the Diner named Chief, who rides with an orange feline copilot named Mister Stinky Cheese. Emily and Mister Cheese bond in the hour it takes to get from the Diner to the rest stop. He's rubbing himself against her face, and she's more than content resting her cheek against his soft fur. When Chief pulls off into the rest stop, Emily looks as though she's going to cry. I have a feeling all the emotional baggage she's carrying right now is being transferred to that little cat.

I drop down my backpack and slide out of the truck so I can help Emily down. Watching her slide out of that big rig, I remind myself it's only been twenty-four hours since I found her in the bathroom. The bruises give her a punk look. She looks more like a teen boy than a twenty-three-year-old woman. The baggy clothes that cover her small frame hide most of her visible wounds. The invisible ones will take longer to recover from. The good news is, even if we come face to face with Jonny freaking law, I doubt he'd recognize her.

All that gorgeous dark hair is now in the trash can in the motel bathroom. It was her idea, and it makes sense, but I know it had to hurt. Hair like that, thick and glossy and the color of European chocolate, must be a thing of pride. When this is over, and she is trying to be 'normal' again, will she mourn it? I know she's going to grieve the life she had before more than the hair, but hair is a physical manifestation of who she is—or rather, was. What used to make her feel beautiful may now be tied to terrible pain.

Why do I think things like this? Do regular people imagine the inner lives of others? *Stop, Angel, stop.*

I stroke Mister Stinky Cheese's silky soft fur one last time, thank Chief, and watch them rejoin traffic on I40. We stand in the shadows, getting our bearings. The rest stop is quiet. Two rigs are idling, drivers asleep, clueless that evil has visited here. A young couple laughs as they race from their hand-me-down Subaru to the bathroom. No sheriff's vehicles. No police cars. Nothing scary or suspicious.

We walk toward the picnic shelter to the right of the main building. Concrete pylons hold a metal roof above a couple of cheery baby blue metal tables with attached benches. Emily leans into one of the pillars, so small she nearly disappears.

"You're sure this is the right rest area?" I ask, although I know it is.

She points to the fenced-in dog park just to the west of us. "A nice older lady had an adorable golden retriever named Brandee. I threw a ball for her."

And then she gasps and stares at me, eyes wide. "How are we going to get back to the motel?"

Oh, shit. I really *am* tired. I was so deep in the plan to get us here, I never thought about how to get back. *Shit, shit, shit.* Even I'm not stupid enough to try to run across the interstate so we can hitch a ride east. A cab would be crazy expensive, not that it matters. I brought my wallet, but left my cash at the motel because, again, I'm an idiot. Maybe we can talk someone into taking us to the next exit, then we can walk across to the east on-ramp, where we can try to hitch back. "For now, let's just take things one bite at a time."

"Bite?" Emily laughs, surprised.

"You know that old question—how do you eat an elephant? One

bite at a time." One of CB's many sayings.

The young couple is now holding hands as they head back to their Subaru, all sweet and lovey-dovey. Life goes on around us. No one has a clue there's a monster on the loose, and he's driving a government-issued vehicle.

A Toyota Camry pulls in as they pull out. It draws my attention because of the fancy paint job—gloss black with two broad red stripes running from the windshield down the hood. A tall, gangly man clambers out. I can't tell his age, or anything about him, really, other than he has dark hair that falls in long waves around his face. He's not our guy, so he loses my attention—until he turns and comes straight for me.

Emily is still leaning into the pylon, which is the only thing holding her up at this point. She doesn't see him. He's coming at a fast pace, and I can't help but go into a protective stance. I palm my pocketknife and hold up a hand in the universal motion instructing him to stop. He doesn't notice or else ignores me.

Now that he's closer, I see he's got papers in his hand, fliers. The guy looks exhausted but committed, even now that he does see my "stop" command. The good news is, he doesn't look insane. I give him the benefit of the doubt and lower my hand but continue to stare at him in a way that—hopefully—suggests he slows his roll.

"Hey," I say tentatively. Cautiously.

"Hey," he returns and thrusts one of the fliers at me. It's dark and hard to see, with just one light serving the picnic area. He starts talking fast. Is he on drugs? "Do you come here often? That's not a pickup line. I'm looking for two women. They disappeared from here a few weeks ago. One of them is named Emily -" before he can finish whatever he was planning to say, Emily is at his back, kicking and screaming and punching with more energy than I would have thought possible.

"You fucker, you fucker, you fucker!" She is pounding on him, relentless.

I'm not quite sure what's happening, but he's not fighting back, although he does keep his forearms up around his head, half-heartedly trying to protect himself. He's not looking at her. He crouches down, giving her better access, his head dipped low. He's staring at the ground.

I am completely and totally confused, but somehow not afraid for our safety. I'm more scared for him. A few seconds later, I finally think to look at the flier he shoved at me. Now I feel no urge to try to help him. It's Emily and Harper.

Emily stops because she's exhausted, and unsurprisingly, all this activity has riled up her injuries. She walks around so she's in front of him and slaps him hard across the face. Then she whispers, "Oakley, you self-centered prick, you may have gotten Harper killed!"

CHAPTER NINETEEN

Thursday, September 10, 2009, Time Unknown

HARPER

It doesn't seem possible that a body can hurt this bad and still be alive. The light hurts my eyes, even the broken one. If I am going to survive, if I am going to make a run for it—*when, not if*—the opportunity presents itself, I have to know what pieces of me work and what don't. A normal, sane, intelligent person would accept that her chance of success is slim. Unfortunately, I don't have the luxury of being a normal, sane, intelligent person.

That would make me a dead person.

My left arm isn't working. I'm pretty sure it's broken at the shoulder. The good news is, the burning pain ended a while ago, and now I'm numb on that side. The bad news is, the fire in the places where they cut strips of skin from my breasts and belly and upper thighs is working overtime to keep me awake. If I breathe wrong, the pain drags a scream from the bottom of my soul.

How long since his last visit? Has it been hours? Days? No idea, really, but if a gun were held to my head—ha! that'd be a nice change!—I'd guess it's been a day.

I tentatively touch one of the newest cuts. It's gooey, and sticky, and smells—bad. Not like normal blood.

My left eye is swollen shut, and aches. I think maybe my right cheekbone is broken, too. I make a careful, gentle assessment with my right hand, trying not to catch one of my jagged nails on the torn skin. That would hurt. That would hurt a lot. So yeah, my cheekbone is broken, and whatever the bone under my eyebrow is called, that's a goner too. Good thing I'm not going to Hollywood to become an actress. A writer doesn't have to look good. Scars might even add to the mystique. Lord knows I'm going to have a really good origin story after this.

My legs work. They hurt so bad, but they work. Large purple and green bruises cover me like ugly tights.

If I turn just right, I can see the raw, oozy, bloody flesh of my feet. Holy hell. They are going to be a big problem. The crazy bitch has a thing for feet. The tops of my feet are covered with red burns. Angry. Infected.

Also, an accurate summation of my current emotional status.

How, exactly, do I think I can walk? I'm a total wimp. I cry when I take out a splinter. Can I suck through the pain?

One bite at a time, Harpy, one bite at a time.

Speaking of bites, I'm so hungry. I'm almost hungry enough to want to eat the terrible stuff Vero feeds us—*feeds you, Harp. Em is gone*—in the metal bowl. It tastes terrible, and has the texture of canned stew. I'm pretty sure it's some crappy cheap dog food. If it's good enough for Spot, it's good enough for me.

If I can get past Vero, I might be able to make my way outside. Find a car. A bike. A pony, for effs sake. A freaking skateboard. Anything to get away from this horror show.

If I can't get outside, maybe I can find a phone. Call for help. But call—who? Not the cops. Most definitely not the freaking cops.

There is also the tiny fact that I am inappropriately dressed for escaping. I am bare-ass naked. The crazy bitch took our clothes as soon as the Sheriff delivered us into her care. When she stripped me, Vero announced my clothes would look better on her than the "little *putas*." Vero is a stunner, so she might be right.

I'm running out of positive thoughts. My well of determination is close to dry. It is getting damn hard to hold onto hope, especially since he's taken Em away. It was easier to fight when there were two of us. Now I'm alone. I don't know if Em is alive or if she's dead.

Lots of challenges. Lots of obstacles. Not going to lie, Harpy, the odds aren't good.

CHAPTER TWENTY

Thursday, September 10, 2009, Late Night

ANGEL

Well, hell. I'm rarely surprised, but he got me. The infamous Oakley has returned to the scene of the crime. Maybe he's not the total douche I thought he was. Emily sits on the bench of the picnic table and cries soft, soundless tears. She won't look at him.

Oakley is upright, leaning against the column she'd claimed moments ago. He's staring at her, silent, and I'm not sure whether it's because he's shocked he found her, because of the way she looks, or because she tried to beat the holy hell out of him. Probably all of it.

"You have good timing, I guess," I say after a while. I'm sitting on top of the table now. It gives me a better view over the top of Emily's head and puts me in a position that feels protective. Then I realize it's not wise for the three of us to be sitting here together, exposed. But we have another option.

"Come on. We're going to your car," I jump down from the table. Oakley doesn't argue, just tags along behind us. Smart man. Out of the corner of my eye I see him watching Emily's painful movements. He's white as a sheet.

Emily slides into the passenger seat like it's an old friend. Her anger is still there, but the fire of it has mellowed. I slip into the back seat. Once Oakley is in, I instruct him to lock the doors. There's a Gatorade in the cup holder between the front seats, and

Emily grabs it and takes a long drink. Angry as she is, this was her boyfriend—who knows if they can get past this?—and she's still got the muscle memory of him and their life together. This is the most normal I've seen her.

Oakley seems to understand he can't be the first one to speak. If he does something stupid, like ask, "Where have you been?" Emily might very well kill him.

We sit in silence for quite a while. Eventually, Emily tells him in highlights about being kidnapped, taken to the ranch, tortured, and put outside to be hunted. By the time she gets to the part about me and the truck stop bathroom, she's crying. I'm pretty sure he's been crying for a while now. He keeps whispering, "Oh my God, I'm so sorry." I believe he is.

I mean, the fact he's here, looking for them, says a lot. He could have assumed they got to LA on their own and never given it a second thought. Or he could've alerted someone from the convenience of his comfy bed back in Tennessee. He didn't. He's here.

Now that Emily is calm, he's allowed to speak, within reason. It turns out he came back the same night he left them here. He made it to Oklahoma City, realized he'd been a jerk—although that's not exactly what he said to himself—and turned around to pick them up.

They were gone.

He assumed they'd hitchhiked. The idea made him uneasy. He kept calling their phones, but both went right to voice mail. He figured their batteries were dead since they'd all three been sharing his charger. At the butt-crack of dawn (his words), he headed back to Tennessee. By the time he got home, he'd worked himself into a bit of a lather, as the old folks and people from Tennessee say. He was tired after driving 13 hours, and he was pissed, and, if he was honest, feeling like shit for causing all this drama. He went to bed and figured he'd hear from Emily the next day.

Except her phone still went right to voice mail, as did Harper's.

He called their friend in LA, who was going to let them crash until they found their own place. The girls hadn't got there yet, and she hadn't heard from either of them. It was at least a full day's drive from the rest stop to LA if you drove straight through, and they'd probably have to catch a few different rides or find a Greyhound or something. He was worried, but not freaked out yet.

The second day, he was nervous. They still hadn't showed up, and the phones still went to voice mail. On the third day, he couldn't sleep. The fourth day, he told his boss at the car dealership where he worked, he needed to take some personal time. He got fired. Didn't matter. Something was wrong. He headed back to Texas.

Oakley had been here for three weeks. At first, he stayed in a roach motel. He started sleeping in the Camry when cash ran low. He printed fliers, and every night, he came back, around the same time he had dropped Harper and Emily off. He figured if anyone remembered them, it would be a truck driver, because a trucker might come through at about the same time if they were on a regular schedule.

Tonight was going to be his last night. If he didn't find them, he was going to the FBI. He wasn't sure that was exactly the right thing to do, but it was what he was going to do.

"Why wouldn't you just call the local police?" I ask from the back seat. Of course, I think I already know the answer.

"I did. I took fliers to every police and sheriff's department within a couple of hours of here. I even talked to a sheriff right over there." Oakley points to the building. "I gave him a flier. He said he'd keep an eye out, and if they—you—still didn't turn up, I should come in and make a formal report."

CHAPTER TWENTY-ONE

Thursday, September 10, 2009, Time Unknown

HARPER

"Gotta get back," the Sheriff grunts. His voice continues to fascinate me. Someday, I hope, I'll write about it. The slowness of it. The weird sing-songedness. Is that a word? Songedness? Probably not, but I don't happen to have a dictionary handy just now to look it up. The weird thing about his voice, and it took a while to figure it out, is that it's totally different from when he picked us up at the rest stop. That guy was upbeat, friendly, even charming. Yes! That's it. He had been *charming*.

This guy, with his weird voice, is definitely not charming. And his drawl is thicker, more country.

From my cage, with all the overhead lights on, I can see his jeans are wet like he walked through water. Or peed himself. I snicker at that but stop fast when I see Vero's head swivel toward me. I don't want attention from her. Now or ever. She's much worse than he is. I have to be careful. Pain and fear and trauma are making me giddy. *Don't let them win, Harpy. Don't let them win. You have to find Em.*

"You will go back to work. I will look for the dumb bitch. Then, when I find her, if she's not dead, I'll bring her back here for you," Vero says in her thickly-accented English. She's from somewhere south of Texas, but I can't guess where. Mexico? Guadalajara? Venezuela? Brazil? "I'll fatten her up so the next release will be very much fun for you."

The words bounce in my brain. *If she's not dead? They don't know whether she's dead? Wouldn't they know? That means the Sheriff didn't kill her, at least. Em could still be alive somewhere!*

Dear Sheriff, upholder of the law, representative of the great state of Texas, rapist, abuser, and hunter of women, bounces his head once. "You better not end her. That's for me." He swings his head my way, and too late, I try to play dead, but they both know I'm alive and awake. "I need to burn some of this energy 'fore I go home. Get her up."

I have nothing left to resist. My body is so ravaged I have nothing more to fight with. I can't fight, but I can try to survive, and that means protecting my mind. I will not give them the satisfaction of crying. I will not show them my fear. I muster up a smirk. "Oh, are we playing more games? Fun!"

I sing as loudly as I can, *100 bottles of beer on the wall, 100 bottles of beer... Take one down... pass it around...*

At bottle 90, they have me strapped face down on the exam table. It's a custom job, I think, because it's the kind chiropractors use, with a hole for your face, but it also has stirrups at the bottom, like at the gyno. My broken shoulder screams.

At 80 bottles, Vero shoves a hard Styrofoam workout roller under my belly, pushing my hips up. As I sing about 70 bottles, my knees are strapped down, wide apart, all of me exposed. At 60 bottles, I hear something electric come to life.

The bottles fall from the wall and shatter.

CHAPTER TWENTY-TWO

Thursday, September 10, 2009, Late Night

ANGEL

"Are you absolutely sure about this?" Emily asks from the passenger seat of Oakley's Camry. The clock glows in the dark. Eleven-forty-four p.m. We're parked at the far edge of the rest stop, near the lane vehicles use to re-merge into traffic.

Not at all, I think, but I say, forcing confidence, "I'm fine. It'll be fine. It's a good plan." And yet my hand sits, motionless, on the handle of the door.

"It's our only plan," Emily mumbles, and it would be funny if it weren't true.

Oakley is silent, maybe because he realizes none of this would be happening if not for him. Or, maybe he's just the not-so-strong but very silent type. I'm not sure what to make of him yet.

"You have your phone in your pocket, not the backpack," Emily says, not a question, but confirmation. I pull the iPhone from the front left pocket of my men's jeans. No plan will ever be carried out successfully in women's jeans with their tiny, useless pockets.

I push the door open before I can chicken out. The weight of the backpack slung over my shoulder, my constant friend these past few years, is reassuring. I smile, overlarge and intentionally cheesy, at Emily. She looks about to cry. "Once he picks me up, follow from a safe distance. If we somehow get separated, I'll text you landmarks as soon as I can." Oakley's number is now saved on my phone.

"What if he finds the phone? He had his hands all over us." Emily says. Next to her, Oakley winces.

I slide the phone from my jeans and push it into the left side of my sports bra. CB would have a fit, but CB's not here. The Van Halen T-shirt I'm wearing is loose enough to conceal odd bulges in the dark. Once the sun comes up, well, I'll worry about that later. I don't want to think about his hands on me, so I don't.

I slap the roof of the car and step away. "We've got this. We're going to rescue Harper and give this ass hat the justice he deserves."

Emily's grunt of approval is the last thing I hear as I cross the asphalt toward the rest stop. I clutch the straps of the backpack to my chest like a lifeline. I walk in front of the sleeping truckers, along the main concourse of the rest stop, toward a handful of minivans and station wagons and sports cars that have pulled in for snacks or bio breaks or to let the dog water the Texas grass.

This plan is far from perfect. There is no guarantee Jonny Law will show up. Even if he does, it might be hours from now. I may have a lot of time to kill. I think about what an ordinary girl would do if she were sitting alone, at a rest stop overnight. She might try to sleep but would probably be too nervous. Should I sit at one of the picnic tables or find a grassy spot? I won't be able to play games on my phone; gotta keep it safely out of sight. I can't sit here doing nothing, though. That will exacerbate—God, I love that word—my stress. I eventually decide to read. It'll suggest I'm a bit nerdy, which could be good for this particular mission. Besides, it's true.

For nearly an hour, I huddle over the table, a book flattened under my hand. *This is impossible.* My eyes skim the same paragraphs repeatedly, but I can't say whether I'm staring at *War and Peace* or *Flowers in the Attic*. Eventually, I give up, put the book in the backpack, and make a pillow with my forearms to pretend to sleep.

Except somehow, stupidly, I actually fall asleep.

A male voice behind me wakes me with a jolt, and I come all too close to wetting myself.

"Miss? Are you all right?"

I turn, expecting to see a man wearing a uniform, or at least a badge. Instead, I see a smiling, balding dad wearing baggy red nylon shorts and socks with sandals. Two little girls, five or six years old, hover behind him, smiling shyly. They've been traveling a while. Their hair is a mess, and their mismatched clothes have stains from ice cream and car snacks. They look gloriously happy.

I nearly burst out laughing, a cocktail of relief and stress making me giddy. "I'm fine. But thank you!"

The dad smiles again. "You hungry? Need money? A ride? My wife and girls will never forgive me if we leave you here in the middle of nowhere without help."

"My mom is on her way to get me. She should be here any time now." I say, forcing myself to relax. "I'm just tired. It's been a long day!" *Day, week, month, lifetime.*

"Alright, then. Girls! Back to the Jenkins-mobile!" The man grins, and the girls gallop like horses toward a newish, giant-sized SUV. Everything's bigger in Texas. A woman opens the back door to help the kids inside and smiles at me. The man slides into the driver's seat, and I feel a spark of melancholy. If I'd had a family like that when I was small, what would my life be like?

The family pulls out.

A brown Texas Sheriff SUV pulls in.

CHAPTER TWENTY-THREE

Friday, September 11, 2009, Early Morning

ANGEL

I don't bother to hide my gawking. It would be weird if I didn't stare. The sicko chicks who crush on killers and rapists will be all over this guy. He's got thick dark hair that's just a little bit too long, bordering on cool. His skin is tan and not too leathery, except for the laugh lines at the corners of sparkling blue eyes. Apparently local sheriffs don't wear a uniform, because he's dressed in nice fitting jeans, a white button down shirt, and cowboy boots. If it weren't for the sheriff's vehicle, you'd never know he wasn't just any old hunky Texas cowboy. He isn't attractive; he's downright beautiful. Is having women throw themselves at you so difficult you need to torture and kill them to feel special?

"Whatcha doin' out here all by your lonesome, young lady?" He asks, smiling down from his height of six-foot somethin'. His watery-blue eyes are framed by lashes so thick they look fake.

I'm torn. Do I play this sullen or sweet? Thinking about Em, I decide on sweet. "I got a ride from a couple, but the woman got mad and made her boyfriend drop me off here." I keep my voice soft. I'm nobody, just a shy lost girl.

"Well, she was just jealous. You're a pretty little thing, aren't ya." That would sound pervy coming from some, but his tone makes it a statement of fact, not an icky unwanted comment from an older man. He shoves his hands into the front pockets of his jeans, not threatening in the least. "Now, I can't leave you out here in the middle of nowhere on your own. It would go against my ethics as a law man, a human, and a father."

My lower lip quivers. He assumes it's because I'm afraid of being out here alone. *No, asshole, it's because I know girls are much safer out here in the middle of nowhere than if they go with you.*

"Do you have people you can call? Family? Friends?"

Crap. What do I say? If I have someone to call, someone waiting for me, will that change his plans? I decide to go with the truth. "My mom and brother died, and my dad's in prison."

"I'm truly sorry to hear that." He drawls, and he does look sorry. Jonny Law is one hell of an actor. "Well, what say I take you into town and get you a motel room for the night." It's a statement, not a question.

"I don't have money for a motel room." I shake my head.

"Now, don't you worry yourself about that. All taken care of. You're not the first and you won't be the last to find herself in a dire situation. We know how to handle these things here in Waterford County." The words are delivered so cheerfully it nearly makes me puke. How? How can this charming, seemingly kind man hide so much darkness? Is it that easy to hide the monster inside?

And then I think of the man who took me and my brother. *Yes. Yes, it's really that easy.*

I let him lead me to his SUV, branded in big, bold letters, Waterford County Sheriff. He opens the back passenger door and motions for me to get in. As I slide onto the seat, he says, "I'll need that," and quickly takes my backpack from my lap before I can even think to grab it. "Against the rules to allow bags in the back of the vehicle."

My gut threatens a good old heave-ho as I watch the backpack go. I keep one foot on the ground, my butt perched on the seat, not 100% committed to getting inside. I watch him put the pack in the hatch of the SUV, behind a gate I can't get past. God, this is real.

Please, Oakley, don't screw this up.

"Pull your foot on in there," he directs gently and winks. I slide all the way in. Is this my new prison? Have I just made a terrible, terrible mistake?

The sound of the door locking behind me flips a switch I hadn't anticipated. I can't tell you what book I was pretending to read thirty minutes ago, but memories of Jennifer stealing Bud and me from our front yard are suddenly so clear, so crisp, it feels like I'm watching a movie. My body reacts to the same fear of not knowing what is happening, the panic and terror of waking up in a basement apartment. Why did I think this was smart? *I'm a fool! I'm such a fool!*

I fight to control my panic, resist the urge to pound on the windows and scream until someone comes to save me, to let me out before it's too late.

Deep breaths. Deep breaths. You're safe. Emily and Oakley are watching. You still have your phone. It's okay. It's going to be okay. Bud's voice flows through me, and my panic mellows to a more manageable level of concern.

When the driver's door opens, I jump. He slides in, whistling. What is he whistling? The song is familiar. Not modern, not current, but—I know it. Lyrics dance in the back of my brain, and I reach for them, knowing somehow the words are important. It evades me.

He doesn't speak. He keeps whistling the song, over and over. I squeeze into the corner and stare out the window, noting anything that can remotely be considered a landmark, just in case.

Twenty minutes later, lights appear in the distance. There are only a few at first, then lots: street lights, stop lights, neon lights outside stores, the occasional blue light of a TV through a front window.

Emily said he drove them through a town. He just never stopped.

"What town is this?" I ask.

He does not answer.

My gut is gurgling and bubbling. Bud chimes in again. *You've got this. Everything's fine. Emily and Oakley are back there. It's scary right now, but pretty soon, he'll take you to Harper, and you'll save her, and Emily and Harper will tell the good cops about this guy, and he'll never hurt another girl again. Because you're brave. You've got this, Angel. You're okay. Olivia would be proud.*

That almost makes me laugh. Olivia, proud of me? Not likely. Olivia rarely gives me credit for anything, much less being brave or strong. Olivia once said I was the biggest baby she'd ever met. Even after we escaped, mostly due to my actions, she's never taken it back.

If my plan works, I'll prove Olivia wrong once and for all. Maybe I'll go to the trial after all. Sit in the stands. Stare down Alfred.

I'm so caught up envisioning my own braveness it takes me a beat to realize we're pulling up in front of a small, clean motel. "Where are—"

He opens the door for me, and I nearly fall out. He's pulling my backpack from the hatch. I hope to God I don't look as surprised as I feel. He hands me my bag, puts a hand on my back, and gently but firmly navigates me to the door of the motel.

I resist, confused. "What are we doing here?" I jerk away from him. Then I realize I'm stupid. This is what he said he was going to do, so I shouldn't be freaking out. But, I rationalize, bad things happen to girls brought to motels in the middle of the night. Case in point: Winslow, Arizona.

"I promised you a safe place to sleep. The owner is a friend. If she has a spare room, she'll be more than pleased to lend it to you until morning." This Texas lawman, torturer, and abuser of women, a man who likes to hunt humans for fun, smiles down at me and opens the motel office door, making bells jingle.

A grandmotherly woman appears almost instantly, beaming. It has to be two in the morning, yet she looks bright-eyed and rested—and very happy to see him. "Jonny! You handsome thing! And who is this?"

"Good question! I never asked your name." He smiles at me again. What's with all the damn smiling? Who's this freaking happy all the time?

I try to regain my composure. I offer the first name I think of. "Rachel."

"Pretty name for a pretty girl," the woman coos. She pats Jonny's hand then makes a shooing motion toward the door. This isn't the first time he's showed up at her motel late at night with a stray. "We've got this. You get back to protecting citizens from the bad guys! Go on now. I'll be sure to get her what she needs tonight and take care of her in the morning before we send her safely on her way."

And with that reassurance, Jonny Law tips his hat at me, winks at the woman and disappears into the night.

What the hell.

CHAPTER TWENTY-FOUR

Friday, September 11, 2009, Early Morning

ANGEL

For the first ten minutes, I sat on the edge of the motel bed, fuming and confused. Now I'm up and pacing. I know I should be happy that a freaking pervert didn't kidnap me. But *why* didn't he? What's different about me than what he saw in Emily and Harper?

That woman at the front desk acted like this has happened before, right? She wasn't surprised by him showing up with me.

For a minute I lose my mind and go on a little rant. *Am I ugly? Why didn't he want to take me and rape me and hunt me? Why? What's wrong with me?*

Bud chimes in. *Good God, Angel, don't be an egomaniac. You're pretty, and you know it. Even he said so. That's not why. It's something else.*

Well, hell, that's kind of mean. Fair, but mean.

Maybe I popped up on the wrong night of his schedule. That makes sense. Plus, he already has at least one girl. As far as he knows, he has two. If I were a monster, I would limit myself to be sure I didn't take on too much.

The vibration of my cellphone, buried so deep in my bra it's creeping into my arm pit, jerks me out of my thoughts. It's a Tennessee number. Emily on Oakley's phone. "Are you going to stay in there? Do you want us to come in? Do you want to come out?"

"I'm coming out. Park across the street, away from lights. Just in case someone's watching, I don't want to make it easy." I drop the key on the table by the door and slip out, trying to get my anger and, if I'm honest, my embarrassment, under control.

"Was that the guy?" I slip into the back seat of Oakley's Toyota, hauling my backpack in behind me. It gets caught in the door, and I growl and jerk it inside, then slam the door harder than I need to, as if the door is the one that rejected me. I didn't use to have a temper, but I've grown one in the last couple of years. CB isn't a fan. I lean into the space between the front seats. "Was that the right cop?"

Emily nods. "It looked like him from where we were. Tall, dark hair, good looking, laugh lines around his eyes?"

"Did he have a name tag?" Oakley asks.

I grunt. "No, no badge or tag or even a star. If he hadn't got out of the sheriff's car he could've been anyone."

We sit in silence for a minute.

Finally, Emily asks, "Why didn't he take you?" It has an entirely different meaning for her. What was it about Emily and Harper that made them okay to take? What made it all right to pick them off the street, damage them, and even end their lives?

Empathy triumphs over my bruised ego. "Maybe he's working a shift that doesn't give him time to drive to the ranch. Or maybe he only takes one or two girls at a time. Who you are has nothing to do with it. You were just in the wrong place at the wrong time."

Except that hadn't been the case with her, or Olivia, or Grace. Alfred had sought them out, chosen them specifically, planned for each of them. Except Bud. Bud was an accident.

But this was different. Strictly a crime of opportunity.

"What do we do now?" Emily asks, her voice stronger but fake, too, like she's making herself sound tougher and healthier than she is. For Oakley? Or for herself?

"We regroup," I say confidently. I'm channeling CB here. She believes she will succeed, always, whether it's getting a job, picking a short-term romantic interest, or riding in to save the day. It isn't always easy, but in the end, she always wins.

We head back to our motel in Erick, Oklahoma. Oakley and Em squabble during the hour-long drive, although she's doing most of the squabbling because he's focused on absorbing everything that happened to her. Guilt is flowing off him like waves.

Once we get back to the motel, we need a Plan B. Time is not our friend.

Harper has been alone for two days.

CHAPTER TWENTY FIVE

Friday, September 11, 2009, Time Unknown

HARPER

Vero is in a good mood. I can hear her singing loudly in Spanish, and every once in a while she clicks her boots against the floor like she's doing a flamenco dance or something.

Maybe she's mad she can't find Em, or maybe she's happy she has me all to herself. Either way, I know it's not going to be good for me. Sometimes, when Dear Sheriff is gone for a few days, Vero sneaks in a game all her own. She's careful not to leave marks like his games do. I thought about telling him but since she's here all the time, and he's not, that seems like a bad idea.

Usually, after Dear Sheriff has his way with me, especially if he lets her participate, she's relatively quiet for a few days. Last night, she was participating all over the damn place. It was her idea to remove my eyelids so I can't hide from what they're doing to me. And it was her damned hand that slipped with the scalpel and sliced deep across my cornea and iris after she took the left lid. She'd be furious to know, if I felt like telling her, that I don't need my eyelid any longer. Thanks to her, I'm blind in that eye. Dear Sheriff got angry at her for the slip, so she never made it to my right eye.

I hear her humming, and the humming is getting closer.

She's at the cage door, grinning. In her hand she holds a thin metal wand. It's long, more than a foot, about an inch in diameter. At one end, there are two prongs. "You ever see one of these before?"

She asks, eagerly, smiling at the thing like it's her lover.

I don't bother to respond.

"This is my friend, picana. It's one of my most favoritest toys," she says in her thick accent. "You know why? Because it causes oh-so-much pain," she tips her head, and turns the smile from the wand to me, "but it doesn't kill you! Isn't that magnifico? And the very best part? It leaves no marks. At least, not if you use it in places that are dark."

And she laughs, and laughs, and laughs.

CHAPTER TWENTY-SIX

Friday, September 11, 2009, Early Morning

ANGEL

'Middle of the night' is relative. In a suburban neighborhood, 2:00 a.m. is sleepy time for most people. At a motel on a busy transportation interstate, not so much. Trucks move in and out as their drivers start or end a driving shift. People traveling to visit family, or moving from one side of the country to another, try to push through. It's never quiet where people are moving.

As I stand at the ice machine, refilling the bucket for the third time, I watch two cars leave in front of the Diner and another two take their spots. Interstates never sleep.

The guests in Room 111 are wide awake.

At this point, I'm pretty sure Em is back to running on adrenalin. No way a person could go through everything she's been through and still be upright unless there's unfiltered stress juice running through her veins.

Oakley needs to convince the woman to get some rest. She won't be good to anyone if she collapses.

I'd propped the door open with a shoe when I left, so I knock it out of the way with my bare foot, then kick it closed behind me. I hand the ice bucket to Em and offer a cold drink to Oakley. He continues to look miserable. I'm starting to feel a little sorry for him. Not sorry enough to give him a pass, but sorry enough to check my tone when I speak to him. I slip into one of the chairs at the table and pull the laptop over.

"We need to figure out who this asshole is," I say, keys clicking under my fingers. Now we know which Sheriff's office he's with, thanks to the state of Texas branding the SUV.

I search for news about the Waterford County Sheriff. Most of the stories that come up have photos of crime scenes and cruisers, but very few actual law enforcement officers. A couple of officers received awards or did something in the community that brought them fame and glory, and their photo in the paper. I type in the name "Johnny" and change the search from all results to images and turn the screen toward Emily. There are five Johnnys at the Waterford County Sheriff's office. One, in particular, seems to participate in every bake sale and fund-raising event offered. I turn the screen toward Emily.

"That's him!" Emily gasps.

I agree. "That's the asshole."

"Which?" Oakley asks since there are a couple of men on the screen, "This fat guy? He doesn't look the one I talked to at the rest stop."

"No! The stupidly good-looking one. That's him!" Em nearly yells.

I'm not surprised, but I am sad. Our friend is not a deputy; he's the actual elected sheriff. As far as the townspeople know, he's a do-gooder who looks out for them and keeps them safe in their beds at night. That's why the motel lady was so chipper.

If only they knew their beloved do-gooder is really the worst kind of evil doer. I turn the laptop back and click to go deeper. "Jonny has no H—oh Lord—his full name is Jonny Johnson. That could make anyone mean."

I instantly feel bad. Tired or not, I shouldn't make jokes. "He was a high school football star. Lost his parents while still in school. Now he's married to a Realtor who was a beauty queen, and her daddy is big in oil or something. They live in Wichita Falls."

Then I swallow hard. The saliva in my mouth turns bitter. "Each year, Sheriff Johnson raises more than $20,000 for the school system by," I pause again, hating the words I read next, "leading specialty hunts."

CHAPTER TWENTY-SEVEN

Friday, September 11, 2009, Early Morning

ANGEL

"Tell me what she was like before." I ask Oakley while we listen to the sound of running water in the bathroom.

The question makes Oakley look almost happy. It's the first time I've seen any sort of lightness in him since we've met. It's so clear he loves her; I can't help but wonder about the momentary stupidity that caused all of this. He doesn't seem the type to think he's entitled to sex. I suspect the threesome was an idea planted in his head by someone else.

He looks at me, and his eyes get a little bright, and I'm not sure if it's pride or tears or a bit of both. "She was really something. She *is* really something. Everybody loves her because she's sweet and funny and generous. She's an incredible singer. People come from all over just to watch her perform, and that's saying something when you're in Nashville. It's funny because she didn't want to leave Nashville—that was kind of Harper's idea. Harper wants to go to LA to be a writer, and she talked Emily into coming along. Some would say it's silly to leave Nashville, Tennessee, the music capital of the world, to go to LA if you want a music career. But Emily will do anything for Harper. And to be fair, Harper will do anything for Emily."

Except have a threesome, I think, but I let him continue.

"If she stayed in Nashville, Harper's right, Emily would've ended up working somewhere, maybe her parents' company, and would never have given music a serious shot. I'm not upset with Harper for wanting more for her friend."

I get the feeling that wasn't always the case. I have a feeling he was very upset about it initially. Maybe the proposed threesome was a lash-out of sorts.

"Emily isn't the bravest person or the strongest person. Her parents had problems, and it touched her. But she's trying. She works hard to overcome her anxiety. That doesn't mean she doesn't fail. She's got some ridiculous fears. She's afraid of spiders, but I guess a lot of people are. She's also afraid of small dogs. Not big ones, just the really little ones, like Chihuahuas and shitzus. They terrify her." Oakley smiles. "She's not great at public speaking. She gets really shy. But put her on a stage with music, nothing will stop her. She's just an amazing human. Not the *most* amazing human in the world but an amazing human. I love her. I would do anything to undo what I caused. I can't, I know, so I've got to try and fix it as best I can now."

Neither of us notice Emily in the bathroom doorway right away. No idea how much she heard. I hope Oakley's belief in her fills her back up, gives her the confidence she'll need to get through this and come out the other side with some semblance of herself intact.

CHAPTER TWENTY-EIGHT

Friday, September 11, 2009, Early Morning

ANGEL

When I first left Peter Baden's house, I planned to disappear completely. I'd let them get on with their lives while I got on with mine. Then CB and I had a conversation one night, where she pointed out they have a right to care about me and it's really pretty selfish of me not to at least let them know I'm okay once in a while. I created one of those free web-based email accounts to reassure Peter and Nick Winston, my personal FBI agent, that I'm alive. Nick sends dad jokes, mostly, even though he's not married, much less a dad. Peter is more conversational. He gives updates on Olivia and sends photos and stories about my niece, Rosie B. I let them know things are good, not to worry. About a year ago, I told them about CB but made them swear they wouldn't try to connect with her. I was afraid one of them would freak her out, and she'd stop letting me ride with her. They both promised, and I trust them... mostly.

There's no set cadence to when we connect. I drop them emails a couple of times a year. Nick is random about how often he reaches out. Peter, in true dad form, has a schedule. I hear from him once a month or so.

Peter has been a lot chattier in the last few months. Alfred's final trial is coming up, and he wants me to be there. He tries to bury that in the rest of the email with stories about Olivia's engagement, and his son Ben's first year of college, stuff like that. But each time, there's a single sentence at the bottom. "You coming back in November?" I never acknowledge it.

Em and Oakley are asleep. I'm staring at the laptop screen, debating whether to contact Nick. To give myself more time, I click the 'get mail' button, and a slew of ads for all sorts of crap sweep in. I don't understand how I get so much junk since I don't sign up for anything. I don't have a YouTube account or Facebook or shop online. It's annoying.

The first real email is a funny cat meme from Nick. I reply with an eye roll—really, a rolling eye—meme.

There are two emails from Peter. One has pictures of Rosie B's first kindergarten show-and-tell and doesn't mention the trial. That's because he saved it all for the second email. No more pussy footing around, I guess.

> *"Hey, kid,*
>
> *I know you don't want to think about this, much less talk about it, but the last (! Yay!) trial is coming up in early November. It would be great if you could come and be with us. You can see Rosie B, and Ben will be in town. Grace and Marnie are going to be here, too. The whole gang. I know this isn't your 'thing' (or is it 'thang'?). I can see that eyebrow of yours jumping up and down (grin). I miss that eyebrow.*
>
> *Fine, I'll stop beating around the proverbial bush. The reason I want you here is so I can be sure you're safe. We've had some weird mail lately from the fan club. I'm pretty confident they're all talk, but still, I'd feel soooo much better if you were with us. Marnie too. You know what a worrier she is. Think about it? Please?*
>
> *Your friend always, Peter."*

I'm a little nauseated but not surprised. From the beginning, Alfred has had a fan club. All the best serial killers have them. Men want to be them; women want to have their babies and breed future generations of death. Nick, and the FBI shrinks, say it's depressingly normal. It's disgusting and horrifying. It's also reality.

This is another reason I'm grateful to be on the road with CB. As far as the media and public are concerned, Peter is my guardian, and I am hidden away in a private, unnamed boarding school somewhere in North America. They have no idea I'm in a truck driving car and computer parts back and forth across the country. It would be impossible for the wackadoos to track me down. First, they'd have to know about CB. Then, they'd have to figure out our schedule, which changes weekly. If they got that far, they might find the house in Pittsboro, but there's so much security inside and out, we'd know they were there before they were even sure they'd found the right place.

I appreciate how much Peter cares and that he wants me to be where he can keep me safe, but I don't think I will be any safer anywhere than I am with CB. Well, present circumstances notwithstanding.

That's not the only reason I don't want to go back. I've thought about it quite a lot, and it comes down to: I am not me when I'm with them. I revert to being the girl I was in the Dollhouse, and that pisses me off. It's taken me a while to figure out who Angel is and I like her, most of the time. I'm comfortable in my skin, most of the time. I'm almost kinda happy... most of the time.

If I go back to LA, all of that changes.

I'm aware I'm being selfish. It's not fair to any of them for me to be a jerk about going back for the trial. But this is one of those times I like to point out I'm only seventeen years old. I'm allowed moments of childishness. Much as I hate that about myself, when it comes to anything related to my time in the Dollhouse, I'm not just a kid; I'm a goddamn toddler. A whiny, whimpering, selfish toddler.

I click the **Reply** button. "Thanks for the pics. I'll think about it." I hit **send**.

CHAPTER TWENTY-NINE

Friday, September 11, 2009, Early Morning

ANGEL

I need some fresh air and perspective. While this situation with Emily is stressful, Peter's email has taken over the worry zones in my mind. I've been hiding things from CB. Well, not hiding, really. But not being 100% truthful. There's a difference, I think. I haven't told her Alfred's last trial is coming up, because I have zero intention of going.

I slip through the gate around the pool, ignoring the "Closed 10 pm to 8 am" sign. If they meant it, they'd lock it. I pick a plastic lounge chair in a dark corner and stretch out, staring up. There are stars, obviously, but the lights from the city block them. One of my favorite things is when we pull into a rest stop in the middle of nowhere on a clear night. I'll climb onto *Casita's* roof and lay on my back, looking up at the sky.

That's where Bud is, twinkling bright, watching over me.

Yeah, yeah, I know that isn't true, but I need a Bud stand-in, and a star is the easiest way to carry him. So tonight—I suppose it's really morning—I struggle until I finally find a bright dot far up and to the west. I'll pretend I don't know it's probably a satellite.

Bud would be mad at me. He'd say it isn't fair to make Olivia go it alone. She's been to all the other trials—in Indiana, and Wyoming, and the civil case where we were awarded money from Alfred's estate.

Olivia would say I'm a baby, like always. Peter would tell me, *of course* he understands, but deep down, he'll resent me for turning my back on his daughter. At least that's how I'd be if I were him.

I feel angry and defensive, even though no one has actually said any of these things to me. CB would say I've got a case of MSU— "making shit up." Yeah, she's probably right. Still, I want to talk with Bud. He's got good insight.

Hey, Bud.

Hey, A.

Miss ya.

Same.

Need your brotherly advice—I don't even get the thought out before I hear his voice, frustrated and annoyed, in my head.

You need to chill out. Take a couple of deep breaths. Think it through and tell yourself the truth. Why don't you want to go to LA?

I don't want to see Alfred.

That's bullshit. He can't hurt you. Hell, you might not even see him. Spill it.

I take in a deep breath, then blow it out, long and slow. *This is going to make me sound like an asshole. I don't want to see Olivia. Or Peter. Or... Rosie B.*

In my head, he's pissed. *Of course you want to see her. Don't be a fool. That's my kid. Your flesh and blood. Our flesh and blood. The last piece of me. Peter adopted her, but she's the last Evanston. Do not turn your back on her. That, I will not forgive.*

Maybe he really is talking to me from that star-slash-satellite. That's exactly what he'd say.

It feels as though it's starting to rain. Then I realize no, it's just tears falling onto my hand. *Damn it.* I hate being such a baby. *She really is the cutest kid on the planet. And smart, and funny, and sweet. She's just like you—except for the sweet part. Peter sent a picture of her standing on the seat of her trike. Daredevil.*

The star-slash-satellite I call my brother says, *It would be way better if you'd see her instead of watching her grow up through pictures. My kid needs her Aunt Angel, so she knows she comes from Evanston stock. Can't have her growing up thinking she's just another California rich kid.*

As if it's better to be a poor Indiana kid? I roll my eyes. Yes, yes, I understand I'm actually sassing my own damn self. When you've been through what I've been through, you're allowed to be a little wacky. These little convos with my bro are a coping mechanism. I'm pretty sure that's what a shrink would say, anyway.

Back to the trial. Why don't you want to see Olivia and Peter? Bud star asks.

It pisses me off. It hurts. I whisper the last part because admitting it gives the pain more strength. *It makes me so angry. I know it's not fair, not right, but it's what I feel, and because I know it's not right or fair, I'm embarrassed that I feel that way, which makes me madder. Circle of doom.*

What exactly pisses you off?

The tears are really coming now. *Them. Their happy little family. Olivia got to keep her father and her brother. She has a part of you with Rosie B. She has everything. Everything I lost, she still has. So she can have the ugly part, too.*

I kind of get that. It sure sucks that you lost mom and me. It's not fair, not at all. But it's not Olivia's fault, either. She lost things, too. Now she's losing you—even though you're still here. And that's your choice.

Wow, you're preachy for a dead guy.

Bud Star laughs. *I'm just your mouthpiece. You're the preachy one.*

Did I tell you she's engaged? And she wrote a book about the Doll-house? She's barely nineteen. That seems like a lot of grown up stuff.

I think I may have heard mention during a previous rant, Bud Star says.

How do you feel about that?

Happy. About her being engaged, anyway. She deserves love. Not so sure about the book, but that's up to her, I guess. Maybe that's how she needs to process it.

Once that book is out, they're never going to leave us alone. The people. The press. The Christmas Miracle will never fade away. I hate her for that.

Bud Star grunts. *You do not hate her. Stop being dramatic. Do you honestly think they'd let it fade away, even without a book? You know better.*

I watch a soft white cloud drift across the dark sky, temporarily blocking my line of sight to the Bud Star. What kind of person has conversations with stars, like they're real people? Maybe I caught some of Alfred's crazy while we were locked in that damn basement.

Right now, I want to focus on Emily, and saving Harper. I'll think about the trial later.

Bud Star isn't done yet, though. *Don't take it out on CB. She loves you, and you love her, and no lie, without her, you'd be dead by now. So you treat that woman with the respect she deserves, get your head out of your ass, and don't be a jerk.*

I stop looking at the star-slash-satellite and close my eyes. It's cold. I shove myself out of the plastic chair, swearing when my foot gets caught between strips of vinyl. When I get back to the room, Emily is asleep.

Oakley asks, "Feel better?"

I nod and hide in the bathroom.

CHAPTER THIRTY

Friday, September 11, 2009, Early Morning

ANGEL

"Since I wasn't good enough," I say, trying for a joking tone, but pretty sure I miss, "we're going to have to find another way to get to this ranch."

Oakley is sitting in one of the hard wood chairs, and Em and I are on the beds. I drum my fingers on my thigh. "I kind of have a connection at the FBI. On the one hand, it would be great to have that resource to ride in and bust Harper out. On the other hand, it seems like there are more potential problems calling him right now than there are solutions."

They're both looking at me, waiting to hear these potential problems. "He can't just drop everything and fly here to help us, for one." That's kind of a bullshit response because I know for a fact Nick would drop everything for me if I asked him to. "More importantly, it would take him a while to get up to speed, and we don't have a while."

Emily nods vigorously at that. Her mental anguish seems to be increasing. Right now, neither her body nor her mind is in a particularly good spot. Who could blame her?

"And, if Nick comes in with guns blazing, Jonny Law will know we're onto him. The Feds aren't exactly subtle. So, Nick shows up and starts asking questions, and our officer of the law has his crazy girlfriend do something to dispose of the evidence before we can figure out where he's keeping Harper. There's no time for a subtle sting operation here." I shake my head. "Unless I'm missing something, I don't think I can call Nick. Not yet."

Oakley says, "I get the impression you have another idea."

I nod. "We follow Jonny Law. Safely, from a distance. At some point, he's going to go to the ranch, and we'll be there to see where he goes."

All kinds of nerves cross Emily's face. I hold up a hand. "I said, from a distance. He won't even notice us." Which reminds me of something, and I turn to Oakley. "Except he will, if we're in a car with flaming red stripes across the hood."

Oakley looks confused, and then his mouth drops open like he's going to object. He closes it.

Even Emily looks upset at the idea of something happening to his pretty car. "What are you thinking? It won't be easy to make that just go away…"

"We can't make it go away. You'll need a different car. A common, boring car," I say with an apologetic look, still watching Oakley. Impressively, he doesn't flinch—much. I can tell it hurts, but he's up for a bit of hurt. "You'll need to find one of those quick sale lots, sell your car, and buy something else—fast."

Oakley swallows hard. He wants to protest. It's written all over his face. Instead he nods.

"Once we have a car, we'll stake out the sheriff's office. Because he's the actual sheriff and not a deputy, I'm hoping he keeps regular office hours. I'm going to call in the morning, act like I'm just a regular citizen. I don't think we need to sit outside all day. We can probably start watching after lunch." I look at Emily. She nods.

"It's 5:00 a.m. You two try to get a couple more hours of sleep." I suggest.

I start to toss the comforter from my bed to Oakley so he can sleep in the chair, but Emily says, "Come on, Oak." And with red-rimmed eyes, he stretches out next to her on the bed, and she rolls into the circle of his arms.

CHAPTER THIRTY-ONE

Friday, September 11, 2009, Morning

CB

The drop is quick and easy, in reality, although my nerves are shot to shit. *Casita* and I arrived in San Diego city limits at 7:30 a.m., and I had a text at 7:34 a.m. telling me where to park. My legit destination is a warehouse in the Grand Avenue area, but they send me to a truly unsavory motel at the east end of San Diego, direct me to park at a specific spot in the back, and tell me to wait.

My little pink and silver revolver is in my lap, tucked nice and safe between my thighs, just in case.

If not for the sound of the door raising, and then closing eight minutes later, I would never have known anyone entered my trailer. They were quiet as mice once they got their extorting asses inside.

A few minutes later, I get a text. "You did good. The photos will stay safe."

What the hell have I been carrying? And how am I going to keep these guys from turning me into a regular mule? No idea yet, but I will figure it out. This went way too smooth for them not to try and play the Lexi card again.

It's nearly 8:00 a.m. on Friday. I have to dump my legit load and get my ass back to Oklahoma City. The good news is, because I own my truck, I control my truck and my records. I followed the rules to get here, because I didn't want to aggravate my invisible companions. Rules or no rules, I'm not stopping for 10 useless hours on the way back. I'll drive until I need to fill up, then I'll power nap for a couple hours and get back on the road.

Chica one is safe, and now I need to get back to *chica* two so we can save *chicas* three and four. Time to burn like a roman candle and explode like stars across the sky.

CHAPTER THIRTY-TWO

Friday, September 11, 2009, Evening

ANGEL

Jonny Law isn't a 'clock out at five' kinda guy. We're still sitting in the car at quarter after eight. I know he's in today because I called this morning. I said I was a student and wanted to interview him for a school project.

We are sitting across from the cop shop in a dark blue Ford Taurus with paper plates. It's the most forgettable car they had at the lot, according to Oakley, and I believe him since he's a car guy. I feel kind of bad for him. His Camry was fully and lovingly customized. In a normal situation, he would've taken his time to sell it. He'd have made a lot more than he got in a fast trade for the Taurus. But the Ford has low miles and is a nice, boring color.

I could never be a cop. Stake-outs go against my tendency to fidget. And I can see how you might gain a pound or two. There's not much else to do except eat when you're this bored. In the five hours we've been parked here, we've had donuts, Mickey Ds, and now we're debating whether pizza or fried chicken is up next.

"That super-sized pop might not have been a good idea," Emily says, nibbling her lip.

"We should've kept CB's SuzieLoo." I'm slumped across the back seat, legs stretched out, eyes on the back door of the cop shop. There's a parking lot with a mix of personal and official vehicles.

"Her what?"

"SuzieLoo. It's a plastic funnel-type thing. She can pull down her pants and pee into it without stopping *Casita*. It's gross but effective in emergencies." I straighten, thinking I spot him, but it's another deputy with a similar build and coloring. My butt is going numb, and I'm having to fight to stay awake. I haven't slept more than an hour or two at a time since we met Emily.

"Very gross." Em agrees. "How long have you been a truck driver?"

"I'm not a driver. Legally you have to be twenty-one, and I'm only seventeen and a half. I just ride along with CB." I open and close, open and close the red-handled pocketknife.

"Why?" Emily asks after a pause. "Shouldn't you be in high school? Or college? You and CB aren't related."

"We are not related by blood, but we're family. You could say I'm in a home-schooling program. My home just has 18 wheels and moves around a lot."

"You'd rather be in a truck than at a real school?"

I wonder if Oakley's asleep. Then I see his eyes moving back and forth, scanning the parking lot, the front door, side doors. He's just the quiet type. "I have the freedom to be where I want to be, which is in *Casita*."

"I'm sorry I keep asking questions. But we've been here all day, and I can't talk about movies any longer," Emily says. She's not wrong. There are only so many hours you can discuss who made a better Batman. Christian Bale, of course. "Do you have a house somewhere? Or do you live in *Casita* all the time?"

"CB has a little house in Pittsboro, North Carolina. It's close to Durham, which is where most of the loads originate." I almost said 'we' have a little house, and 'our' loads, but I'm not comfortable saying that after our earlier argument.

"You're not from North Carolina, right? Wasn't it Indiana?" Oakley asks.

"Yes, but I had nothing to go back to there. Olivia's father, Peter, took me in, wanted to adopt me. I couldn't. Nothing felt right. Their family is very different from mine. They are still a unit, and I'd lost everything. I didn't fit. It didn't make sense. Or, rather, they didn't make sense to me. So, I left."

I rub my eyes, which are starting to burn. I need to remember to blink. "No matter how smart you think you are, heading out on your own is full of risks."

Emily grunts in agreement. "Where did you and CB meet?"

"In Winslow, Arizona." I laugh now, but it sure wasn't funny then. "Yep, that Winslow. She came to my rescue, and we've been riding together ever since."

CB is gonna be five-foot-two inches of pissed-off Latina. I expect I'll learn some new cuss words when we're in the same room again. I'm pretty sure she knows we're not exactly staying put the way she told us, but so far, I'm doing an okay job playing it cool. Emily even held it together when CB insisted on speaking with her at the motel. We didn't mention Oakley because CB's no dummy, and she'd figure out real quick that we're mobile, and lack of transport was one of the things that gave her the confidence to leave our butts in Erick. I wouldn't put it past her to sic some of her trucker buddies on us to be sure we stayed in our room.

I figure if she can keep secrets, so can I. I'm still pissed she won't tell me why she has to finish the load and couldn't get a friend to pick it up. Something feels—wrong. I can't think of a single thing that would make her choose a run over me or even Emily. CB's just not built that way. Someone needs help; she's there, probably taking off her shirt to keep you warm.

Our pending come-to-Jesus is going to be a two-way conversation.

CHAPTER THIRTY-THREE

Friday, September 11, 2009, Evening

C B

The phone in room 111 rings, and rings, and rings some more. I wouldn't be worried, except this is the second time I've called with no answer. I waited an hour between calls, so even if the girls went to the Diner for food, they should be back now.

Nope, they're off doing something they shouldn't be doing.

Damn it!

I dial Angel's cell. She answers on the second ring.

"How's it going?" I ask.

"Okay." She sounds guilty.

"How's Emily feeling?"

"Okay." Angel grunts. One-word answers. Oh yeah, she's up to something.

"She still in bed?" So far, she hasn't officially lied to me.

"No, she's up and around."

I bite down a smile. "Did you eat?"

"Yeah."

"Have you figured out the *pendejo's* name?"

"Yes! And you are not going to believe this!" She finally sounds normal.

I don't interrupt because once I let her know that I know she's not where I left her, there may be yelling. Who am I kidding? There definitely will be yelling. "Tell me!"

"He's the freaking Sheriff of Waterford County! He has three teen-age kids, including two daughters. So gross!"

Very gross. His two little princesses are safe at home while daddy rapes and tortures someone else's daughters.

"He's married to some ex-beauty queen. They live in Wichita Falls. He's won all these awards for his do-gooder work. Get this—he leads charity hunts." In her excitement she sounds exactly like the seventeen year old she is.

I slam my hand on the steering wheel. "Bastard! Anything else?"

"That's pretty much it." She's back to sounding evasive.

"Angel?" I keep my tone light.

"Yes?"

"Where are you right now?" I can't help it; there's a growl in the question.

She's silent for a long, long moment, then admits, "In a car outside the sheriff's station."

"What? Why? And where did you get a car? And—why? I told you to stay put until I get there. Whose car? You didn't steal a car, did you?" I taught her how once. Well, not exactly how to steal a car, but how to hot-wire one.

"Stop yelling!" Angel yells. Most of the time, it's easy to forget she's seventeen and not twenty-seven, but when she's in trouble—and she is most definitely in trouble—she's 100% teenager. "We're going to follow him when he leaves work and see if he goes to the ranch. It's Oakley's car -"

"Who the fuck is Oakley?"

"The guy who left Emily and Harper at the rest stop." She says this quietly as if she feels bad he'll hear her confess his sin.

"The asshole that wanted the threesome?"

"He's nice, actually. He's been looking for them since that night -"

"We will discuss Oatley's supposed virtues later. For now, get your asses back to the motel right this minute!" I'm yelling so loud my voice is bouncing back at me.

She's silent. I can picture her, one eyebrow up in defiance, staring at the phone. I've seen her do it with that foster dad of hers when she calls him and he says something she doesn't like. She will not pull that shit with me.

"Angel Evanston, you will instruct Oatley—"

"Oakley. With a K."

"I don't care if it's with a flying hyena. You will instruct Oat-Oakley to take you back to the motel. You and Emily will go inside and lock the door. He is welcome to sit outside and keep watch, but he may not enter the room. Do you hear me?" Yes, I realize this is stupid. We're not in a 50's sitcom. But I'm pissed and when I'm pissed I'm not always rational.

Angel is silent again. I picture the eyebrow.

"We have trust between us, Angel, and you broke that trust," I bring out the big guns. On the very few occasions we've battled, this always works.

Until today.

"Trust goes both ways. You couldn't stay with us, and now I can't stay in the motel room. This will work. We'll be safe. We'll follow him to the ranch, and as soon as we know where it is, we'll let you know, and you can meet us there. Then we'll all be together, and we can decide what to do next." She waits for a beat, then adds, "It'll get us much closer to finding Harper. If we have to wait for you and then start the stake-out all over again, it'll be at least another day, maybe two, before we even find the ranch, if we're lucky. You know I'm right."

I am silent now.

She says, "You asked me to trust you. I did. I do. And I'm asking you to trust me. Please, CB."

Fuck. Fuckity fuck.

"All right. But you stay the hell away from him. Do not get close.

Do not put yourself in his way. You promise me! On Bud! You promise me!"

The reference to her brother gets her. "I promise."

"You text me when you have some idea of which direction you're going—north, south, east, west. I'm driving as fast as I can. I will have to turn off 40 at some point." I take a breath. "Did you call Nick?"

"There's not anything he can do at this point except get snippy like you are." Angel says, and before I can snap at her for calling me snippy, she says, "I'll call him when we find the ranch. Have him send in the cavalry while we have Jonny Law in our sights."

That makes sense, I have to admit. I'm still pissed. And I'm nervous about getting anywhere near her pet FBI agent. No choice, though. This is worth the risk. "All right. And Angel?"

"Yes?" I can hear she knows what I'm going to say next.

"We're going to have one hell of a talk when this is over."

"I know." And she hangs up.

CHAPTER THIRTY-FOUR

Friday, September 11, 2009, Evening

ANGEL

"That girl ain't right." The woman's words were a badge of honor for me. The waitress hadn't meant for me to hear. She probably didn't think it was a good thing to not 'be right.' I already knew I wasn't 'right' and would never be 'right,' and I certainly didn't care if I fit into someone else's idea of what was 'right.'

I used to remember the woman's name, but not anymore. That was what, more than two years ago? The day I left the Baden house. I have a battered picture of that diner in a small wood memory box. The first photo I took with my fancy new Apple iPhone, a gift from Peter, my foster father, Olivia's dad. CB had it printed for me. That photo represents the first day of my new life. The day I left the Baden household, not because I felt unwanted, but because I didn't fit. I wasn't part of their world. I knew I had to find my own place, my own world without Bud. Without Shine, my mother. Just me. No longer afraid. Well, at least not always afraid.

I left LA and headed south and then east, with only a vague destination in mind. The first couple of weeks weren't half bad. I had money because Peter constantly shoved cash at me. He wanted me to have security, to know I could buy anything I needed or wanted. That was a new experience for sure. Before the Dollhouse, we were dirt poor. Junior, my father, is in prison for attempting to rob a bank. Bud and I lived with our mom, Sunshine, in a trailer at the edge of our small bumpkin town in the middle of nowhere, Indiana.

Having money in my pocket—lots of it—was a new feeling and one I didn't entirely trust. I split those bills up and hid them everywhere. A few singles and five dollar bills in the deep front pocket of my boy's Levi's. Not enough to draw attention, but enough to buy a Coke or sandwich. There were $20s folded and tucked into each sock, in the space under the arch. That took a bit of getting used to. I kept ten one-hundred-dollar bills rolled up in a plastic tampon applicator—clean, of course. Another $1,000 in the padding of my extra bra. Altogether, I had just over two thousand dollars. I figured it would last at least four or five months. Once I was a safe distance from LA, I'd look for work at a fast food joint until I figured out what was next. Teens can always get a job working fast food. Maybe I'd spend some time in New Mexico. Or Texas. Or, maybe I'd head north, and check out Montana.

That was the plan.

Two weeks into my new life, I stopped at the Tumbleweed Inn on the outskirts of Winslow, Arizona. All of Winslow was pretty much outskirts. If not for the Eagles song, would the town even exist? One of those bear/woods philosophy questions. But it is handily situated near Interstate 40, a major trucking route, and since my means of transport was the thumb, it suited me.

The old man at the desk gave me a metal door key with a plastic circle stamped 129 and nodded wordlessly in the direction of the room. The rooms opened directly onto the parking lot, which seemed the standard layout for places in my price range. No elevators or breakfast buffets here. I knew to ask for a room away from the ice machine and away from the pool if there was one.

Room 129 was around the back of the building. The floor was tile instead of carpet. A living room with a kitchenette, a wool-upholstered sofa in an ugly orange plaid, a folding card table with a torn vinyl top, and an old TV and VCR. A door opened to a bedroom with a queen bed. The bathroom was clean but needed updating.

I refused to look at the kitchenette. It reminded me too much of the kitchen in the Dollhouse.

I was exhausted, and it was late. There was only one door into the unit. After a couple of hours' rest, I'd move on. Winslow wasn't a place I felt like hanging around.

The shower was musty-smelling, so I stripped off my dirty road clothes and gave myself a quick wipe down with one of the thin, scratchy towels on the counter. I'd shower at a truck stop tomorrow.

I changed into a clean T-shirt and boxers and sat cross-legged on the bed. I pulled my beloved Rand-McNally road atlas from my pack. It was battered and dog-eared. I'd found it at a used bookstore in Lake Meade. Each night I explored its pages, wondering about the person or people who had studied it before, noticing their marks, scratches, and occasional notes. "Marcy's Donuts! Yum!"

Tomorrow I'd head east, maybe get to New Mexico if I lucked out and found the right ride. If not, I'd stop where I stopped and continue on the next day. I'd used exactly $337. Lots of time to find the next place.

Each motel night, before I went to sleep, I folded the next day's clothes, sat them on the nightstand next to the bed, and tucked my dirty clothes into the backpack. Then I put the backpack next to me, on the outside edge, like a crib guard. I'd spent months chained to a wall at night. I couldn't roll over because of the cable that tethered me. Now I luxuriated in the freedom to move, but recurring night terrors resulted in more than one fall to the floor before I worked out the backpack trick.

I put a chair under the doorknob and set a small, ugly vase on the chair seat. If someone shook it, the vase would fall to the tile floor and make a noise. I was probably paranoid. But after Alfred, I'd rather be paranoid than sorry.

I turned off the light in the main room, turned on the light in the bathroom, and left the door cracked just a bit, creating a night light of sorts. Then I went to the window and raised the sash, letting coolish air into the room. At the edge of the back lot, I saw a couple of rigs parked, lights off, drivers sleeping as I should be. The ceiling fan turned on with a wheezy rattle, and I half-wondered if it would come crashing down on me in the night. Just in case, I adjusted myself, my clothes, and the backpack to be a safe distance away.

I woke up early—I wasn't great at sleeping, always half-listening of the sound of a door sliding open—so I packed up my stuff and headed across the parking lot to the diner. Diner food was and is my favorite. Pancakes the size of your head, strong coffee that's either really good or really really bad, fast service from servers who don't ask a lot of questions, and always cheap.

Most of the time, I'd eat and be out in thirty minutes, and no one even noticed me. Not in Winslow. A fat old man with a stained white T-shirt and a grimy red baseball cap pushed his way into my booth, adjusting his big belly to fit. When he smiled, I had an unfortunate glimpse of black cavities and missing teeth, accompanied by rancid breath that made me lose my appetite instantly.

"How about I buy your hotcakes and you show your appreciation," he winked, and nodded toward the trucks at the edge of the lot.

"Fuck you, asshole." What is it with these sorts of men who think they can just take whatever they want?

I started to slide out of the booth, but he put his foot up on my bench to block me. I glared at him. "Move your foot, or you'll wish you had."

He smirked. "Maybe I should call the law on ya. You look like a runaway."

I was pretty sure 'the law' had better things to do than help this perv harass me, but I wasn't going to stick around and find out. I picked up my plastic glass of ice water, smiled at him, and threw it in his face.

His roar got the attention of the whole place, but shock also brought his foot down. I was out of the booth in seconds. I tossed $20 at the hostess and was out the door. Screw that.

Note to self: never sit in a booth again. Tables only.

The diner door opened behind me and I prepared to run, even though I was pretty sure I could stay well ahead of him with a simple skip, the fat turd. But it wasn't the old man. Instead, it was a tiny Latina woman dressed in a pink bomber jacket, skin tight jeans and 4" wedge espadrilles.

She pointed to a semi with a bright pink cab and said, "Let's go."

The fat guy was huffing behind her now, with a couple of equally gross friends.

The woman spun around on those crazy shoes, and told the man, "Stop right there, you *goddamn mothafuckin sonofaputo,* or I will take great joy blowing your balls into the next county." She raised a pretty pink and silver revolver to make her point.

I looked at the man and his friends, then the woman. *To the truck or keep running? To the truck or keep running?*

"Go to the effing truck!" Wonder Woman in pink yelled, reading my mind.

I went to the truck.

The man came at the woman and she shot the ground between his feet, kicking up a chunk of tarmac. "You get only one warning, *amigo.* Be wise."

She walked backwards toward me and the truck, stepped onto the running rail and opened the door. She motioned for me to go ahead. I hauled myself in, clumsily and without dignity, much less grace. I knelt on the driver's seat of the semi and watched as the man stared at the woman for quite a while. He finally raised his hands in surrender, turned, and retreated.

That is how CB and I met.

CHAPTER THIRTY-FIVE

Friday, September 11, 2009, Evening

ANGEL

"Does Peter know where you are?"

"He does. Just because I don't want to live with him doesn't mean I want to cause him extra stress or pain." I don't tell her that wasn't always the case. "Me being here is not his first choice, but he leaves me be, as long as I check in once in a while."

"What about Olivia? Do you talk?" Oakley asked.

How to explain my relationship with Olivia? It's complicated. We survived something no one should have to survive. There are things we've experienced that no one else could ever understand. I love her and I know she loves me. We don't always like each other, though. As far as I know, she still believes I'm immature. And I can't stop feeling as though she took my brother from me and made me feel alone in that creepy basement. On the other hand, she is the birth mother of Rosie B, the only living connection I have to Bud. I'm grateful for that.

We don't talk often. She has my number, of course, since her father gave me my iPhone and pays the bills… Holy crap. I just realized Peter has always been able to find out where I am. How did I never realize it before? He pays the bill for my cellphone so if he wanted, he could get records any time. I wonder if he has?

Emily interrupts my silent freak out when she asks a big question. "Are you happy?"

I think about it for a minute. "I'm never going to be Suzy Sunshine, but there are varying stages of all right, and I'm solidly in the middle, so I'm good."

When Em and Oakley head into the library for the fourth time, I stay in the back seat with the keys clutched in my hand. If Jonny Law picks now to head out, I'll start the car, text Oakley, and hope to God they run fast. Fortunately, we don't have to test Emily's sprinting abilities.

Em is ever curious. "How come you don't have to pee as often as we do?"

"We were locked up overnight in the Dollhouse. When you're chained to a bed and know that if you can't hold your bladder, you'll be sleeping in a cold, wet spot all night and have hell to pay in the morning, you learn to control it."

"Damn," Oakley says, shaking his head. "That's crazy. What's the Dollhouse?"

"That's what the guy that kidnapped me called the apartment he set up in his basement. He made us his 'dolls' so we could reenact scenes from his childhood that were kind of messed up. He thought if he could retell the past in a different way, he'd be happier in the present. Don't think it worked out for him. He's sitting in a California prison waiting for his final trial."

Emily frowned. "I mean, I get wanting to change the past. I'm pretty sure I'm going to want to forget this bit of my life eventually. But that seems like a crazy way to do it."

"He has a few mental health issues," I say. That's an understatement. "The last trial is coming up and I can't wait for it to be over. Then this whole thing will finally be marked done."

"How many trials have there been?" Em asks, frowning.

"There were four kidnapping charges, and two murder charges. There were four trials: one in Indiana, one in Texas, and a civil case. This last one is the federal case."

"Wait..." Oakley chews his lip, then meets my eyes in the rear-view mirror. "The Christmas Miracle case? That's you?"

I nod. I hate that name so much. There was no miracle. There was death and destruction, and nothing will ever be the same. That's not a miracle.

"There he is!" Emily shouts and immediately slides low into the seat. That's not necessary since she looks different with short hair and a cap. She's wearing a pair of my old jeans, with a belt buckled tight to keep them on her hips, and CB's navy blue zip-front sweatshirt over one of my T-shirts. If Jonny Law notices the car at all, he'll think it's two young men. But emotional responses aren't always logical.

"Calm down, babe," Oakley says, and I see his hand snake across the console to hold hers. "If it looks like he's coming for us, even for a minute, I will hit the gas, and he'll be chasing us back to Tennessee. I promise. He's not going to hurt you again as long as I'm around."

I believe him. He's not physically impressive, but he's genuinely nice, one or two missteps aside. He loves Em, and she loves him, despite his temporary stupidity. He won't be winning any fights on her behalf, but he'll die trying. Let's hope he doesn't have to.

I lean between the seats toward the windshield. The sun is starting to set to the west, but there's still enough vibrancy to bounce off the glass and muddle my vision. "We're 100% sure that's him. Right?"

Emily adjusts the brim of her baseball cap to give her a better view. "It is!"

I look at Oakley, who already has his fingers on the key in the ignition. "You ready for this?"

Emily doesn't give him a chance to speak. "We can't leave Harper another day."

"You know, she could already be..." I hate myself for saying it, but

I have to. I'm thinking of another day, a few years ago. Timing is everything, and the universe has a cruel sense of humor.

"I know. Even if she's dead, I can't leave her there. She deserves the respect of a real burial. Her mother, mean as she is, can't be left not knowing. *I* can't be left not knowing." Emily is angry. She slaps the dashboard. "But I don't think she's dead. I'd know. We're as close as sisters. I'd feel it. And I don't feel it. Start the car. Start the damn car!"

CHAPTER THIRTY-SIX

Friday, September 11, 2009, Evening

ANGEL

"Let's not get too excited. I mean, he could be going to get dinner or something," I say, as we follow Jonny Law's big government SUV.

"He could," Emily agrees.

Oakley is silent. He may be the one of us who has a future in law enforcement. He stays behind the Sheriff's vehicle, pulls into the next lane for a bit, then, on a stretch with nowhere else to go, he takes the lead for a while. *I'm not following you, pal.* I'm impressed.

"Anything look familiar?" I have the Rand-McNally open on my lap, my finger acting as a perpetual 'you are here' dot. When Jonny Law makes a turn onto an in-town highway, I move my finger. We're two cars back now, and the car between us is a damned law abider. We could have legally made a right on red, but instead, the old man in the sedan ahead of us sits and waits until the light changes, then makes the turn onto the highway. I suck down sour frustration. Road rage will not do any good. Besides, we can easily see the SUV a hundred yards ahead, in the right lane, so there's no rush, no hurry.

"Nothing," Emily says, apologetic. "It was pitch black when we were here. I don't know if I'll recognize anything with the sun still up."

"It'll be dark very soon." We are clearly headed out of town now, northeast. "I think he's going there. To the ranch. We've headed the right way if it's where we think it is."

We stay in the right lane, maintaining a steady 82 mph, same as Jonny Law. There are other vehicles on the road, so he's not likely to notice us or think anything is out of the ordinary. The sun is moving closer to the horizon on our left, layers of orange, red, and pink sinking behind the distant hills.

"Apparently, we're turning. Text CB we're headed east on Highway 33."

Emily checks the phone screen and says, "We've been driving a bit more than an hour. She says she's in west Texas. That's not so far. Are you sure we shouldn't wait?" Apparently, she doesn't feel the same adrenalin rush I'm enjoying.

"West Texas is two New England states away. What if he gets off 33 somewhere? We'd have no idea. We have to stay on his tail."

"Right. Right." Emily agrees.

Oakley says, "No turning back now."

"No turning back now."

CHAPTER THIRTY-SEVEN

Friday, September 11, 2009, Evening

ANGEL

Sheriff Jonny Johnson adjusts his speed downward as we approach the outskirts of a small town where the posted limit is 55. He hovers between 55 and 60. That's silly, since it's unlikely one LEO would pull over another, especially in a marked vehicle. But whatever makes him happy.

"Can I ask a question?" Emily looks back at me. It's been about fifteen minutes since our little caravan turned east.

"Another one?" I tease. She doesn't smile. "Sure."

"Are you scared? You don't seem afraid."

I'm not anything, really, at least not right now. It's like someone hit 'pause' on me. Maybe this is how actors and athletes feel; you know what you're going to do, but you don't think about it too much until it's your turn on the stage or the field, because if you burn up all your energy before the moment that matters, what's left? I am intentionally avoiding thinking about what might happen when we find the ranch. If I let those kinds of thoughts in, well, it might be all over.

I don't want to freak Emily out by saying that. Instead, I say, "I'm not *not* afraid. I'm just... forcing myself and my emotions to be in this moment. Right now, we're okay. I don't want to think about what might happen later because that could get me worked up, and control is important. Need to be able to think clearly."

Then I add, looking at both Em and Oakley, who is watching in the rear view mirror, "It's absolutely all right to be scared. We're in a scary situation. But we're being smart about it, right?"

Em gives a half-hearted nod and glances down at the phone screen. "CB is still yelling."

We both smile.

"Oh, shit, we're stopping," Oakley says. Jonny Law is pulling into a mom-and-pop type convenience store. "Should we pull in too?"

I try to see our tank over his shoulder. "Do we need gas?"

"We have a quarter tank." He says.

"What are you doing?" Em gasps when Oakley takes my question as instruction and turns into the station.

"It's either this or wait for him up ahead and hope for the best," I say.

Jonny Law pulls into a spot in front of the store and hops out, cheerful and friendly, touching the brim of his hat at the men, holding the door for a couple of older women. Jonny Johnson's photo could be in the dictionary as the definition of southern charmer.

Oakley pulls the Taurus up to a pump, then slams his fist on the wheel, engine still running. "Crap."

"What?" Emily hisses.

"I only have cash. If I go in, I could come face to face with him. He might remember me from before, at the rest stop. And you two can't go in." Oakley says.

"No. Pull over to the air pumps," I order. Once the Taurus is parked, Oakley slips out and puts a quarter in the machine, and it roars to life. He squats low and presses the air gun to the rear driver side tire's valve. We're all watching Jonny.

From the back seat, I see him amble out of the store, not a care in the world. He has a giant soda in one hand, a bag of chips in another. No worries pestering his mind.

Oakley replaces the hose when the time runs out but doesn't

hurry to get in the car.

Jonny won't notice me tucked down into the back seat. He probably won't notice us at all. I just don't want him to get a look at Oakley.

Jonny Law is leaning against his SUV, talking on the phone. His wife? Or that crazy woman Emily told us about?

We can't leave before him in case he doesn't get on the highway and continue in the same direction. If we guess wrong, we could lose him, and we'd have to start all over.

That can't happen.

"I feel like my heart is going to jump out of my chest," Emily says in a near-whisper. She has slouched down in the seat again, baseball cap low over her eyes. Her hands are clenched in her lap. Fear radiates off her like heat. She's not looking at Jonny. Fear has her gaze locked straight ahead toward the dumpsters behind the building.

Oakley is fiddling with something since he doesn't want to get back into the car yet.

"Emily, you know you can stay here. As soon as we see which direction he's headed, you get out and wait here for CB. That would be really helpful." I suggest quietly.

"No!" Emily snaps, then looks embarrassed and says more gently, "No. I'm staying with you. I'm just nervous. I'm fine. Okay, I'm not fine, but I'll be fine—someday."

Oakley says, "He's pulling out!" and practically dives into the driver's seat.

We wait a couple of beats before starting the car. Sheriff Jonny Johnson heads east on highway 33, then turns onto highway 283, still heading slightly north. Oakley lets two vehicles go ahead of us, then follows. "Better tell CB we've turned again."

I'm secretly glad Emily refused to stay behind. Oakley is cool and all, but Em and I have kind of bonded over this. I feel like we will both be weaker on our own.

And then I wonder if I really am the coward I claim not to be.

CHAPTER THIRTY-EIGHT

Friday, September 11, 2009, Time Unknown

HARPER

I'm dying, plain and simple. My body has fought the good fight, but now it's ready for rest.

Vero is getting angrier and angrier that she can't find Em on the cameras. She takes her anger out on me.

It's been two days? Three? Since Emily was turned loose. Dear Sheriff stuck around for a day trying to find her, then announced he had to go back to work. Vero told him she'd keep watch on the cameras and let him know when she found the little *puta*. I hope she never finds Em. I hope Em somehow got out, and that's why they can't find her, or, at the very least, she curled up somewhere and died a relatively painless death.

If that's what happened, though, it's really unfair. Em's parents will care. My sweet mama won't notice my absence one way or the other, but Mr. and Mrs. Bright, they'll be heartbroken.

I don't know what time it is. Keeping us in the dark is just another method of torture. They're so gleeful about it, Vero especially. I kind of feel like something terrible happened to the Sheriff once, and that's why he's the way he is. Every once in a while I get a very brief glimpse of the man who picked us up, and then he's gone. Vero, though? I think she was born a monster. I think she rejoices in it.

It's pitch dark. There is only a small blue glow from the camera pointed at the cages. The blue dot tells me it's on. I stretch out, as flat on my back as I can stand. This is the most comfortable position. So much of the damage they've done is on the front of me. Broken ribs; burns and cuts all over my belly and breasts. My vagina is so torn I doubt I'll ever have sex if I survive. Not sure I'll want to, but I'd like that decision to be mine. I think the reason they feed us so little is so that we quickly lose control of our muscle and bodily functions. With everything they do to us, nothing will ever work the same again.

Has anyone made it out alive? I doubt it. I really do. Frustration makes me shout, "Fuck you! I will be the first to escape this hell hole and tell the tale! Fuck you, you insane bitch!"

I nearly jump when Vero's mechanical voice comes at me. This is the first time I've been made aware there is a speaker system. Of course there is. "You're a fool. A pathetic, ugly, dried-up fool. You think you'll escape? No one has gotten out. Jonny has been doing this since he was a boy. His father taught him. You might say it's the family business."

"Fuck you, bitch!" I yell, except my throat is so raw it's hardly more than a whisper. Still, the emotional intent is clear.

Vero laughs. "There was one girl, Daphne, she was called. Another white girl like you. She was a blond, like you, too. She was the first after I came. Did you know I was supposed to be one of you? But Jonny saw me for who I am and understood I would be a help to him. Plus, I like the things he does, so it's not as interesting to hurt me. Anyway, this Daphne. She was the oldest one that's come while I've been with my Jonny. Twenty-eight. Petite, but what a rack! I was a bit jealous, truth be told! That silly girl thought she could bat her eyelashes at my Jonny, and he'd take care of her. He took care of her, all right. One thing you and your *puta* friend never understood: the fun is in the prey's reaction. If you're silent, like your friend, it's not very fun. You, though, you're mouthy, and you fight. Well, you did. Not so much anymore. You're losing your fun-ness, and he's getting bored."

I whisper "Fuck you!" again. I don't know if the words make it out of my head, though.

"Daphne, she was extra stupid, even more stupid than you. She tried to flirt her way out. Offered Jonny *whatever* he wanted." She says it in a simpering voice, mimicking the girl named Daphne. "*Anything*, she'd say in her stupid high voice. Except she didn't really mean it. She meant anything *vanilla*. Anything that doesn't hurt. Jonny, though, he took her up on it. She said 'anything,' and so he did *everything*. The more she tried to manipulate, the more he enjoyed it. That girl, by the time he turned her loose, was walking death. He usually tries to leave a little something to make the hunt fun, but with her, he went too far for that. She barely made it out the barn door. He gave her the usual hour, and when he went out, excited to get started, there she was, not twenty feet away, face down in the dirt." Vero laughed.

That is not where he will find me, I swear! I'm not going to acknowledge her anymore. Fuck that. I don't want her to know she's getting to me.

"You know he's got a three-step system for the meat?" Vero says.

My brain twitches. What? What meat?

"Yeah. First, we strip the parts we want from the bone. That goes into the freezer until we need it. Then we leave the rest for nature to process. It's already kind of slimy but it gets worse if it sits around too long. "

"You eat—the meat?" I can't help it. I thought I'd maxed out on what could horrify me but I was wrong.

Vero snorts. "Fuck, no. *We* don't eat the meat." She bays like a dog at the moon, then laughs and laughs.

CHAPTER THIRTY-NINE

Friday, September 11, 2009, Night

ANGEL

"That sign..." Emily mumbles so quietly I'm not sure she's talking to herself, or us. We've been on US-283, heading northeast for a while now, with absolutely nothing happening to break the monotony. It's almost dull enough to lull me into a sense of normalcy. *Nah, we're not following a Sheriff. No, we're not worried that he's known to have a fondness for torturing and killing young women just like us. Nope, we're not the least bit foolish, driving right up to knock on the door of his lair.*

"Which sign?" I ask, looking left, looking right, and seeing not much but trees and fence lines. Then I spot it. How could I miss it? A giant faded "Jesus loves you" billboard sits all lonely and sad in the middle of a wheat field. "Oh, *that* sign."

"Let me think a sec. I saw the sign, had a second of relief, thinking maybe Sheriff Johnson was taking us to a church of some sort. Maybe some sort of 'runaway therapy' even though we weren't runaways, and we're both adults. At that point, I was desperately looking for any idea that wasn't terrifying." She fidgets with the phone in her hand. "I think... I think we kept going awhile more, but we must be close."

Em tries to hand me the phone. The hood covers most of her face so I can't tell what she's thinking. I push her hand and the phone away. "You text her. She doesn't yell as much at you."

"So you're saying I should start the text with, 'It's Emily,'" and she actually laughs.

I nod extra enthusiastically.

Emily's fingers fly over the keyboard. She reads out loud as she's typing. "CB, it's Em. We're getting close. I saw a sign I recognized. We'll keep you updated."

Then she waits.

"Did she yell?" I chew my lower lip.

Emily shakes her head. "Not yet. No response."

That doesn't help my nerves.

Emily feels them too. When she eventually announces, "She's yelling!" she sounds as relieved as I feel. "She says to pull our asses over and stay put until she's nearby."

I shake my head, no. "We can't. We'll lose him. Tell her we will keep a safe distance, and she needs to drive fast."

Emily relays the message and grimaces at the response.

"Well?"

"I think you probably know what she said about that."

I smile. "Good thing she has a lead foot." The adrenalin pumping through me at the idea of being separated from CB is good. If things are too calm for too long, the nerves can build up and become debilitating. No time for that.

Emily looks up from the phone. "CB says she's getting closer and we are absolutely positively not allowed to go near that ranch without her." A ping indicates another text on the digital heels of the first. "And then she said, has anyone thought about what we'll do when we get there?"

We're all silent.

"I guess I really hadn't. Thought about it, I mean," Emily finally admits.

I've thought quite a bit about it for the last few miles. Nothing good or that I want to share. Mostly the "Oh, well, we're in deep doo-doo" sorts of thoughts.

The phone rings and Emily stabs the answer button. Before she can say a word, CB's voice blares through the speaker. "That's what I thought. Fortunately, I *did* think about it. Once we have the location, I will sit outside the gate. You will head to the nearest police department with Emily and my camera as evidence. They won't be able to ignore you."

I start to say that's a good plan, but CB shuts me down. "That's *the* only plan. Like it or not, I do not care a single bit. I went along with your part, and you will give me the respect I deserve by following my part without argument."

Well, hell. I can't disagree with that without being an asshole.

"I will take your silence as agreement," CB says, and it isn't lost on me that her accent is much less thick. She's still a private-school girl at her core whether she'll admit it or not. "Your gas station stop let me shorten the gap a small bit. I'll need to fuel up soon, and I'm going to grab a cat nap since I haven't slept in 24 hours. I don't have any interest in running down innocent civilians because I can't see straight. Do you have anything to say?"

I shake my head no, realize CB can't see me, and grunt, "No, ma'am."

CB chuckles at the 'ma'am.' "That's more like it. Emily? Are we in agreement?"

"Yes, ma'am." She's no fool.

Oakley wisely keeps his mouth shut.

"Good. Just a few more hours, and Harper will be in safe hands, and this so-called officer will be on the other side of the bars."

I hope to God she's right.

CHAPTER FORTY

Friday, September 11, 2009, Late Night

ANGEL

Emily's navigational skills aren't particularly accurate. It's been more than an hour, and we're still on US 283. "Hey, there's a mile marker! Text CB that number. I wonder how far we are from Oklahoma City. Knowing that would help us triangulate." I say.

"I haven't seen any directional signs yet," Emily says.

"Me either."

Emily swears. "The phone is dead." She shakes my phone like that's going to do anything. Exhaustion has broken her brain.

I tap Oakley on the shoulder. "Have a charger?"

Oakley hasn't said a word in at least twenty minutes. If the Ford wasn't still pointed in the right direction, I'd think he was asleep. "It's in my bag back at the motel." Then he says, "Here, you can use my phone -"

I feel the "oh shit" before he says the words.

"What's the matter?" Emily and I demand at the same time.

A string of swearing comes rapid-fire. It's the most syllables I've heard Oakley utter at once in the hours I've known him, and they are not syllables I want to be hearing right now. I try to keep my voice calm. "Oakley? What's wrong?"

"Oak! What the hell!" Emily doesn't feel the need to be calm. She snaps, her voice shrill.

"I was holding my phone when I was filling the tires with air.

128

Sheriff Johnson looked my way, so I ducked, and I think I set it down next to the air machine—and forgot to pick it up again." He slams the steering wheel, once, twice, with a flat palm, then fists, and shouts, furious with himself. "How many times can I be an idiot? Seriously! How many goddamn times?"

Emily touches his arm, trying to calm him. He's no good to us if he's a mess.

Then I realize how truly screwed we are. Without his phone and with my battery dead, we have no way to tell CB where we are. We are alone. That is absolutely not okay.

"Guys," I say, my brain doing back-flips and front-flips trying to come up with a solution. "We've got a pretty serious problem. How are we going to tell CB where we are when we find the ranch?"

Oakley slams the steering wheel again until Emily yells at him to stop. "You don't get to have a meltdown now. You absolutely do not. Pull yourself together! We need you!"

That ends his fit of self-flagellation, but it doesn't solve our problem. I say the only thing I can think of, hoping one of them will have a better idea, or at least shoot me down. Because I really don't like that one thing I can think of. Not at all.

"When we find the ranch, you're going to leave me there and then bust your asses getting back to the convenience store where you left your phone. Hopefully, the phone will still be there, but even if it's not, they'll have a pay phone you can use to call her."

There are no better ideas, and neither of them shoots me down.

CHAPTER FORTY-ONE

Friday, September 11, 2009, Late Night

ANGEL

All three of us are so tense we're ready to slap something, or someone. For the last twenty minutes, we've been the only car on the road behind Jonny Law. I have to keep my lips pressed together so I don't tell Oakley to slow down. Jonny Law would notice, probably, if the car that's been behind him for quite a while suddenly slows for no apparent reason. His law enforcement side might kick in, sending him back to check on us. At the very least, it would make him wonder what's happening.

Emily has recognized two more details—a quilt on the front of a barn, and a beautifully restored Ford pickup parked with a handwritten *For Sale* sign at a side road. The only reason we can see the Ford is it's under a big spotlight at what appears to be a park-and-ride lot.

Jonny Law's SUV disappears over a rise, and suddenly I'm having a panic attack. What if he's noticed us and is waiting on the other side of the hill? I swallow and say this out loud. "If he noticed us, he might be waiting just over the hill."

"That's very paranoid thinking," Emily says. And then she adds. "But you're not wrong."

Oakley slows the car just a bit as we approach the crest. "If he has pulled over and is waiting for us, do I stop? Or hit the gas?"

"Hit the gas. Definitely hit the gas." Emily instructs.

"Yeah, that's what I think too. If he's already suspicious, and he pulls us over, he'll recognize one or both of us. We'll have no choice but to run for it." I agree. "No way he'll think it is just a coincidence."

"Jesus," Oakley says.

I agree again. I take a deep breath, and hold it, then let the air out slowly, trying to steady my nerves. It's not freaking working. The fear seated firmly in the unknowing is trying to take me back to the Dollhouse. I resist. Bud isn't waiting for me with a running circular saw dangling above him.

It feels as if it takes minutes to get to the top of the hill, even though Oakley is going 75. In reality, it's seconds. We hit the crest. No sheriff's SUV waiting for us.

And then Emily shrieks, and the relief goes away. "That's it! Right here! Make a right here!" She points to a dirt road at the bottom of the hill.

Three more minutes of driving, and we've arrived.

We are at the ranch.

CHAPTER FORTY-TWO

Saturday, September 12, 2009, Early Morning

ANGEL

Oakley is almost as intense as CB. He's got his hands on his skinny hips and his eyes are flashing in a way that suggests we should take him seriously. It would be funny, under other circumstances.

"Now we know where it is, we're all going to ride back together to get the phone," he announces.

I shake my head. "We need to know if Jonny Law leaves. I'll be fine. I'll just make myself a little camping spot in the trees and keep an eye on things while you two go back to get the phone and find CB. Plus, you're almost out of gas, remember?"

"So?"

"There weren't any gas stations after we got out of town. If you run out of gas before you get the phone, that's just another problem to deal with. Seriously. I think I will melt down if one more thing goes wrong. Just leave me here." Jonny Law is not going to leave this place without me knowing it. I'm determined.

Unfortunately, so is Emily. She refuses to leave me here alone.

Oakley throws his hands in the air. "Fine! Y'all are gonna sit right here, together. You are gonna wait for me to come back with CB. You will *not* go off investigating on your own," Oakley orders. He knows full well we're no more likely to listen to him than we did CB, but at least he gave it a shot.

He doesn't really need to worry. I'm confident neither of us is going to suggest that we try to bust down the gate of the ranch and charge in. We're brave, not crazy.

The ranch gates are at a T where the gravel road we turned onto off the highway meets another road. The sign above the ranch says "Hunters' Haven." My stomach flips. The gates are made of heavy steel, and roll open and closed. There's a padlock the size of my foot, for extra measure. We're not going near it. If Jonny Law is smart, he probably has cameras monitoring the gates. Unfortunately, he seems smart enough.

We've made a little hideaway spot in a copse of trees to wait. Oakley found a blanket in the trunk of the Ford, and we tuck it into a pile of leaves at the base of a large old oak a few yards in from the road. We have a clear view of the gate through all the scrub trees, but no one will spot us unless they have reason to look. We have a bottle of water, and a box of tissues in case we need to pee. I have my pocketknife, and we have a flashlight. That's it. Nothing to see here. Just two girls, in the woods, doing nothing.

If there's anything I am really bad at, it's doing nothing. I spent a lot of time doing nothing in the Dollhouse, and now it's a unique form of torture for me. But I'll deal with my fidgets once Oakley is on the road, pointed back to the convenience store in the town no one thought to remember the name of, somewhere in Oklahoma.

Damn it. We are digging ourselves in deeper and deeper.

By the time we're settled, the clock in Oakley's car says it's 3:00 a.m. Can that really be right? We've calculated it will take him two hours to get to the gas station. Then, he'll somehow find CB.

Please God.

And then it will be another two hours for them to get back here.

Four hours round trip *if* everything goes perfectly. Not freaking likely.

Oakley gives us one more stern look to remind us to stay put, then heads off on his mission to find CB.

"You should sleep," I tell Em. "I'm wired. I couldn't sleep if I wanted to. And also, I'm not a hot mess like some people," I try to tease but just sound tense.

Surprisingly, she agrees. "I need all the energy I can suck up. I wish I'd brought CB's magic juice." Then she looks at me, eyes big. "Do not leave me. You wake me the minute you see or hear anything."

"I promise." I take off my hoodie because I've got layers on, and it's not especially cold. I fold it and hand it to her so she can use it as a pillow. "Sleep."

Exhaustion wins, and she falls asleep almost instantly. The sound of her nasal breaths through her broken nose is oddly comforting. One, she's alive, and two, I'm not alone.

What the fuck am I even doing here? If I was smart, I would have spotted her in the bathroom, reported it to the truck stop manager, and high-tailed it out to the safety of CB and *Casita*. Not my circus, not my monkeys, as the saying goes. I've already been on another bonkers ride and paid a very high price. According to some, I'm a coward. My cowardly ass should have run at the first sign of trouble. I don't want to think they're right, but... I'm not sure I'm up for this... whatever "this" is going to be.

The only thing I *am* sure of is there will be blood, as the other saying goes. But whose blood?

Wouldn't it be ironic if I survived the Dollhouse and died here, on a middle-of-nowhere Oklahoma ranch, helping a woman I met just days ago try to save another woman I've never even met?

I'm not suicidal—far from it. I feel obligated to live a hellaciously good life—in part for myself, to say "screw you" to Alfred, but also to honor Bud. He can't have died for nothing.

I can't do anything interesting if I let myself get dead.

CB's plan is a good one. We just have to be patient. Oakley will find her at the gas station and bring her back here.

That's when I'll call Nick. He won't have time to come to the rescue himself, but if I tell him what's going on, he can send LEOs he trusts. With Emily outside and Harper inside, they have to give us the benefit of the doubt and check things out, right? And then they'll see.

Unless Nick just happens to contact the wrong cop somehow, and that person gives Jonny Law a head's up. It wouldn't take him and his woman friend much time to hide Harper, or worse. I really think we need to surprise him, be completely sure he has no idea we're coming.

I'm still going to tell Nick. That way, if things go sideways, he'll know where to look for my body. Poor Nick. Please don't let him have to look for my body.

Damn, Peter will be pissed if I get myself killed. Olivia too. And Rosie B... she's so little. I really do want to see her grow up. And CB. Oh, God, if something happens to me, she's going to fall apart from the guilt and grief. That sounds egotistical, but I know her, and it's true. That's how I'd feel if our situations were reversed.

Krikey! If something happens to me, something might also happen to CB. Am I going to get her killed? Holy hell! I have to stop thinking!

So, here's how it will go. Oakley will find CB, and they'll be here before the sun is up. I'll call Nick, and he'll send the guys on white horses—wait, it's guys with white hats. Okay, whatever. Honestly, I don't think we can knock at the gate and ask politely and Jonny will give himself up. Although, hell, it would be nice if we did, and he did.

Nothing can go wrong because I can't bear the idea of anyone, especially CB, getting hurt.

Emily asked if CB is my mom. She's not, of course, but also, she kind of is. She's my mother, my sister, my best friend, my teacher, my shrink, my boss, my priest. She's my everything, in the greatest way. She's the place I feel most at home. She's the place I feel most like me.

That's a lot of pressure, I know. For a while, when I first thought I might stay with her, and that she wanted me to stay, I felt guilty. But also surprised. Peter wanted me with him, but that felt like it was out of obligation. CB wants me around because she enjoys my company, even when I'm a pain in the ass. I don't think she'd ever admit it, but she needs family as much as I do. The stars—maybe Bud—brought us together because we both needed something that the other had and wanted to give.

Jeez, my cheeks are wet. I'm teary. Why am I bawling? I'm tired, that's why. Tired and stressed, and okay, scared shitless.

I want to talk to Bud, but I don't want to wake Em, and I don't want to move to a place where I can see the stars. I tip my head back and squint until I fool myself into thinking there's a bright spot in the sky. It's probably bird shit on a leaf, but it'll do.

Yo, I say in my mind.

Yo yourself, Bud says back.

Is this the stupidest thing I've ever done? I ask.

Stupidest? Not even close. Stupid? Yeah, it's pretty stupid. He was never one to soften things up.

I should call Nick, right?

Silence. Then, *Yeah. Call him when CB gets here.*

Will you be mad if I get dead and don't get to see Rosie B grow up?

Fuck, yes. You're not supposed to die. You're not even an official adult yet. Achieve the goal of having a legal beer, then worry about the rest.

I almost laugh. Sometimes, I forget I'm not old enough to vote, buy a lottery ticket, or be an organ donor. Oh, damn. That's something I'd want. If things go awry, I want my body to be used for good, but I'm not even allowed to make that choice. Some adult has the ultimate say and has to give their permission.

That's the last thought I have before I doze off.

CHAPTER FORTY-THREE

Saturday, September 12, 2009, Time Unknown

HARPER

"My dear, I have exciting news! The time has come." Typically, I hear him come in, but not this time. Maybe I'm slow to react because the overhead lights aren't on. Usually, he turns them on the minute he steps into this area of the barn. I think he likes that the brightness burns our eyes after we've been in the dark for so long. Any little thing he can do to add to the discomfort of his captives...

I try to move into the corner, even as I wonder why I'm bothering as I drag myself across the concrete. There's nowhere to go, nothing to protect me. I can't even hide behind my attitude anymore. I'm fresh out of piss and vinegar.

A part of me hopes it's almost over. That part is bigger than I'd like to admit. Only a tiny piece of my mind clings to hope. It's been so very long. Em must be dead. I might as well be, and soon will be, I'm guessing. "Exciting" for him is going to be deadly for me.

He unlocks the cage gate and steps inside. No idea where Vero is, the crazy bitch.

As if on cue, the lights blast on. There she is.

Dear Sheriff squats next to me and runs his hands over my body, surprisingly gentle. "You're pretty banged up. That's going to slow you down. Tell you what. Because you've made the past weeks a real fun time, I'll give you one last gift."

The words are offensive, but I don't have the energy to spit on him the way I want to.

"I'm going to give you a one-hour head start." He beams, and it strikes me again how disgustingly handsome he is. It's unfair that so much rot and malice can be wrapped in such a pretty package.

"Gee, that's generous of you. I'm pretty sure you give that same gift to everyone." I cough, and my chest blazes fire. I'm positive I have broken ribs, and I think something inside my chest just might be poking at a lung. It's hard to take a breath, deep or otherwise. "I know about the cameras."

Vero chuckles, and I spot her near the wall of hunting equipment. In my mind she is being lit up from the inside, as if someone's plugged her into a wall socket and her veins are neon cables. Clearly I'm entering the delirious phase of this nightmare.

"That you do, that you do." He pauses a beat, then says, "How 'bout I make it a true gift. We'll keep the cameras off for that hour. But at 61 minutes, cameras go back on, and the fun begins!"

I suppose, in this situation, that really is a gift. I have an hour to drag my broken, battered, tortured body somewhere to die. If I can figure out a way to kill myself, I might do it. There'd be a lot of satisfaction in taking that away from him.

That thought gives me a small burst of energy.

The sheriff is gentle when he lifts me to my feet. He brushes my hair out of my face like a father soothing a sick child. I wonder if he has children. I can't imagine he does. That would be an affront to God. He slips an arm around my waist and helps me hobble out of the cage, past the torture room, and into the central part of the barn, which is a literal dump. There is junk everywhere. The big barn doors are wide open. I haven't seen the sun in—weeks? It's not bright, so it might be sunrise, or sunset. I blink. It hurts. But the air smells fresh and feels nice against my bare skin.

He sets me on my feet and ignores my gasp of pain when my bad knee screams at me. While I struggle to stay upright, he pulls keys from his pocket and unlocks the dog collar that has been around my neck since the night we arrived. It falls to the dirt, and he leaves it where it lands.

"May I have a drink of water before I go?" I ask, meeting his eyes but not begging. Is there anything human in there? Anything left? Anything at all?

Another long pause. "There's a hose." He nods toward the front of the barn, turns on his heel, and disappears into the barn. His voice drifts back to me. "Use your time wisely. See you soon."

Motherfucker. Something is definitely wrong with my knee. I was a track runner back in high school, and I once tripped over a weight someone on the football team left on the field. My kneecap popped, and this is exactly what it felt like. This just keeps getting better.

I take a minute I don't have to argue with myself about the water. I need it. I force myself to hop awkwardly to the hose, with the bad knee stuck in a bent position. I'll need to find a crutch or something to lean on ASAP. For now, I turn on the spigot and take a long drink. I start to turn off the tap and then think, screw it! Maybe it'll make a muddy mess, and he'll slip in it.

I take another long minute to orient myself. The barn and the deceptively cute cottage-type house are at the edges of a circular dirt parking area. His SUV is parked at the edge of it, between the house and barn. I try to remember how far it was from the gates to the house. Too far. Too damn far. And I can see from here it's mostly open fields. Nowhere to hide. No tree to find to hang myself from. Although what am I going to use to do the hanging? No idea. I'll figure it out.

I'm not going to let him win. He's won everything else. Not this. *Not fucking this.*

The idea of getting anywhere near the house is terrifying. I'm not sure why. Maybe because it's filled with Vero's aura, and that means it's a Hellmouth.

To the left of the barn is a long, narrow building with six fenced-in exterior kennels. I volunteered at a small country shelter one summer, and I know the outdoor areas have a small door that can be opened for the dogs to go in and out. Currently, there are no dogs in the outside areas. One small bright spot.

I can't move fast with one functional leg. I hear a weird sound nearby, and it freaks me out. Then I realize it's me, grunting in pain with each step. I concentrate on keeping quiet. I don't want to stir the dogs. Granted, I'm bleeding enough they'll probably smell me. Jesus. Is he going to hunt me with dogs? I don't want to be killed by dogs. I love dogs. I want to die still loving dogs.

I get past the kennel. It feels as though it took me the whole hour, even though it's only thirty feet. The sun is creeping up, slowly, so it's early morning. Behind the buildings, there is another large, open pasture, surrounded on all sides by thick scrubby woods. I decide on the woods. If I could run, the field would be a quicker way to the back of the property. But I can't run. And I don't want to be caught in the open.

More shuffling. It hits me that I'm naked. My mind is going. I start talking to myself. At this point, I'm sure I'm beyond delirious, I'm downright cray cray. "Emily has done this. I bet she didn't go toward the gates either. She's too smart for him. She's back here somewhere. Since he didn't find her, maybe she had the same thought as me. Maybe she found some poisonous berries—the poison ones are always red, right? Note to self, look for red berries—and she ate them and crawled into a pile of logs and died. If she's dead, I hope that's how it happened. I hope to God so. Please don't let her have died in pain."

The trees are really thick here. Mother Nature is a slob, littering the forest floor with tree branches, shrubs, grasses, rocks. Staying upright becomes an Olympic event for me. I find a limb that makes a decent crutch, and I cling to it.

I'm thirsty. I don't know how long it's been since I drank the water. I'm sure it's more than an hour now. I can't see any of the buildings, so that's good. But he will have benefit of the cameras soon if he doesn't already. I need to hide.

I hear rushing water, and then I see it. A creek. A good-sized one. There's even a naturally formed pool. If I can make it to the pool, I can swim to the other side. That will be easier than walking. I'll give my poor body a small break. *You've been a good body, body. You didn't deserve this.*

I really am losing it.

One of the advantages of going through the woods is that I haven't left footprints, although I bet Dear Sheriff is a good tracker. He'll spot the broken twigs and such.

Doesn't matter. This is my only option.

I keep going until I'm at the edge of the pool, which is surrounded by rocks and boulders. I can see it's deep, because it's dark, and not too murky. I don't bother being graceful. I step off the edge and drop down, hoping it's not deep enough that I will jam my bad leg on the bottom. It's even deeper than I'd expected, and I let myself sink. The cool water feels so good I don't immediately try to push to the top. Maybe I should stay here. Maybe this is how I end it.

Finding peace in that thought, I open my eyes. Through the clear water, I see—bones. The bottom of the pool is thick with them, two or three feet deep in places.

In my head, I scream, and I use the last of my energy to kick to the top. I burst through the surface of the water. I don't care if he's standing right there and sees me. I will never get the sight of those bones out of my mind. Not ever.

There's no one around. I force the image out of my head and focus on getting to the other side of the pool. I drag myself out. It's a steeper bank and hard to navigate. I have to crawl. By the time

I reach the top, I'm covered in mud. That's good, though. When I'm flat on top of the bank, I shove my hands deep into the rusty mud and grab handfuls. I rub it all over my body, my face. I pull it through my hair. Camouflage.

I'm completely spent. I need to find somewhere safe to rest. Where, though? I look around. I remember the word 'riffle' because my grandfather's farm has a creek, and he was very into biology and botany. He told me lots of things about plants and water and animals. The pool feeds a part of the creek where the water runs fast and shallow. That's the riffle. Further downstream, where the water moves fast and rough, it becomes a rapids. I think I see a waterfall.

Where the pool flows into the riffle, there is a grouping of boulders and larger rocks. I drag myself toward it. I see an outcrop. I roll under it. I have to rest. Or die. There are worse things than being lulled to your end by the sound of water.

CHAPTER FORTY-FOUR

Saturday, September 12, 2009, Early Morning

ANGEL

When I wake, the sun is inching above the grass across the road.

Emily is sitting up, although her eyes are closed. I can tell she's awake because her breathing is easier than when she sleeps. Not as nasally. "Hi."

"Hi." I yawn and push up and take a small sip of water from the bottle she passes to me. The bottle is two-thirds empty.

"I've been thinking."

"Ut-oh." I smile and sit up next to her, our backs against the mighty oak. It's cooled significantly. I unfold the hoodie and slip my arms into the sleeves.

"My muscles are stiff, and the pain is already getting worse because I'm not moving."

I don't like where I think this is going. I shoot her a sideways glance but don't say anything.

"I've been studying the road, and I think the place where I got in the truck is maybe a half mile that way," she points across the gravel. "There's a corner up there. If we go right—don't ask me if it's east or west—and keep going for a little bit, I think we'll find the spot where I was washed under the fence."

Yeah, that's where I thought she was going. How did I sleep through her getting up and moving around? That's not good. "I understand what you're saying, but we really need to sit here and wait. You're still hurt, remember? And I'm exhausted. Plus we promised Oakley and CB we wouldn't do anything stupid. This—what you're suggesting—is pretty damn stupid."

Emily doesn't respond with words. Instead, she carefully gets to her feet and looks down at me. She's moving better. Not great, but better. "I can't sit here anymore. I just can't. It's eating me alive, the not knowing." She sucks in a breath. "After all you've done already, it's asking too much to expect you to come with me. I know that and it's okay. You wait here for Oak and CB and then you come and you find me. Promise you won't leave me—won't leave us—in there!" Her voice has a tinge of hysteria just below the surface. She's going, with or without me, even though she's terrified.

I consider. It would take us, what, an hour in her condition? Is she even capable of walking that far? I'm not confident. We'd need to stay in the woods as much as possible in case Jonny does have cameras. I certainly would if I were a creepy son-of-a-bitch like him. Judging by the sun's location, we still have an hour or two until Oakley and CB get here. I suppose we can walk the fence, see if we spot an entry point, and then get back here before they realize we were gone.

Plus, it'll take my mind off how thirsty I am. Em needs the last of the water more than I do.

And I think she'll go whether I agree or not.

"We'll leave the stuff here, because we're coming back." I shoot her a glare to tell her I mean business. "And just in case, I want to leave a note." Nobody thought about paper and pen, but I can make do. I peel leaves off twigs and arrange the twigs to say, "Gone fishing. Back soon."

CHAPTER FORTY-FIVE

Saturday, September 12, 2009, Early Morning

C B

It's amazing what you can do with a lead foot and a bad attitude. Of course, running with an empty trailer doesn't hurt, either. But now I'm freaking out. Angel's cell is going right to voice mail. Why isn't she answering? At least a dozen explanations race through my mind. Most of them are more suited to that *Silence of the Lambs* movie than real life, but this whole situation is kinda like *Silence of the Lambs*.

The last time we texted, they were at the gas station. Somewhere in Oklahoma, off Highway 33—no, Emily said they turned onto 283. I don't even know for sure whether they were headed east or west. I assume east, but what if I'm wrong? There have to be dozens of gas stations and convenience stores along that stretch.

I slam the steering wheel with my fist. *Fuck fuck fuck!* Why aren't they answering?

The last couple of days have aged me 10 years, at least. I left North Carolina a 42-year-old woman, and now I'm ready to file for Medicare. Sons of bitches. I'm too hot for this kinda stress! It's not good for a girl's complexion!

I hop on the radio and send an SOS of sorts. "Hey, anyone know of a mom & pop C-store along highway 33 before you get to highway 283? Probably eastbound but not 100%."

A couple of voices come back. "That's a long stretch. More

145

specific?" and "I can think of at least three. What do you need?"

"My kid called from one of them, and now she's not answering her phone. I'm headed that way to find her. I think she had car trouble."

"Shit, sorry. Where was she coming from?" Trucker One asks.

"Waterford County, Texas."

"And you think headed east? It might've been one of two, then. Mom & Pops." Trucker One again.

"Yeah, that's what I'm thinking." I agree.

He sounds amused. "No, I mean, one of them is actually called that—Mom & Pops."

"Oh! My bad."

"There's also the Circle S. That's not what we call it, but that's what's on the sign." Trucker Two chuckles. I can just imagine what he calls it. Jerk.

"Great. Thanks. Hopefully, it's one of those. Any idea which comes first?"

"The lucky one!" Trucker Two laughs.

Trucker One grunts, no more amused than I am. "You'll see the Circle S first, then Mom & Pops is about 40 minutes past that headed east. Good luck!"

I press a little harder on the gas. It's been hours since Angel told me they were behind the Sheriff, and at that point, I was still in Texas. But I've been on this stretch for a good while. I should be getting close.

What if they're not there? What if Jonny Law, as Angel calls him, spotted the tail and grabbed them? It doesn't sound like this Oatley—Oakley—guy is especially imposing. He could be lying dead in a ditch somewhere, and Jonny Law and his girlfriend could have two more toys to play with.

Jesus. I'm sweating like a motherfucker. My girl has been through so much trauma in her short life. She can't go there again. Not again.

I could call Nick. Angel gave me his number once, just in case.

The very idea terrifies me. Even though Angel has been riding with me for two plus years, by her own choice, if someone was in a bad mood and had resources, they could accuse me of kidnapping. She was barely fifteen when we started riding together, and she's not legally an adult now. Peter Baden definitely has resources. I looked him up once after Angel told me her story. It wasn't hard to find more info. The Christmas Miracle was all over the media. She doesn't talk about it very much, but I know she's pulling a freight car of baggage from that time. No one will blame her if she pulls it forever but I really hope she can let it go someday.

I spot the first station, Circle S, up on the right. It's a small, clean place, with three rows of pumps, half of which are full. There are four vehicles pulled up in front of the store, away from the pumps. None of them are a Ford Taurus. I don't see Angel or Emily.

I maneuver *Casita* off to the side so I don't block anyone's movement or vision and jump down. I walk around the store, even around back, just in case. Nothing. I go inside. There are a couple of people debating beer brands. One guy is in line for lottery tickets and smokes. A woman has a pizza and a gallon of milk. I grab a Red Bull and get in line. When it's my turn, as I pay, I ask the cashier if she's seen a tall blond girl today and show her Angel's photo on my phone. The woman shakes her head, no, and turns to the next customer.

Fuck! I go back outside and look at the pumps again. They're mostly empty now. Still no Taurus, no Angel, no one who looks like an Oatley. *Oakley.* Damn it. What a stupid name.

I get back in *Casita*, point her east. I'm fidgeting, my hands playing drums on the steering wheel even though I've got the radio off. The only song I hear anyway is "Fuck fuck fuck fuck." It has a lousy beat, and the lyrics are for shit.

Forty minutes feels like days, but finally, I spot the Mom & Pops sign and pull in. It's busier than the Circle S was. I park to the side and hop down. There are a lot of cars at the pumps. But no Taurus. No Angel or Emily, either. I go inside, grab a big water and some Red Vines, and ask the cashier if she's seen, Angel. Again, no.

Where the hell is my girl?

CHAPTER FORTY-SIX

Saturday, September 12, 2009, Early Morning

CB

With no luck at either of the gas stations, my stress level is officially off the charts. When I catch up with Angel, I think I will beat her. She acts so tough sometimes and I know it's because of the Dollhouse, and especially the way Olivia suggested she's a baby, and a coward. Honestly, it's Olivia I should beat. That girl has done almost as much psychological harm as Alfred.

Angel keeps all of the goodness deep inside, protected by a hard outer shell very few are allowed to see. I get it. Of course I do. We're not that different, Angel and me. My protective shell is made of humor; hers is hidden in disinterest.

Some might be surprised Emily cracked Angel's shell open in mere seconds. Not me. Empathy is Angel's super power. What terrifies me is that it's also got the potential to be her kryptonite. Take a need to help, and combine it with the fear that you're a coward, and you've got potential for extreme risk-taking and misadventure.

If Nick Winston, FBI agent, doesn't throw me in jail, we need to have a conversation about how we can help Angel channel that empathy in a safe way that lets her own who she is without putting her in freaking danger.

Damn it!

If I keep slamming the steering wheel, I'm going to have a bruise the size of Texas on my hand. I refuse to let myself think about what could happen if I don't find Angel and Emily.

It's been forty-five minutes since I left the last convenience store on Highway 33 and now I'm coming up on highway 283. I turn onto it, continuing my northeast trajectory, and send up a prayer to the Gods of Trucks. I'm in the middle of nowhere, it seems, with very few vehicles passing me in either direction. The sun is up now, so I can keep an eye out for anything that might be a clue about which way they've gone. I pray someone sends me a sign that points me in the right direction.

Out of nowhere, a figure jumps into the road. It doesn't walk, or saunter, or even run; it literally jumps, up and down, up and down, like a freaking kangaroo, across the ancient blacktop, crossing two lanes and a grassy median. The fool is waving his or her arms like a maniac.

I am full up on crazy. No more. They can wait for the next good Samaritan because I'm not the one. "Get out of the way!" I think. Then I scream it, because I am not 100% confident I can stop *Casita* before she turns the person into roadkill. The person doesn't seem to care that they have a 35,000 pound semi barreling down on them. Instead, the idiot jumps up and down again, arms waving like one of those people directing planes at the airport.

I step on the clutch, throw *Casita* into neutral, and push hard on the brakes. I mutter a prayer that she can slow before we turn the idiot into cream of idiot. The air brakes whine and *Casita* shivers in protest as we get closer, closer, closer.

Still the fool stays put. What the hell is wrong with them?

Oh, Jesus, it's not Angel, is it?

That thought has me standing on the brakes as we are nearly upon the person.

Just before I jerk the wheel to the right to avoid plowing into them at five miles an hour, I understand who it is. "Oakley?"

When *Casita* comes to a stop, I see the idiot has turned his back to oncoming traffic. He has his hands pressed to his face so he doesn't have to watch his own demise. Except now I'm on the side of the road, and he's still standing in the middle of the road like a fool, and at some point, there will be another car or truck barreling down on his scrawny ass.

"Oakley!" I yell out the open window, and he turns, somehow looking surprised that I know his name, and also that I'm on the shoulder. The idiot starts smiling. What the hell is wrong with this kid?

"What are you freaking doing?" I demand as my feet touch the ground. "Get out of the friggin' road. Where are the girls?"

CHAPTER FORTY-SEVEN

Saturday, September 12, 2009, Early Morning

HARPER

I barely fit under the overhang of stone. Small, sharp rocks are stabbing into my back and shoulders. I pull into a fetal position, as much as my body will allow. It's still early in the day. I doze for a bit.

The Sheriff's voice startles me awake, and I cram a hand into my mouth so I don't shriek.

"Everything on this land is fed by the blood. The blood runs in the soil of the fields, in the water of the creek. It's absorbed in the trees and grass. It colors everything I see, everything I touch. There isn't a thing on this ranch that isn't tinged red when I look at it."

I don't think he knows exactly where I am, but he knows I'm nearby. His voice is different. Somewhere between the charming Sheriff we first met and the monster who has tortured us for weeks.

"How desperately I wish it didn't have to be this way. I tried to end it. I tried to be different. To be better. To be the man I dreamed of as a boy."

My leg cramps, and I want to move, but I don't dare. I try to reach down, to massage the knot. Pain reminds me who is boss.

"If I had understood then how very deep the blood runs, I would have left this place, I would have gone far away, to California, or the east coast. I wouldn't have stayed on this land. This hellacious, soul-eating, terrible land."

His voice changes, softens. The calmness, the rationality, the heart of the words he utters is more terrifying than anything that has happened so far.

"When I was a young boy, just six or seven, my father told us this land was a gift from God. These 684 acres were given to our family to live our destiny, to fulfill our promise. My father's pride was contagious. Sam and I, just kids, still looked up to our old man as the most interesting thing in this beautiful country. We had not yet learned that the land we worshipped, and the man we idolized, would take our souls, and in Sam's case, his life."

"Sam isn't alone in the dirt." When he says *Sam*, his voice cracks. What happened to Sam? Was it his brother? Or sister? It sounds as though they died here. How?

His voice is heavy with sorrow. "How many lives have been lost here? That's not right. 'Lost' implies there was hope, and there was never, ever hope. Once you set foot on this land, it's too late. Your fate is sealed. You will go one of two ways, and neither choice is yours to make: you'll be the hunter, or you'll be the prey."

I can hear leaves crunching under his heavy boots, and I hold my breath and put my good hand over my eyes since I can't really cover them. I don't want to see him coming for me.

"There's a narrow band of rock that crosses the wide part of the creek. Perhaps you saw it. If it's been a wet year like this one, and you slip to the right, you'll be dragged downstream through the rapids. If you survive the rapids, you'll be caught up in the old chain-link fence the first John put up to separate our property from Donovan's land next door." The first John? Is he talking about himself in the third person, or someone else?

As if reading my mind, he says, "The first John was my father. I'm named after him. It's supposed to be an honor, but for me, it's a curse."

He sighs deeply. "As I was saying, if you're trying to cross and you fall in and you're really unfortunate, you'll be pulled under the fencing. There's a run of barbed wire and it'll tear you to shreds. It might even catch you and keep you down until you drown."

"On the other hand, if you're trying to cross, and you happen to slip to the left, you'll find the bones."

I want to scream, "I know all about the bones!" but I resist.

"And if your foot happens to go in at the just the right angle—or, I suppose, just the wrong angle—you may find yourself stuck. Your feet can get tangled in the bones, and the rocks that circle them." He pauses again. "Should that happen, someone might come upon you and take the opportunity to hold you under the water until the pain stops."

It's clear those last words are important, but I don't understand. I wait for more, but that's it. I've almost stopped breathing during his soliloquy. Now, all I hear are birds and water and other nature sounds. Is he gone? Is he standing there, waiting for me to pop my head out? The uncertainty is paralyzing.

CHAPTER FORTY-EIGHT

Saturday, September 12, 2009, Early Morning

ANGEL

Emily is moving much better. CB's magic in action. Em still needs a damned doctor, but she's not dead, and none of her body parts have fallen off. I call that a win.

I count paces as we move north through the woods from our hiding place to the corner where we'll head east. Eight hundred and forty steps. This part really doesn't matter as much as the next part, but I want to train my brain now, so it starts tracking. Just in case.

The entire property is fenced with tall steel panels that look like they should be surrounding a prison, not ranch land. The weave is tight, with holes less than an inch. Nothing to slip fingers through to help a person climb. A V-shaped piece of metal is at the top of each panel where it joins the next panel. Sharp-looking wire is strung from V to V, so even if you were somehow able to climb to the top, you'd be cut to shreds when you attempted to cross over.

Don't the neighbors wonder why their buddy Jonny Johnson has such an intricate and lethal fencing system? Are the deer and rabbits really that badass in Oklahoma?

It's incredible that Emily made it out through that, through any of this. If I didn't hate the word, I might call it a miracle.

Now that we're on the new road, we've lost the cover of trees. Instead, there's an open field on the opposite side of the gravel, punctuated by tall windmill towers with what look like airplane propellers at the top. The good news is that on Jonny's side, he's recessed the fence ten or so feet, and there are trees everywhere, hopefully blocking his view of the road if he does, in fact, have cameras.

Emily is not talkative. She hasn't made a sound since we turned onto this stretch. She's focused on the ranch side of the road, nervous we'll get spotted, but also, she's studying the landscape intently, trying to remember. She's got to be exhausted. This is quite the hike for someone in her condition. Is she going to be able to make it back to our hidey-hole by the oak? Why did I agree to this?

Like Oakley, I don't always make the best decisions.

We're in about 1000 feet when she stops. "I think it's over there," she whispers and points ahead and to the right. It looks the same at everything else to me, but I trust her. She swivels her head left and points to a specific windmill. "That's the one the man in the truck was working on."

I start to ask how she knows since they all look the same, but then I see a red utility flag stuck in the dirt at the edge of a ditch that divides the road from the wind farm property. It's the only flag I've noticed. In my experience when utility or construction companies plant those little flags in the ground, they rarely come back to retrieve them.

"Which way now?" I ask, keeping my voice low. I'm no real estate expert, but we've walked nearly a mile on this piece of road. If the fencing is the boundary of Jonny Law's property, the boy has some serious land available for his hunting pleasure.

Fucker.

Emily tilts her head and peers through a gap in the trees. She points. "There, I think." She takes the lead, but she's in no rush. I don't know whether that's because she's tired, or scared, or smart. Probably all three.

We walk through a thick cushion of fallen leaves and branches, trying not to trip. The trees are so dense it's hard to see the sun rising and even harder to tell what's past them. Vines have taken over the fence along this part, and for a few minutes, I think we've moved beyond the edge of it. Then it reappears, dull silver peeking through green vines.

"Here!" Emily says triumphantly and comes to a stop. We can clearly see the corner of the fence, where it jogs south again. The contrast between Jonny Law's ranch and the neighbors' property is clear. Whereas Jonny's area is wild and overgrown, the neighbor has some kind of maintenance program. The scrub trees aren't as thick, and the ground isn't shin-deep with woodland debris. Most of all, the sun shines in, and the impact of that one thing is the difference between heaven and hell.

We move onto the neighbor's land, careful and slow. This wasn't part of the plan. We shouldn't be going in; we should mark this spot and return to our hidey-hole to wait for reinforcements. This is dangerous. This is insane.

Emily is moving forward, almost in a fugue state. She's ignoring the burrs and sticks poking at her ankles. We're about twenty yards in when she stops and points again. "Here it is."

And yes, here it is. The creek. To me, uneducated to the names of things of the natural sort, it looks more like a river. It's easily thirty feet wide and the water is moving fast. The bank on either side is a small beach of mud, then there's a steep hill before the landscape is again grasses and trees and fallen branches.

"That's where I woke up," she says and points. Handprints are still visible in the mud. Emily's handprints. There's too much nature on the ground beyond the beach to show footprints. I suppose that's good.

The fence stretches completely across the top of the water, anchored in the banks on either side. Although the fence is simple chain link, not fancy like the other parts, it's still topped with the same V's with the razor-edged wires running between them. The water is wild and loud where it meets the fence. On Jonny's side, there's a significant drop in the creek, with a series of smaller drops close together in the forty feet approaching the fence. The rocks that create the rapids are football sized and sharp-looking, when you can see them through the rushing water. It reminds me of the water raft ride at Magic Mountain in LA. We went there once when I was living with Peter and Olivia.

The idea of being washed through all of that makes me cringe, even without the barbed wire.

On this side of the fence, the water runs fast and clear. I can see large, flat rocks on the bottom. But, just a few feet downstream, I can't see a thing. I think that means it's much deeper there. Rocky outcroppings hang over the water in some spots. I imagine little schools of fish partying in dens underneath. There's a whole other world in this creek.

I wonder how much blood has flowed through it.

"Look," Emily says, pointing. It's just another dead tree, as far as I can tell. It's 20 feet tall and leafless, its root ball half raised out of the soil. It takes me a minute to understand what she's so interested in. Then I see it. The tree branches have fallen into a cradle of healthy leaf growth from another tree...a tree on Jonny's side of the fence.

My tone is sharp and final. "No. Absolutely not."

"We can do it. I know we can." She's moving toward the fallen tree. She stops at the base and strokes it like it's a beloved pet.

"No." We can't. We cannot, on purpose and with intent, go onto the ranch alone. Just us. No backup. No weapons. That's just stupid! "We are going to go back to the blanket and wait for Oakley and CB—"

A quick movement from a rock formation on the other side of the fence catches my attention but it's so brief I wonder if I imagined it. I look around trying to identify the source. But Emily saw it too. She hobble-runs to the fence. Her eyes scan. When she finds what she's looking for, her fingers press against the fence.

The word comes out a whisper. "Harper!"

159

CHAPTER FORTY-NINE

Saturday, September 12, 2009, Morning

HARPER

I don't know where Dear Sheriff went after he got done telling me his tale of woe. The quiet lulled me back to sleep for a while. Now I'm half-dozing, pondering what moves, if any, should be next. Can I just stay here, with these peaceful sounds accompanying me as I shuffle off this mortal coil? I like that idea.

Something catches my eye, and I look to the left, expecting to find him looming over me. Instead, a hundred feet away, I see a fence stretched across the creek. That must be what he was muttering about. But what's got my attention is that there are people there.

People who are not Vero and are not Dear Sheriff.

There are two people. They're wearing jeans and hoodies. They're young, I think. I don't think they're connected to the Sheriff. I believe they are—someone else. I have to take a chance. I wave my hand, afraid to make a sound in case Dear Sheriff is still near the creek. I don't think he'd see my hand if he's still there... but I guess I'll find out if he does.

The people are arguing and don't notice me.

I wave again, more frantically.

They both look my way. Between my mud bodysuit and the rock overhang, I'm well hidden. I wiggle my hand again. One of them gasps and starts clawing at the fence.

I must be hallucinating. Or maybe I'm already dead. It almost looks like Emily. I can't make out features so well with just one working eye. But the body is the right height. The person is dressed in clothes Em would never wear. The hood falls back as they attack the fence, and I see short, dark hair cut in a shag. That's not Emily's hair. She'd never ever cut her beautiful hair. But, it is the right color.

Maybe I'm not dead. Did she really escape? Did she get out? Is Emily alive?

My reserves of piss and vinegar are refilling. I wave again, frenzied, to be sure they see me.

The girl that might be Emily puts a foot on a half-fallen tree and starts to climb, first walking up the trunk, then wrapping her legs around it to shimmy her way up. That is definitely my Emily. She was the best tree climber in our whole elementary school!

The girl is halfway up the tree before the other person starts after her. The second person isn't much of a tree climber but seems to be stronger. The one who might be Emily is slow and careful. The other person is a bit faster but less confident. I watch as please-be-Emily reaches the part of the tree that crosses over the fence and moves carefully. That's when I see the nasty-looking wires strung along the top of the fence. They look lethal. Please don't fall, please don't fall. Please-be-Emily scoots, inch by inch, to the top of the tree, and I understand the plan. The climbing tree's upper branches are supported by a healthy, mostly straight tree on this side of the fence. If please-be-Emily can get to the healthy tree, she can climb down and come get me, and we will get out of this fucking hell hole and go to the good cops, and Dear Sheriff and Vero will be in jail forever, and we'll start our California lives off with a bang, selling our incredible story of survival—

The person who is not Emily drops from the healthy tree like an apple and lands on the ground. She yelps in fear as she falls. She grunts when she lands on the hard, rocky soil. I start to call out and then look where she's looking. Dear Sheriff is standing on the other

161

side of the creek, and he's got both a rifle, and his bow and arrow. *Run!* I scream in my head. *Run!*

CHAPTER FIFTY

Saturday, September 12, 2009, Morning

C B

I don't want to do this. I really, really don't. But I trust my gut, and my gut says, *Call Nick now. Deal with the consequences later.*

Nick's number is in my phone as *Cielo.* That's Spanish for heaven. Angel told me when she first met him, she thought she was in Heaven and he was welcoming her. I know a half dozen Nicks, but I don't know a single Cielo. I've also never met an angel in Heaven.

I find the number and hit send. I press the speaker button so I can be hands-free. I'm driving too fast to divide my attention.

Oatley-Oakley is in the seat beside me. He is not a conversationalist, so I'm not concerned about him chiming in.

The phone rings and goes to voice mail. Makes sense. Nick has no idea who I am, and this is his personal cell. I don't leave a message. That would make our connection official. Instead, I hit redial. If I call enough times, he'll pick up.

On the third round of redialing, he answers. "Who is this?" His voice is sharp and deep. I suppose that's what an FBI agent should sound like.

"My name is CB. I'm a friend of Angel's." I say. My voice is annoyingly weak. I put more power into it and repeat. "I'm a friend of Angel's. She needs you."

"Tell me." It's a command, and I don't like it or him.

"It's a complicated story, but we met a young woman who claims to have been abducted, tortured, and hunted by a local Sheriff—" I begin, but he cuts me off.

"Where are you?"

"In Oklahoma, headed to the ranch where another girl is still being held. The girl we found says her friend is still on the ranch."

"Angel's with you? Put her on!" Now he sounds angry.

"She's waiting for me at the ranch. Outside the ranch." I say and then make the mistake of muttering, "I hope."

"What the hell, lady? You're supposed to keep her safe, and you're not with her?" He's not angry. He's furious.

What does he mean, 'you're supposed to keep her safe'? That sounds like he knows who I am. Angel has never even hinted she's told him about me. *Shut up, CB. Now is not the time to get caught up in that.*

"It is complicated. And don't yell at me," I say, not hiding my own anger. "Help now, and we can both yell later. I'm headed there. We haven't called the local LEOs because we didn't know which agency he was with and didn't want to tip him off. Now we know he's with Waterford County Sheriff." I look to Oatley-Oakley for confirmation, and he nods. "He *is* the Waterford County Sheriff. But he's probably chummy with all the other cop shops. Our plan is to contact the locals when we're physically outside the ranch. We'll have Emily—that's the first girl—on the outside to tell her story and show her wounds, and he won't have time to hide Harper—that's the second girl—once the law gets there. I need you to contact the appropriate authorities, so they don't waste time thinking we're off our rockers."

"Where is this ranch?" Nick demands.

"I don't know exactly." He makes a huffy noise, but I continue. "I'm headed there now. I have a guide, but we don't have a specific address or coordinates. I just know it's off of US 283 in Oklahoma."

Nick is silent for a moment. "I'm confused."

"You and me both, honey."

Oatley-Oakley snorts in amusement.

"Who was that?" Nick demands.

"Oat—Oakley. He's the guide."

"Riddle me this. Since it's complicated and you don't know where you are, how exactly am I going to send in the cavalry?" He's mocking, and I don't like that at all. If I didn't need him, I'd hang up on his holier-than-thou ass, but I do need him. I'll find a way to make him aware of my displeasure later. Perhaps as he's loading me into a police car in handcuffs.

"As soon as I find the ranch, I will message you the location. You will find the best, nearest law enforcement and send in the cavalry." I would never have guessed I'd use the word 'cavalry' in conversation once a year, much less multiple times in a single day. "You will make sure they know this is 100% legit, and they need to come with their believer caps on. Not just two officers. A whole cavalry. You get me?"

"You know the FBI are not always the most popular folks, right?"

"Hmm, I wonder why." I can't resist. "Are you going to help or not?"

"Don't be stupid. But when this is over, and Angel is safe, you and I are going to have a conversation and set some ground rules." Back to the commanding. What an ass.

I roll my eyes. "Whatever. We'll be in touch soon."

With all the come-to-Jesus conversations gonna happen, we're going to need to rent a church.

CHAPTER FIFTY-ONE

Saturday, September 12, 2009, Morning

ANGEL

It takes me a minute to catch up. Emily's moving with such confidence I wonder if she was an arborist in her past life. I watch her hug the thick trunk with her thighs and make little upward jumps until she's at the top.

I refocus on the area where the waving hands were. I don't see anything right away. Then I see it, hands flapping. I squint as if that will help, and surprisingly, it does. There's an eye peeking out from under a rocky overhang. Harper. It has to be! She's alive. *Holy hell, she's alive.*

Which means I have to follow Em up the damn tree. I am not a tree climber. I never was. Bud was one hell of a tree climber. Bud is not here.

Fuck, shit, damn.

Okay, tree. Be gentle. I've never done this before. Don't go breaking while I'm halfway up and dump my ass into that nasty-looking razor wire!

I see Emily disappear into the full leafy canopy of the healthy tree on Jonny's side. *Well, shit. How did she start?* I climb carefully onto the root ball, my shoes slipping a little bit on the dusty bark. I take a tentative step upward, bent at the waist so my fingers can grasp the rough trunk. This is not a flattering view. Splinters are in my future, I'm pretty sure. I'm also sure I look like a damn fool, but that's fine, as long as I'm not a fall-on-my-ass fool. The tree trunk is getting narrower and the ground is getting farther away. This is where Emily sat down and wrapped her legs around the trunk.

Whose stupid idea was this? Not mine. *Not mine.*

I scoot up the branch, fighting gravity and fear. I am not about to look down. I'm pretty sure I'm fifty feet up, at least. Okay, fifteen. Same difference if you're falling. Falling is gonna hurt. *Don't fall.*

I'm getting close to the fence and the razor wire. *No falling, no falling, no falling.* I pull my feet up onto the branch behind me so they don't dangle and get caught. If I get the hang of this, maybe I'll try riding a bull. Same basic concept, I'm sure.

Focus, Angel. Bud's chiming in. Things are getting serious now.

Look, pal, I'm either going to laugh, or I'm going to think about what the hell I'm actually doing, and then I'll be frozen with fear. You manage stress your way. I'm choosing jokes.

That shuts him up. I am now safely above and past the fence, nearly to the bushy tree on the other side. I wasn't paying attention to how Emily got from one tree to the other, and the trunk bronco I'm riding is getting really, really thin. I can feel it bowing under my weight as I move closer to the thick leafy canopy. I can't see inside the tree to know where to put my feet. *Shit, shit, shit.*

"Em!" I whisper-hiss.

She doesn't answer.

"Emily!" I try again, a tiny bit louder.

No answer.

I take a breath and stretch one leg, pointing my toes down, searching for something to land on. My foot finds something hard. A branch. Good. Okay. I take another breath and balance while I shift most of my weight from the leaning tree to the solid tree -

I nearly lose my balance. I grab for anything I can to keep myself safe in the tree. Finally, I find a solid, sturdy branch in my hand and I cling to it until I'm standing on a substantial limb. I'm still much too high in the sky for my comfort, but I can look down, even though I'd much rather not.

I carefully squat, clinging to the branches around me for dear life, and find a place where I can see through the leaves.

Oh, shit. Sheriff Jonny Johnson is on the other side of the creek. He's got a rifle in one hand and a bow in the other. A quiver of arrows is strapped to his back. He's looking toward the place where Harper is hiding.

Don't do it, don't do it, don't -

I do it. I monkey swing down branches like I've been climbing trees all my life, and when I reach a branch eight feet off the ground, I take a deep breath, and let go. I land hard on my ass, and it hurts, but I don't have time to think about it.

"Well, now, you're the funniest looking 'coon I've ever come across." He says with a drawl. He sounds happy and relaxed, not like a man who is hunting women. Then his tone changes as he recognizes me. "The girl from the rest stop. Rachel, was it? I have many questions. Why don't we go up to the house and have a nice glass of sweet tea and a chat."

I get to my feet and launch double middle fingers at him. "Fuck you, ya bastard!" Have I lost my ever-loving mind? I take off at a run, headed west, away from the tree, past Harper. I don't look at her, just move as fast as I can through the fallen branches and shrubs, leading Jonny Law away from Harper and away from Emily.

I glance back once to see if he's following, if he's keeping up. He's on the other side of the creek, not running, just taking quick, long strides. He's confident he's going to win this game. He's whistling that song again. This time I recognize it.

Teach your children well...

CHAPTER FIFTY-TWO

Saturday, September 12, 2009, Morning

HARPER

I watch a girl race past me. Who is she? Why is she here? My brain is foggy. I know she saw me, although she didn't look at me. And why did she flip off the Sheriff? That seems like a poor decision.

Oh. I understand. She's trying to buy me time. To do what, though? Where can I go in this condition? I can't climb a tree. I definitely can't climb that fence. He's already told me what's underneath if I'm stupid enough to try to swim out.

Does she know what he does to women like us? Will he capture her and torture her? Or will he simply hunt her? Who is she? What is she thinking?

And what happened to the other person that might be Emily?

So many things I don't know, but I do know I can't stay here. I don't hear the running girl anymore or Dear Sheriff. They've moved to some other part of the property. I need to go now. I need to get up and help her. She won't survive alone.

I dig my fingers into the mud and claw my way out from under the rock. My right hand screams in protest. Oh, yeah. Broken fingers. How could I forgot.

The sun is warm on my back, but the mud I rubbed over my skin earlier has dried, and now it's cracking and itchy. *Wonder if this spa has a hot stone massage.* I lay on my belly on the muddy ground and take calming breaths.

I hear the sound of footsteps coming toward me from the direction of the fence. Do I try to run? Or is it a friend? I have no idea what to do. It could be the person who might be Emily. Or maybe someone was chasing the running girl, and that's why she fell out of the tree, which means I'm now facing a new kind of danger. Maybe the person is in league with Dear Sheriff.

I consider sliding into the pool, and then remember the bones. The bones.

I decide to have faith. I lay still, my forehead resting on my arm, and wait.

"Harpy!" At the sound of my name, I turn my head. Emily, my friend, the keeper of my hope, is kneeling next to me. She is very much not dead, although she is also not in great shape. Her beautiful hair is gone. She's still a stunner, even with bruises and cuts all over her face. It strikes me that she's not naked. She's wearing clothes. Has she been outside all this time? Why didn't she stay outside where it's safe?

She kneels beside me and touches my face. "You're alive. You're alive." She's sobbing. "I can't believe you're alive."

"Me, either," I say, trying for a joke.

Emily is here! Best friends with rhyming names and big dreams, ready to conquer the world.

"There are cameras," I tell her, and I have to force the words out. My throat is on fire. I don't think she heard, or if she did, she doesn't understand.

She grimaces when she looks at my face and moves her eyes down my body. "It was really smart to cover yourself in mud. Can you move? If I help?"

I work myself into a seated position that leaves my injured knee bent and less painful, as if it matters. I'm naked, but at this point, I don't give a damn. "Who is that other girl? He's hunting her. We have to help."

"First, I have to put you somewhere you'll be safe." Emily supports me while I try to sit. "Did you see any buildings? Besides the barn and the house, I mean?"

I stare at her. Is she real? Or a ghost? Is she the ghost of the bones?

"How did you get in here? How did you get out?" I look back the way they came. "Can we go that way?"

"You don't want to go out the way I did, and you're in no condition to climb a tree," Emily says. Her voice is scratchy too. She looks bad, but not as bad as the last time I saw her. The bruises on her face are green and yellow, not blue and black. Her split cheekbone and matching brow bone are scabbed over. Her mouth is still an ugly mess, but even that looks better—like she lost a boxing match. I have to focus.

"I don't know what's that way," I point in the direction the girl ran. I glance at the pool, keeping my eyes above the waterline. "I only saw the barn, the house, and a dog kennel. And the driveway that leads to the gate."

"How did you get across the creek?" Emily asks.

"I swam. But I don't—I can't do that again." I *won't* do that again. Those bones will grab me and pull me down. I have no right to be living when they're dead.

"We'll find another way," Emily assures me, but her face tells a different story. She props me against the boulder that was my hidey-hole. "I'm going to look. I won't go far. If you hear me shout, get back under your rock."

I'm not going to argue. My brain is busy anyway. Who is the other girl? Where did she go? Did she escape him? I haven't heard a gunshot, or the scream that would come from an arrow piercing flesh. I want to believe we're going to get out of this, both of us—all three of us—alive! I want to believe that with everything I am. I push hard at doubt and dread. I tell hopelessness to fuck right off. My Emily is back. It will be alright. The dark feelings don't

THE HUNTED: SINS OF THE FATHER

disappear entirely, but they're at the margins now.

"Found a way. Come on." Emily says as she hobbles back. I hadn't noticed before how slowly she's moving. Her face may look—well, better—but she's still hurt. Of course, she is. I know what they did to her before they turned her loose.

Emily takes off the hoodie. Underneath, she's wearing a Def Leppard T-shirt, the *Pyromania* one. I love that album. "Put this on." She guides my arms through, then zips the front. It falls to just above my knees. I feel better, being covered. It's warm, too. I hadn't realized I was cold until now.

"Thank you." I smile. "I missed you."

She hugs me gingerly. "I'm so glad you're alive."

I see her see my bad eye. She looks queasy. I try to laugh. "It's bad, I know. You don't look so good yourself."

She smiles at that, then turns back to business. "Before we head across, we need to get our bearings. Once we're on the other side, we will have to move as fast as possible and that's not saying much for either of us. Do you remember which way we go to get to the buildings?"

I frown. "We want to go *to* the buildings?"

She nods. "That's the last place they'll look for us, right? Especially since they don't know about me."

She's already forgotten about the cameras. I don't remind her. What's the point?

"And also, it's the best place to hide you. More people are coming. Oakley," she sucks on her lower lip when she sees my eyes flare, "and another friend, CB. Maybe more. We need to get somewhere and stay safe until the guys in white hats arrive."

Oakley! How the hell did he—whatever. I'll think about that later. Now, I look across the creek. All I see are trees. Trees, trees, and more trees. "I don't know. I came through the woods across from the pool. The woods were to the left of the buildings if I was facing them. There was an open field I could have gone through, and it would have been more direct, but also more exposed."

Emily is thinking. "We're going to cross, and then we'll stick to the trees to get to the back of the buildings. Okay?"

I nod.

Then she says in a small voice, "Harp, I'm fucking terrified." I think she's going to add something reassuring, but she doesn't.

"I know. I've been trying to wake up from this nightmare but can't seem to do it," I say, keeping my tone as light as I can manage. My throat is so sore, it's on fire, but at least I sound like a human person again. I am desperate for something to drink. A drink and staying alive to see the sunset are my primary goals at the moment. "So, before we can do anything else, we have to do something about my knee."

CHAPTER FIFTY-THREE

Saturday, September 12, 2009, Morning

HARPER

I don't remember where or when, exactly, but I have a vague memory of someone having a dislocated shoulder. I think it was a TV show, actually. So anyway, this person had popped their shoulder somehow, and they went somewhere to get it fixed. Immediately after, they were good as new.

Bull-freaking-shit. I remember from the last time. It hurts like a mother when they pop it back, and it hurts for weeks after. Maybe the difference is a shoulder, that you can sling and rest, versus a knee, which is sort of required equipment for all walking activities.

Now, as I instruct Em on what to do, I'm psyching myself up and trying to convince myself it'll be better this time. Right. I press myself flat into the mud, the good leg straight out in front of me, the bad knee bent because it won't do anything else. I try to help by straightening it as best I can, but it's not going very well. "Okay, you're going to have to pull my ankle straight toward you. Be sure not to twist or jerk. Do it as fast as you can. Fast, hard, and straight. Got it?"

"It's going to hurt!" Emily always was a bit of a wimp. But it's hard to be annoyed when she's worried about me.

"Yes, it is. I'm going to bite down on this nasty-tasting stick, so I don't scream. Your one and only job is to do this so I have a decent chance of getting somewhere that's not here. Okay?" I'm using my bossy voice. It's the same voice I used to talk her into going to college parties when we were freshmen. Into making a secret road trip to Memphis when our parents thought we were at church camp. Into moving to LA. That last one may not have been such a great idea.

She's crying, but she's in the right position, kneeling with my foot between her legs. I clamp down on a branch and nearly howl with the pain biting down sends through my damaged teeth and lips. Once she starts tugging on my knee I might not even notice!

Emily makes a face and squeezes her eyes closed, then pulls hard on the leg. I swear I hear a pop as it goes back into place. Or maybe that's the fireworks of pain exploding in my head. Either way, the leg is aligned and mostly straight.

We're both crying now, although my tear ducts are so dried up nothing actually comes out.

"Five minutes. I need five minutes. You look for a couple of sticks that are the right length to splint my leg." I order. Miss Bossy Pants, I am.

Emily doesn't go far, but it's not hard to find suitable sticks here. The ground is thick with them. She brings two back, equal length, straight and long enough to start at my mid-thigh and end at the top of my shin. They'll work. I pull the cord from the hoodie's neck and give it to her. Again, it's not much, but it's long, and if we can break it in two, it might hold for a while.

Splinted, badly, I give myself a few more minutes to breathe.

"That's not going to hold." Em points out. She peels off the belt that was holding her jeans up, and they drop down dramatically. She wraps the belt around the sticks, around and around, and takes the two pieces of cord back. She slides them through two loops on the front of the jeans and pulls tight to gather the material together. Then she knots the ends. Neither of our make-do solutions will last long, but they're all we've got.

"Ready?" Emily finally asks, and I nod. She slips her arm around me, and lifts me into a standing position. She's carrying more of my weight than I am. For a while, we shuffle along in the direction the girl ran. My knee hurts like a sonofabitch but I have to push the pain away. Emily navigates us through a mess of shrubs and woodsy detritus toward the creek. We're far enough from the pool I can't see it, thank God. I'm so exhausted and such an emotional mess I'm pretty sure I hear the voices of the bones calling to me to join them.

I push the sound away and study the creek. Here it's just a small riffle feeding rapids. If I have to walk through the water, at least I don't have to worry about stepping on what used to be someone's face.

That thought digs in, and I suck down a sob, and Emily turns her head to check on me. "What?"

"Nothing, sorry, I just—something hurt. Sorry." I stammer. I stop to look at the part of the creek she's brought us to. It's narrower here, just ten feet wide, and not very deep. I can see rocks under the blue water. They're probably slippery. My feet are muddy and hurt. I'm going to fall, even with her help. *Stop it. You've made it this far. Emily is here. You'll get across.*

Emily takes off her shoes, steps into the water, and tests the rocks. "Not crazy but slick enough. Are your feet bad?"

"Bad? Well, assuming you mean sliced and burned." I look down and her eyes follow mine. Her face tells me it's worse than I think. It terrifies me that I've become numb.

She takes my hands in hers, and I step in, too. I almost lose my balance on the very first rock, but I recover and stand still for a second to settle my nerves and center myself. Then I take a breath and move to the next rock. And the next. Emily is walking backward so she can hold my hands and keep me steady.

A gunshot breaks the quiet, and we both release tiny shrieks. I hear Em whisper, "Angel. Oh no." I push my way through the pain and move quicker, and she tugs me up the bank of the creek and toward the trees.

CHAPTER FIFTY-FOUR

Saturday, September 12, 2009, Morning

ANGEL

I get the feeling he's toying with me. That gunshot should have hit me. I should be wounded at the very least. He's a law man, for God sake. He doesn't seem like the type to miss. He wants me alive.

I'm tucked into a ball behind a pile of dead tree branches, tears streaming down my face. What the hell did I do? I'm not ready for this! I'm not a fighter! My little red pocketknife isn't going to do much for me against a bow and arrow or a rifle, much less a hunting knife. Between sniffles, I seriously consider running back toward the tree we came in on, except I'm sure they'll be watching that area. I would be if I were them.

'Them'—is it just Jonny Law and Vero? Or are there more?

And where are the girls? I'm assuming—hoping!—Emily went to Harper as soon as I led Jonny away. Unless she fell out of the tree and broke her freaking neck. That's a possibility, too. Then this was all for nothing!

I'm overwhelmed and under-prepared and scared shitless, and we're all going to end up dead.

You're an idiot, Angel Evanston. That's what you are. An absolute idiot. You got yourself into a giant mess, and now you have to figure a way out. Stop freaking out and think! This time it's not Bud's voice. It's Olivia's. She didn't call me a coward, but the implication is there.

Okay, okay. Deep breaths. In through the nose, out through the mouth. It's going to be okay.

Be calm like Olivia. Think like CB. Be strong like me. Be fast like yourself. Now it is Bud. Yeah. He's exactly right. I can do this. I. Can. Do. This.

Really, if I condense it all down to one thing, one simple goal, it's to get to the front gate and open it for CB and Oakley. They must be close. They may even be out there right now, looking for us. Furious that we left. I can't wait for CB to yell at me. I've never wanted anything more.

There it is, that's my plan. I'm going to run like holy hell toward where I think the gate is, and when I get there, I'm going to scream my head off until someone hears me. I'm going to believe that Emily and Harper are tucked away safe somewhere, and they'll be okay until help arrives.

I've moved away from the stream, but I haven't crossed it. I listen and don't hear anything but the faint rush of water. If my calculations are correct, I am about 1000 feet from the northwest corner of the property. I could stick to the perimeter and follow the fence line of the ranch all the way around to the gate, couldn't I? Except... if I were an asshole like Jonny Law, I'd want to keep my prey away from the fences, where a passerby might see or hear them. I'd set up cameras to alert me and maybe even boobie traps to keep my prey from getting too close. Since Johnson Law is a fan of hunting, I can only imagine what those traps are like.

A picture of my ankle in the jaws of a vicious bear trap flashes through my brain. *Stop it, Angel!* It's CB yelling at me this time.

I stand up and brush leaves and dirt from my butt. I need to move now before I paralyze myself by thinking about what could be.

CHAPTER FIFTY-FIVE

Saturday, September 12, 2009, Morning

HARPER

Seeing Emily's condition gives me an odd perspective. She's hurt bad, but because she was turned out sooner, she hasn't been tortured to the same extent I have. I guess there are advantages to being boring. I should have been smart enough to realize that being a wise-ass wasn't helping me. Except then he might have turned us both out, and we'd both be dead.

Now, I'm trying to seem confident, ever hopeful, and all that. It's hard. I have no idea where the girl Angel is, but that freaking gunshot has me shook. For Emily's and my sake, I've convinced myself he was just playing with her. It can't end like this.

The only 'good' news, and it's really not good at all, is that the shot sounded like it came from the other side of the ranch. But it's been a while now, so for all we know, he's headed right toward us.

It feels as though we've been staggering through the woods toward the buildings for hours. I'd guess it's approaching noon, based on the sun above us. I've lost the small reserve of energy I started with, and Emily is practically carrying me now. Twice, I've tripped over fallen logs and landed on my hip as I twist to avoid landing on the bad knee. It's swollen and painful. Each time I trip, it takes minutes we can't spare as I struggle to get back up. Each time I seriously consider whether I should just stay here and become part of the compost at the bottom of the forest floor.

I get up because Emily put herself back in danger to come for me. I can't forget that.

Thankfully, I see a flash of red through the trees. The barn. I'll ponder later why so many barns are red. At least, I hope I'll have the time and opportunity to consider things like that. "See it?" I whisper.

"The house is over there, I think, and the dog kennel is that way," Emily points.

I don't see anything, but I believe her. Because we're closer to the buildings, I move slower. Under the canopy of the dense trees, there are all sorts of wild plants growing. Fluffy green ferns, and something with bouquets of tiny white flowers. Tall grasses. As we get to the edge of the woods, where it meets the pasture, there are wide strips of a plant with pretty purple flowers. Beyond that, it's all field grass. I don't want to cross the grass. There's no protection.

I imagine muscular European hunting dogs the size of ponies with giant fangs and raised hackles charging at us across that pasture. Interestingly, he hasn't released them yet. I whisper, "Did you ever actually hear dogs?"

Emily thinks, then says, "No. I didn't."

"Me either." We're getting close enough I can just make out the kennel building. My left eye, sans lid, is pretty much useless. I think it's infected because it aches, but there's no vision. Unfortunately, my right 'good' eye is fading fast. Things are blurry, and any kind of direct light burns. How long until I'm totally blind? I'll be completely useless at that point.

The kennel is directly ahead. There are no dog sounds and no dog smells. I don't think there are actually any dogs. Where's the human door? It's got to be at one of the ends, doesn't it? Or maybe on the other side of the building. We lurch to the right, away from the barn.

We're in a sunnier area, and although my vision is no clearer, I can see Emily looks worse, much worse, than when she found me. I want to collapse on the ground and give in to the grief that is washing over me.

"Hang in there, please. Please, Harp, you have to hold on," she whispers. I guess I'm not doing a very good job of masking my emotions. I wrap an arm around her, and we hobble like contestants in a three-legged race toward the kennels. I'm shaking so hard I can hear my teeth rattle. I don't know whether I'm shaking because I'm scared to find out I'm wrong about the dogs or because my body is giving up. *But, please don't let us die here. Please, please, oh please.*

We don't get too close, just move to the very edge of the trees to have a better view. There's a human door at the end of the kennel building. I'm sure there are cameras nearby, but where? I don't see any on this end of the building. I squint and look into the trees with my almost working eye. Again, I don't see anything that looks like a camera. Maybe it's at the other end of the building, closer to the barn. Maybe. The next question is, will the door be unlocked?

Carefully, together, we stumble-hop the twenty feet across the strip of grass that is between us and the kennel. *Please don't trip, please don't trip.* If either of us goes down now, we're both going down, and I'm not sure we can get back up. Finally, we reach the door, moving carefully because the ground is carpeted in leaves and crunching leaves are noisy. I'm gasping for breath. I look one more time for cameras, and this time I see one. It's on the front of the kennels, facing the barn. "Look," I whisper and point up. Emily sees it and gasps.

"Now we know what they look like." I test the handle. It's covered with a layer of dust, and it sticks, but we both shove, and the door swings open with a small squeak. There's a horrible smell, but a bad smell isn't going to kill us, so we'll deal with it. I use the edge of the sweatshirt to wipe the dust from the handle so my handprint doesn't show. Then I realize that looks as obvious as a handprint. I point to the dusty ground. "Get some dirt and throw it on the knob." It likely won't pass close examination, but it's less noticeable than a sparkling clean knob.

We step into the darkness, and Emily pulls the door closed almost all of the way, stopping just before the squeak. For just a minute, we need to catch our breath and figure out our next steps.

CHAPTER FIFTY-SIX

Saturday, September 12, 2009, Midday

ANGEL

I need to cross the creek. As far as I can see, in either direction, it looks pretty wild. It's totally open to the west, with no protection, nowhere to hide. It will make me a sitting duck if Jonny Law comes up on me while I'm trying to cross that way. But, if I try to find a 'bright side' I suppose I'd see him coming, too, if I don't feel a bullet or arrow first.

To the east, there's a steep embankment that's more mud than dirt. There are deep tire tracks in the soil, and it looks like it gets regular use. Someone must drive down here for something. There are thick woods on either side of the dirt track. If I wade across here, I can use that road to get started up the hill and then cut into the trees. I need to be careful. One false step and I'll fall into the pool. My best chance is to fall into the shallow part, if I have to fall at all.

I take off my sneakers and roll my jeans to my knee so they don't get soaked. It seems a little stupid to be worrying about wet jeans right now, but it's also weirdly comforting to control anything I can. I tie the strings of my shoes together and loop them around my neck to keep them high and dry and my hands free.

I take another deep breath, in through my nose, out through my mouth. I don't remember which shrink taught me this simple trick, but it works. Most of the time, anyway.

No time like the present, Ange. Get your ass moving! It's Bud. Was he this much of a nag when he was alive? I don't remember, and that makes me sort of sad.

My first tentative peek around the woodpile shows no movement of any sort. I hear birds. The only other sound is the swoosh of moving water. I slowly step out of my hiding spot and wait to see if my appearance brings any reaction. Nope. Nothing. Jonny Law must be busy with something else. Or someone else.

There really is no best place to cross, so I take careful steps down the bank. The mud and soft grasses are much easier on my bare feet than the sticks and branches and brambles were, but they're also slick. Jesus, the water is moving fast. I see stones below, so it's not very deep, but this isn't going to be easy. I take a careful step in. Damn, it's colder than I was expecting. The rocks under my feet are sharp and uneven, but it's only ten, maybe fifteen feet to the other side. I've got this.

Once I get across, it's easy peasy. Just run like the devil's after me, because he is.

I'm halfway to the bank when I hear a sound. It makes me jerk, and I almost lose my balance. Once I'm stable, I scan the other side. I don't see a damn thing except for fallen trees, branches, shrubs, and grasses. Wait. What's that? A flash of reddish tan moves through a cluster of tall grass, and I see sparkling eyes, too low in the grass to be human.

Whatever it is looks interested but not scary. It's not barking. A dog would bark, right? If it was one of the dogs from the kennel Emily told me about, it would be a hunting dog, and it would alert, wouldn't it? Maybe it's a wolf, but wouldn't a wolf growl?

I decide it's a coyote. I feel like I could win a battle with a coyote. Or at least not end up dead. CB says coyotes are her spirit animal because they're playful and adaptable when they're not sick or scared. I like that. Okay. It's definitely a coyote.

I take another step, and the coyote watches, then the eyes

disappear into the grasses.

A few more steps, and I'm on the bank, and then I'm on the road. It's not a steep hill, but it's hard to climb with the mud slick and sucking at my bare feet. I want to put my shoes back on, but not here, not in such an open space. Maybe I should follow the coyote. Does it live here? Does it know a way out? Some secret tunnel that goes to the safety of the outside world? Maybe to the Acme Corporation?

Once I'm in the grass, taller than my head when I'm sitting on my butt, I wipe the mud and leaves from my feet, tug my shoes on, lace them tight, and listen again. Nothing but birds and water. Good. Now, which way do I go? I think the gate is south, and if that's right, I'm nearing the northwest corner of the property. But what if I'm wrong? What if I waste time running the wrong direction, or worse, in circles, or even worse yet, right into Jonny Law's clutches?

Angel, calm down. Use your brain. You know how to do this. Look up. Bud's voice lectures.

I look up. The sun is high in the sky now, and if I think of where it was when we started this insane adventure, I know where to go.

Thanks. I tell my brother. I start running in the same direction the coyote went, not full out, more of a jog through the trees that look like bald pencils. Their leaves have already started to fall, carpeting the ground.

Where are the cameras? I'm sure they're everywhere. It would be good if I spotted one, so I could recognize and avoid the rest. But nothing jumps out at me, and I have to keep my eyes on the ground so I don't trip on a log and break my face.

I'm nearing the end of the spindly woods. The carpet of leaves has composted, so it's been quiet to run through. This new area is full of dead branches and shrubs. Crunchy, in other words, which means *loud* if you're running through it. No choice.

I speed up, figuring if I'm going to be loud, I better also be fast. This is just a bizarre track event, I tell myself. Jump a hurdle, dodge a tree, don't catch your foot in that nest of broken branches.

It's getting hot, and I'm sweating at my hairline and between my boobs. If this were a typical run, I'd take off my hoodie and wrap it around my waist, but I want all the padding I can get. Plus, I think the black hoodie is better camouflage than my Stones T-shirt.

I'm five minutes into the new topography when I hear it.

"Teach your children well..."

I stop, drop to my knees, and crawl between two tree trunks. Both are wrapped in vines, and my internal alarm system is screaming at me. Is that poison ivy?

Aw, come on.

CHAPTER FIFTY-SEVEN

Saturday, September 12, 2009, Midday

HARPER

Once we're inside, I put a finger to my lips in the universal "shhh" sign. No dogs. Nothing to be afraid of except that terrible smell. Whatever it is, we're both gagging. My insides rumble in protest. It smells like a sewage leak, but it also smells weirdly sweet. What the freaking hell is the goddamn smell, and where is it coming from?

"What is it? God, it's awful," Emily whispers and gags again.

"Shhh!" I warn. "I don't know."

There's a bench against a wall. We stagger to it and sit. We're both desperate for rest.

"Where have you been?" I whisper.

"It's a long story, so I'll tell you most of it later. But the girl, that's Angel. Another woman is coming soon, with Oakley. That's the good news." Emily closes her eyes. "The bad news is, they don't know exactly where we are. We were supposed to wait outside for them and then call the cops and bust down the gate to save you. But I got impatient. Now..."

Neither of us says anything as we look around. It's shadowy, the only light from filthy skylights above us. The panes are so buried under leaf debris and dirt they hardly allow in any light at all. There are no other windows, which is good, I guess. I make out the shape of another door at the other end, which is bad.

On the wall opposite the bench, there are four pegs. A large dusty leather dog collar hangs from each. The collars have names branded into the leather: Titus. Elvis. Hank. Pepper. Someone has carved crosses into the wall in the center of each collar. This is an altar for beloved pets. Did Dear Sheriff once have a soul? Or is there, or was there, someone else who loved these animals?

I'm about to whisper to Emily to peek outside when we hear crunching leaves. They're close, but not too close. I press my back against the wall, find Emily's hand, and hold my breath.

Fear turns my guts into liquid. I look around to see if there's anywhere to hide. There's not. But I finally understand what the smell is. My body arches and lurches and vomit rises in my throat, but I swallow it back down before it shoots out of my mouth, which is terrible and horrible and burns. I can't let Emily see or know until whoever is outside is gone. It's too late for me.

I know. Before there are bones in the pool, there is this place.

To my right, between me and the second door, there's a low concrete tub, the kind you wash dogs in. In the tub is a mass of something green and slimy. Parts of the green mass are sliding—no, dripping. In other places, the green has turned black and there are areas of white just visible. The thing used to be a person.

Jesus, if things don't go right, that thing could be any of us.

Keep your shit together, Harpy.

On the other side of the door, Vero says, "There's a third girl. I think it's that *puta* that came here with the blond girl."

"Whadya mean? The dead one?" Sheriff Johnson grunts. I'm pretty sure the fact that he's standing here means he didn't kill Angel. She got away!

"I don't think she's dead." Vero says.

"The hell you say. There's no way she got out and she sure as hell didn't last all this time in here without you spotting her on the cameras."

"After that strange one fell out of the tree, and you went after her, a second girl dropped down from the same tree. She headed after you. I lost her in the area by the creek where the owl took out the camera. But she's on the ranch somewhere." Vero sounds pissed. "And I think it's the second girl we haven't been able to find."

Dear Sheriff isn't pissed; he's thrilled. "Well, now! That means I have three deer to hunt! Ain't life amazin'! I'm gonna call Mildred and tell her to let the deputies know I'm taking a couple of days' vacation. Then I'll call Mrs. Johnson and tell her I'm working a case and won't be home for a bit. We are going to have us a fine ol' time, Veronique! Yessiree, we are!"

Vero sounds just as gleeful now that she knows he's not angry. "Since there are three, can I have one of the cunts? Please?"

"They're mine." The Sheriff snaps. It's the first time I've heard him show anger toward her. "I might let you play with one before I finish her. But I do the finishing. Always."

She's suitably chastised. She sounds grateful, the evil bitch. "Of course. Thank you."

The implications of their conversation almost overtake the stress from the smell. Almost.

Emily has her eyes squeezed tightly shut, and she's pushing so hard against the wall she's about to become one with it. I touch her hand. I'd squeeze, but I haven't been able to feel parts of that hand for a while now.

"I'm going back to the house to make those calls. You watch the cameras and figure out where our Bambis are. Hot damn, this is going to be a day of days!"

Crunching leaves suggest they've left, but I hold a finger to my mouth and shake my head at Emily. *Not yet. Keep quiet. Wait.*

"What is that goddamn smell?" Emily finally whispers, unable to control herself. She's swallowing convulsively.

"Don't look," I say quietly. "There's part of a body over there. It's been there a while. That's the smell."

Despite what I tell her not to do, I can't help but look myself. A few feet from the concrete tub, there is a hook hanging from the ceiling. A butcher shop hook. There's a box freezer. And on top of the freezer, there's a meat grinder.

Vero's comment about processing the meat comes back to me in bright neon letters. I gag. I cannot tell Em. Not ever.

Em completely ignores my warning, looks, and starts to scream. I slap my working hand over her mouth to shut her up. I can feel her lips and jaw moving against my hand.

"Shut up! Shut up, Emily!" I hiss. "I know it's bad, but do you want to be laying there with it?"

I get the feeling she's on the verge of full-on hysterics. I'm not sure what to do. But if she lets loose, they will absolutely find us, and quick. "Emily! Stop it right now!" and I flick my finger into one of the cuts on her cheek. I instantly regret it because her face is such a battered mess, but it does get her to stop.

"What—what—what -" she stammers and starts to look again at the tub. She's going into shock or something. I put my hand on her cheek and turn it back toward me.

"Forget it's there, ignore it, you have to, you have to."

"I—I—I -" Emily stammers.

"I know. Emily, I know. You have to get yourself together. You found help! You got yourselves here! You're smart and strong. You can do this. We just have to find a way to fight. That's all." I try to soothe her with my voice since the words are not what she wants to hear, which is that we can walk out that door and pretend none of this happened and get on with the lives we planned.

"You're right. Sorry. I—I am fine. What are we going to do?" She whispers.

"For now, we need to stay put and figure out a plan. We're not going to be able to dodge them forever, especially with the cameras." I say. At the idea of staying here, with the mess in the tub, knowing what I know, my gut threatens to blow again.

Emily shakes her head, nearly hysterical. "I can't. I just can't. I have no strength left, no fortitude. Harper, I can't do it—"

Fear makes me lose patience and I snap. "I'm scared too! I'm fucking terrified. But you escaped, and you came back, and now we have to figure this shit out. So let's just sit here and be quiet and think. Okay?"

Eventually, she nods, and I finally unclench. I'm dying, I know that. I'm pretty sure it's too late to fix me. My only mission now is to get Emily out, alive, before I go.

I really need her not to be the thing that gets us killed.

CHAPTER FIFTY-EIGHT

Saturday, September 12, 2009, Late Morning

ANGEL

I never saw the potential for a Crosby, Nash & Young song to be an earworm, but it is. Now it's in my head, I can't get rid of it. Oddly, Jonny Law sings only a few of the lines, and hums the melody in between. Sometimes he sings the key—*If they told you, you would cry*—over and over.

Who broke him?

Jonny Law keeps moving through the woods I just left. I watch him from my spot between the trees. There's a chance he saw me and is trying to fake me out. Nothing I can do if that's the case. I wait until he's totally out of sight, and I don't hear humming or singing. I push through the trees and the evil vines and race toward the pasture.

The pasture is the size of two high school football fields sitting side by side, and absolutely bare of trees. I can either run straight across or cling to the woods, which will give me some cover if he sees me. But it will also slow me down considerably.

I'm debating my choice right up to the edge of the field. *Right to the woods, or straight through? Right to the woods, or straight through?* I shout in my head.

I let my body decide and feel an extra burst of energy as I head onto the turf of the field.

In my head, Bud and Olivia and CB are yelling, *Fuck! Fuck! Fuck!*

Run faster!

There's one slim tree line that is a marker between this pasture and the buildings. I glimpse the top of the barn—at least, I guess that's what it is, judging by its size. I'm at least 100 yards away. Lots of time for someone to take a shot and down me like a deer.

Run, run, run, run

What am I going to do when I get to the barn? Holy crap. I need a plan! Should I stop and see if I can find Emily or Harper? Or keep going to the gate? Or swerve off to the woods and hide and catch my breath?

My legs are pumping so hard it feels like I won't be able to stop even when I want to. At this rate, unless something gets in my way, I'm going to keep running right to the gate.

Never tell the Universe your plans.

I hear a shot, and something stings in the general area of my right hip. I don't slow, at first, just yelp and keep going. That's when I realize he got me. Must not be too serious, because I'm able to keep going. I run as fast as I can manage while I put a hand to my ass and try to figure out how bad it is.

When my fingers brush my hip, the hole in my jeans and a sharp sting tell me I've found the spot. My fingers come up sticky, but there's not a ton of blood. But krikey, it burns! I can't stop running, but I can zig-zag. I don't know if it's an urban myth or whether it really might work to avoid an attacker. I'll try anything that makes me a more difficult target.

I hear his laugh behind me. He's not anywhere close enough to grab me, but he's definitely close enough to shoot again. He shouts, "Damn, girl, you're a feisty little bit! I made a mistake leaving you at the motel!"

That pisses me off. I ignore the pain and put on more speed. I zag left, then right, and feign like I'm going to keep going right toward the woods. At the last second, I swerve left and dodge between two of the buildings. There's the dog kennel, and the barn.

I don't see or hear anyone else, just Jonny Law, who is singing and humming. Now that I'm slowing down, the pain is catching up. Holy hell, it stings! I don't think it will kill me, but I'm still pissed.

The doors to the barn are wide open. Something about it reminds me of the clown rides at amusement parks. The building is two stories, red, and badly in need of paint. I catch a glimpse of stone foundation at the corners. The rest is wood. This all registers as I careen toward the doors. A giant puddle of mud sends me sliding. I somehow manage to stay upright and I burst into the barn.

I pause to look around, getting my bearings. At the back, there's a heavy-looking sliding metal door. I'm sure that leads to where the girls were kept, and I'm also sure I don't want to end up back there for any reason.

The front of the barn is a complete mess. An old green metal desk, missing most of its drawers, sits in the middle of the room. It's piled high with empty soda and booze bottles, telephone books, seed packages, tools, and an old sled is perched on top. The floor is thick with sawdust and junk mail. Hooks, lethal-looking and rusty, hang from the underside of the loft. The hooks hold various items: lanterns, rope, a pair of red and white pom poms...

This is hoarder heaven. The sides walls are stacked high with hunting and farm equipment, TVs, old wood doors and fireplace mantels, a kid's metal pedal car, random furniture, trash bags full of who knows what, boxes of overflowing junk. Along the left wall, hay bales rise eight feet high, nearly buried under winter coats and seed signs. Barely visible through the chaos, there's a ladder to the loft.

I can either find somewhere to hide in all the crap and risk tetanus, or I can go up.

I choose up.

Climbing a ladder with a bullet hole in your tush hurts like hell.

CHAPTER FIFTY-NINE

Saturday, September 12, 2009, Late Morning

ANGEL

The loft is nearly as much of a mess as the ground floor. Up here, I find old screen doors, car and bike tires, terra cotta pots, rubber hoses, and a lot of graffiti. "Jonny was here" and "Sam is king" are two of the dominant ones. It smells dusty and mildewy. There's a roll of orange plastic snow fencing. Piles and piles of dirty magazines are tucked in the corner closest to the ladder, next to a couple of mouse-eaten old-style down pillows and a crusty-looking sleeping bag. Crushed red party cups and a dozen empty bottles of Jack Daniels litter the floor. There's a crumpled pack of Marlboro red cigarettes next to a matchbook from a place called *Daddy's Money*. Great name for a college town bar.

The one thing I am desperately looking for but haven't seen is a telephone. If there is one, it's downstairs. I am nowhere near ready to go back down there.

I don't hear singing, or humming, or anything at all. It's dead quiet. Wrong choice of words. Rephrase. It's too quiet.

Where are Emily and Harper? Where is Jonny Law? And where is the girlfriend, Vero? I haven't caught a glimpse of her yet.

I do a careful waltz through the junk, picking and choosing where I put my feet, praying the floorboards don't squeak. I want to get to the corner farthest from the ladder, where I can see all directions, and then I need to check this damn wound.

The loft is twenty feet front to back by forty feet wide. The vaulted center is probably ten feet high. It's another ten feet down to the floor below. If it was cleared space, it would be a good size. As it is, crammed full of junk, it's claustrophobic.

I finally reach the corner. There's a dusty military trunk, wood with metal straps. It's large enough I can sit on it, but it's so dirty I don't want to. I listen again. Silence. I feel reasonably safe as I carefully slide my jeans down to identify exactly where the sting is coming from. It would suck to get caught with my pants down but I need to assess the damage.

The wound is ugly, but not at all what I expected from getting shot, even if it is just a flesh wound. There's a trench in my flesh the length, width, and depth of my index finger. It curves along the top of my right butt cheek, just below my waist, around my side. It's not bleeding much, but the area is angry red. I realize I'm looking at my flesh, minus its usual covering of pale skin. The pain feels like a burn. If I didn't know I'd been shot, I would say I'd pushed myself into the edge of a hot griddle and split my skin open. It freaking stings.

"Don't you ever ask them why? If they told you, you would cry."

Shit. He's here.

CHAPTER SIXTY

Saturday, September 12, 2009, Late Morning

HARPER

We've been in the dog kennels for a while now, and I'm getting weaker with each minute. I can't stop thinking about Vero telling me about the process for 'the meat.' Fortunately, I can't remember the steps. I don't want to come across anything that makes me remember.

I'm almost used to the goddamn smell, or maybe my brain has stopped recognizing odors. We are both getting very good at whispering.

"Emily, you have to go. Run for the house. Try to find a phone. I'll slow you down, so you have to leave me here."

Emily doesn't respond immediately. She's over the minor freak out she had before. Now she's the woman who talked a complete stranger into helping her save her friend. She reaches across the space between us and carefully touches my face. "Good grief, you're a mess."

I laugh, and it feels good, even though it hurts. "Yeah, well, some of us didn't have time for a salon visit." I can't get over her hair. Even with this funky Goth 'do, she's beautiful.

"If I leave, you have to promise me you will do everything you can to stay alive until I bring help. Do not tell me I came back into this fucking hell hole for nothing. You have to live. We both do. We all do."

Clearly, she's referring to Angel, wherever she is. It hits me that if I meet Angel, she may very well be the last new friend I make. That's a depressing thought. I really want to meet her and thank her and beg her to keep Emily safe after I'm gone. She's going to need a friend who understands all of—this.

I nod. "I'll do my damnedest. And you have to do the same."

"Deal. We haven't heard Vero in a while." Emily points out. "Did they tell you where they watch the cameras? The house? The barn?"

I try to remember, then shake my head. "I never saw her at a computer, so I would bet they're in the house somewhere. You can't go into the house if she's there. You have no way to defend yourself."

"Agreed." Emily starts to chew her lip, then gasps when it hurts.

"There's nothing you can use as a weapon." I've looked. The collars are all that's here, except the thing that was once a body. Not even a leash or brush. "Hey, can you open one of the kennel doors and look inside? Maybe there's a food dish or water bowl. It won't do a lot, but it could be useful to create a distraction."

Emily hobbles obediently to the nearest kennel, the one farthest from the concrete tub, and peers inside. I don't blame her for not rushing in. We've both spent too much time in kennels. When she carefully opens the gate and goes inside, I know she sees something. She comes back out, a large metal dog bowl in her hands. "You're so smart."

"When you've been treated like a dog for weeks, it comes naturally." I try to joke. It falls flat. "Wear it as a helmet. Or throw it at something, so it makes a loud noise to distract Vero and the Sheriff."

Emily takes a deep breath in through her nose, out through her mouth.

"Meditation breathing?" I ask.

"CB taught me."

"CB?"

"She's Angel's—mom sort of? It's complicated. She's a healer type.

She's the reason I'm standing here in such excellent condition," Emily says and tries to curtsy. She nearly crashes to the floor.

We are screwed.

I watch her take slow, careful steps to the door.

"Hey."

Emily turns her head.

"I love you. I know you know, but I need to say it. We've had great adventures. From third grade to now... can't imagine having done it with anyone else." I'd wink if I had two working eyes. It would probably look frightening with just one. I hope I still have lips but that's a question, too. I blow her a kiss.

"Fuck you. Stay alive. Do not die on me. I will kill you." Emily says and slips out the door. I'm alone again.

CHAPTER SIXTY-ONE

Saturday, September 12, 2009, Midday

C B

"Damn her!" I kick at the blanket and the stupid "Gone fishing. Back soon." The message dissolves into a pile of twigs. *Idiota!*

"I bet it was Emily's idea," Oakley says.

"Doesn't matter whose freaking idea it was," I say, furious. "They're both fools. If we're lucky, they're in the woods somewhere, trying to spy through the fence. But so far, there hasn't been all that much luck in this endeavor. I'd bet money they're inside the damn fence, maybe dangling from meat hooks."

His eyes get big at 'meat hooks,' but he doesn't say anything about it. Instead, "What do we do?"

"First, I'm going to call Nick and give him the coordinates. Then... fuck. Let me think." I squat and press my hands into the sides of my head to put some counterpressure on the pounding. *Damn it, damn it, damn it.* "Go figure out where the hell we are."

Oakley nods and trots off.

The minute he's out of sight, and hearing, I break down. I sob, for Angel, for Emily, for my niece Lexi. Mostly for myself. Because I can't stand the idea that I let Angel get into this situation, that I may have made a decision that's put her life in danger. If something happens to her, I'm not sure I will survive it. I'm really not.

That thought snaps me back. *Times up! No more pity parties.* You can cry later after you chew Angel a new one. And hug her for an

201

hour or two. Then you both can cry all you want.

I pull my phone from my pocket and start toward the road. Again, I call Nick, who answers immediately this time. "We've found the ranch." Oakley gives me the numbers on the sign at the intersection, and I repeat them to Nick. "The girls aren't where we put them. Don't bother yelling. Just send everyone you can send, right now."

"What are you going to do?" Nick asks sharply.

I take a deep breath. "I'm the Big Bad Wolf. I'll try asking nicely, and if they don't let me in, I'm going to blow the fucking gate down."

CHAPTER SIXTY-TWO

Saturday, September 12, 2009, Midday

ANGEL

"Well, now, I tell you what. I very much appreciate you accepting my invitation." Jonny Johnson says from the center of the chaos that is the barn. He speaks slowly, the timber of his voice warm Texas honey.

How the hell did he find me so fast? Oh, hell. Muddy footprints, probably. That doesn't mean I'm going to confirm my presence. Maybe he's bluffing.

A blast of his rifle through the floor of the loft indicates he's not bluffing. *Fuck.* I sit on the lid of the dusty trunk and slowly and carefully raise my legs onto the top. Sitting hurts like hell, but it probably hurts worse to have a bullet enter and exit your body instead of just skimming it. A bit of wood and metal between me and the floor seems like a good idea.

"It wasn't supposed to be like this. I thought I ended it when I ended him." Sheriff Jonny Johnson says. "Do you know I have three kids?"

My mouth is moving before I can stop it. "Jake, Jessica, and Juli-anne. And your wife is Melissa. She was a beauty queen. Her father is an old-money oilman." He's quiet, so I add, "Wonder what they'd think if they knew what kind of man their daddy really is."

Something crashes below, and another bullet comes through the floor, on the opposite end of the loft. This time it's clear he's angry but not ready to hurt me—yet. "Well, aren't you miss smarty pants. No matter. The sins of the father end with me. Jake has never been here, and he will never be like his grandpa or me. Never!" He fires another shot up, again, nowhere near me.

"Your father was—like this?" I ask, deciding it may be to my advantage if he's in the mood to talk. I know from past experience, building rapport with your aggressor can be helpful.

"My father, John with an H, was the original hunter on this land. Him and his friends used to pick up girls in Oklahoma City and bring them back here and have their fun. The friends would go on home, and John would finish the game his own special way. Don't know if the friends knew about that part."

I hear him shuffling around below. Then, something else falls, not a crash this time, but a slide. Maybe a pile of magazines. "What about your mother? What did she think?"

He snort-laughs. "My mama wasn't around after I was eight. John told me and my brother Sam she took off on us, didn't want to live in the middle of nowhere on a dusty ranch. But later, after I did the thing, I realized that was a lie. My mama is in the pool, with the rest." He fires another shot up. Again, away from me. "Don't know why I'm running at the mouth today. Maybe it's time. Maybe after we resolve this situation, I'll finally have the guts to end it."

"What's the pool?" I'm not about to ask what he means by having the guts to end it.

"The pool, the pool!" He snaps as if I should know, and BAM! another shot comes through the floor. "In the creek, where the Harper girl was hiding, there's a natural pool. All the bones of all the prey are there. It's a haunted place, but I like to think my mama takes care of them bones."

Jesus. And then I think, how many bullets is that? Five? Six? I'm not sure. I'm also not sure how many rounds a rifle can shoot before it needs to be reloaded. "I'm sorry. What a terrible thing, to think your mother left you and then find out your father actually murdered her."

"Thank you. That's a kindness on your part." Jonny sighs deeply. "That man killed my mother, and Stacy, and my brother Sam. He took my whole family."

"Stacy? Was that your sister?"

Another snort-laugh. "Sister, no. She was Sam's girlfriend. She's the dynamite what blew it all to shit. Dumb Sam shoulda known better than to try and have a girl. John found out, and him and his friends dragged them into the truck one night after a football game. Brought them back here. John and the others teased them and got handsy with her but didn't do their usual, being that she was Sam's girl. Then they got really drunk and started pushing Sam to 'do her, right here, so we can watch.' Stacy freaked out. Sam said hell no and tried to get her out of there. Took her into the house and was trying to figure a plan to get her back to town. He didn't know, John sent his friends home. John came in, dragged Stacy outside, and, well, in the end, Sam died trying to stop him. Then Stacy died, and ... it was just John and me."

I almost feel sorry for him. "How old were you?"

"Twelve."

Holy crap. I do feel sorry for him, the him that was a kid. Then a bullet blasts through the floor, and I decide the man he is now can fuck himself. "That's a terrible story, and I'm so sorry. What happened to your—John?"

He's quiet, too quiet. I hear a click, something falls to the floor and then another click. Reload? Finally, he answers. "Well, one day, he was hunting prey, and he got his foot jammed in between something in the bottom of the pool. I like to think it was the souls of all the bones. I came upon him, and he begged me to save him."

I don't say anything, in part because I don't want to ask whether he saved his father, because I'm pretty sure he didn't, and also I'm thinking. I can't stay where I am. If he's reloading he's not going to let me go. At some point, those bullets will come closer to my corner. I have to move.

I wait for him to start speaking again and carefully, oh so carefully, put my feet on the floor, moving slowly, an inch at a time, to avoid making noise. Now I'm standing, pressed up against the back wall, hoping that's an awkward spot to successfully hit a moving target. Trying to navigate all the junk on the floor makes it slow going.

I have an idea, but I need to ask a question that will keep him talking long enough for me to get to the other side without getting shot. "Clearly, you hate what John did. How did you end up becoming just like him?"

Bullet through the floor, followed quickly by another. Apparently, that is not an acceptable question. "I'm nothing like him! He hunted for pleasure. For me, it's a blood illness. I can't escape it! I have tried, oh how I have tried."

I'll be closer to him, so this plan of mine better work. I hear him pacing, which is good. I move, sideways, pressed flat against the back wall as I scoot toward the sleeping bag and dirty magazines in the opposite corner. Each time I have to raise my foot over a box, or old toy, or tool, I send up a small prayer.

"I swore I'd never hunt. I graduated school and moved to Texas, and joined the sheriff's a few months after he was gone. Never planned to come back here. Wanted nothing to do with it. And then, around the anniversary of his death, I had to come to town to sign papers at the attorneys. Went to a bar, got drunk, and this girl started flirting. I didn't mean to do anything to her. Brought her back here, just like a regular hookup, ya know? But then...well, I couldn't stop it. It was like I wasn't myself. I was John in a Jonny suit. I don't remember none of it. Just found her, dead in the middle of a pasture, the next day. And I knew. I knew it was me."

He doesn't shoot and I realized it's scarier than if he does. But I'm getting closer to my goal. Eight more feet to the sleeping bag. My plan—my survival!—hinges on there being at least one match in that damned Daddy's Money matchbook.

"No use trying to hide it, girl. I know you're moving." He says and shoots at the exact spot where I was just a minute ago. There's a loud PING! When the bullet hits the trunk, I can see a hole blasted through the top. He could've killed me at any time.

My eyes burn with tears, but I keep going. I might as well ask another question. "So just that once? But then—what happened? Are Harper and Emily the first girls since then?" I know they're not, but it might keep him talking for a few more minutes.

"Hell, no. There's been a girl every year around the anniversary of John's death. Until I met Vero. Veronique. You haven't met her yet. You will. You'll like each other. Well, she'll like you. You'll probably hate her, truth be told. She's crazy." He laughs. *Bam!* Another bullet through the floor, this time a foot to my left, like he's herding me toward the ladder.

"Jonny, you said you want to stop. Why don't you stop now, let us all go? Be the good man you wanted to be as a boy? Be the good man your children and wife think you are? Stop, so Jake never learns what he comes from. Let this end with you." I make my voice as soothing and calm as I can, knowing it will either work or he'll fly into a rage. I'm close enough to my target that it's worth a risk. I reach the sleeping bag and pick up one of the pillows. My foot bumps an empty Jack Daniels bottle, and I pick that up, too. My fingers dig into the seam of the pillow, which isn't hard since the mice have had their fun. It's easy to create a hole large enough to shove the bottle in with the feathers.

My eyes are glued to the top of the ladder because, for all I know, he's coming up to get me. With my other hand, I kneel and search the floor for the matchbook. *Pat, pat, pat.*

"It will end with me, girl." He's angry, and at the same time, he's calm. In my experience, when someone is angry and calm at the same time, they have control and will do more harm.

He's at the base of the ladder now, so close I can smell him, a mixture of department store cologne and sweat.

I find the matchbook and clutch the pillow between my knees, ignoring the angry howl from my hip. I fold back the ancient cover. One match. If I don't do this right, my only chance is gone. My eyes scan the space around me. I need to keep him talking. "What's your plan? Kill us, and how many more? When will it end?"

BAM! This one is very close, so close I feel splinters of wood flutter around my face. I see what I need, grab it, and crouch. I rip out pages of *Beaver Hunt* magazine and twist them into a cone. I tear the pages at the top edge to make a rough fringe. The pillow and bottle are at my feet.

"It's almost done. I'm tired. After I take care of this situation," I can hear his feet on the wood rungs, and his voice is getting louder as he nears the loft, "I will make sure it's done, once and for all."

CHAPTER SIXTY-THREE

Saturday, September 12, 2009, Midday

ANGEL

I struggle to keep the cone tight while I open the matchbook and tear out the single precious match. Instead, I drop it. Damn! I squat and feel around with my hand again. *Pat, pat, pat.* I don't find the matchbook, but my hand touches something unexpected. Cool metal. Can it be? Is luck finally turning my way? I don't take my eyes off the place where the ladder joins the loft floor. Yes! It is! I pull out an old gun someone tucked into the sleeping bag. Maybe one of the Johnson brothers, fearful of their father.

I'm starting to believe in miracles after all.

The only exposure to a gun I've ever had is CB's little pink revolver. I know this is a revolver, too, but I couldn't tell you what kind. It's black metal with a wood handle, and it's good sized. I doubt it was new when the reader of the girly magazines hid up here. It looks like it's straight out of an old western. I see the cylinder part but have no idea if there are bullets in it. I've never held a gun in my hand, much less shot one.

"Well, I've enjoyed our little chat, but it's time to get to business," Jonny Law announces as he breaches the top of the ladder and steps onto the loft floor.

Fear floods my body, all my bravado gone in the blink of an eye. I have just enough presence of mind to move the gun behind me, but that's it. I trip on the bottle-spiked pillow in my panic and fall to the ground, landing half on the sleeping bag, half on a pile of empty Jack Daniels bottles. At least one shatters under me when I land, and I feel stabbing pain in my hip near the bullet wound.

Lady Luck gives, and Lady Luck takes.

Jonny Law smiles the same angelic smile he gave me when he dropped me at the motel and walks forward until he's standing over me, one booted foot on either side of my thighs. "Well, now, this isn't at all the way I expected our acquaintance to play out. I thought you were going to force me to kill you early on, and take away the pleasure of getting to know you."

I roll to my side, try to curl into a ball between his legs, which sends shooting pain through my hip. There are no words for how I'm feeling. *I can't be someone else's plaything again. I can't. I'd rather die.*

"Playtime is the most fun of all!" he says. The rifle is no longer aimed at me. Instead, it's hanging down by his side. Jonny Law is feeling confident that he's got the upper hand. I'm afraid he's right.

Angel! Shoot the motherfucker! Bud shouts. In my panic, I'd nearly forgotten the gun!

The revolver feels awkward and alien in my hand. I don't have time to worry whether it's loaded, or if I can aim straight, or if it will blow up, or shoot me instead. I raise the gun and point it straight up toward his head. I whisper a little prayer, and pull the trigger.

Nothing happens.

I'm not sure who is more shocked—him, that I have a gun at all, or me, that it didn't do anything. He recovers quickly, and bends over me, grinning.

I roll onto my back, hold the gun with both hands, and point it at him again. The muzzle is aimed at his face. That's when I see the cock and pull it back, then squeeze the trigger again.

Jonny Law jerks away as the bullet leaves the gun but he doesn't escape entirely. Many things happen at once. There's a *bang*! and he howls and stumbles backward. I crab-walk on my hands and feet through the broken glass, away from him, staring in horror. There's blood. So much blood. But he's still alive!

How can the monster be moving? How can he see me through all that blood? I have no idea, but he can, and he does, and he's angrier than ever.

CHAPTER SIXTY-FOUR

Saturday, September 12, 2009, Midday

HARPER

I meant it when I said I'd slow Em down, but that doesn't mean I'm going to sit here and rot, sucking in the smell of death while I wait to join it. Not knowing whether Em is alive or dead will speed my journey to the afterlife, I have no doubt. I'll keep my promise to stay alive as long as I can, but if I'm going to die, which I'm sure I am, I want to die fighting, not sitting around waiting for the grim reaper to find me.

Just as I am ready to test my courage and open the door, I hear the sound of feet pounding through the leaves outside. Small feet. Vero's feet? No, she'd be the one chasing, not being chased. I understand the first steps are the ones being chased because only a few moments later, I hear heavy feet crashing through the leaves. The Sheriff is after either Angel or Emily. If my sense of direction is working at all, they came toward the buildings. They weren't headed back to the field and woods. It has to be Angel. Emily should already be at the house or near it, shouldn't she?

I wait to hear if there are any more footsteps or if they change direction and head back toward me, but it's silent. I crack the door and peek out. No one. I listen again. Nothing. *Now or never, Harpy. Now or never.*

It feels safer and smarter to go around the back of the kennel since I've already spotted at least one camera on the front. I'm certainly not fast on my feet, but knowing that I'm moving toward a definitive outcome, one way or another has given me a little bit more energy. Unfortunately, having a jacked-up leg does not infuse one with grace, and I feel like I'm lurching Quasimodo-style. Whatever. Probably goes with the rest of my current 'look.'

Once I'm around the back of the kennel, I can see between the buildings. The large circular driveway is currently empty except for Dear Sherriff's SUV by the house. I hear talking coming from the barn. Definitely the Sheriff, but who is he speaking to? It's unclear. He's telling a story with the charmer voice, not the creepy monster voice. Maybe he's telling Angel the story he told me at the creek. We get it, dude. You had a fucked up childhood. Who didn't?

Whoever he's telling is in deep shit. I need to help if I can. That is when I spot the single door in the back of the barn's foundation. It's a start.

CHAPTER SIXTY-FIVE

Saturday, September 12, 2009, Midday

C B

There's no intercom at the gate, no way to communicate with anyone inside. I look up and see two cameras pointed toward the road. If someone is watching, they know we're here.

"We really are going to have to bust through," I say primarily to myself, although Oakley is standing beside me. The gates are the kind commercial businesses have, a sliding cantilever system that rolls on cables. I know *Casita* will be damaged, and I'm okay with that, but I'm not 100% sure she can make it through. The one thing I have going for me is that the gate is at the T of the intersection, so I can get good speed going before we hit. The fastest I've ever run *Casita* without a load is 85. My trailer would typically be full, but I did what Angel begged me to do and had a friend take the load back east for me. We're running empty.

The kid doesn't say much, as usual. I motion with my head to get back in the truck. I maneuver until I can turn us around and head away from the ranch down the straight gravel road. I have to find a way to turn around, and that's not going to be easy. I'm sweating with nerves.

"Kid, you ever shoot?"

"Shoot?"

I sigh and roll my eyes. "A gun."

"Oh. Yeah."

"You any good?"

"Yeah." He actually smiles, and it's the first time I've seen it. I can sort of understand what Emily sees in him, I suppose. He's sweet, definitely. Good looking in a pretty boy way. Quiet, but thoughtful. If he really is any good at shooting, I'll bump him from a 6 to a 9. If not for the stupid threesome thing, he'd go all the way to a 10.

"See my floral bag there," I indicate with my head. "Get it. Look in the side pocket."

He clambers out of his seat and nearly loses his balance. We're going straight, and nowhere near as fast as we soon will be. I drop him from a 6 to a 5.

Bag in hand, he pulls himself back into the passenger seat. "Got it."

"Side pocket, in a satin drawstring case, there's a revolver. Pull it out. Carefully. It's not loaded, but I don't want you dropping it." I spot a dirt road up on the right and slow. I'll turn in and then back out so I'm headed the way I need to be. "The bullets are in the satin bag so keep it out."

Oakley retrieves the satin drawstring case and returns the gym bag to the floor behind him. He loosens the strings of the bag and takes out the small pink and silver revolver. It looks silly in his large hand. Without direction, he loads bullets into the gun. He puts the satin bag with the remaining bullets in the front pocket of his jeans.

I slam on the brakes and he almost slides into the footwell as *Casita* slows. "Sorry. I just had a thought." Once we're stopped I pull to the side of the road, and jump down. I leave my door open and yell, "Stay there."

I hurry to the back and wind down *Casita*'s landing gear until it's touching the ground. Then I exhaust the air out of the air lines, disconnect the air and electrical lines that connect the cab and the trailer, and stow the lines in the dummy coupler on the back of the tractor. The last step is to pull the pin from the fifth wheel. I squat down and check that the jaws are open, then haul my butt back into the cab.

"What're you doing?" Oakley asks. I'm sure he notices I'm now splotched with grease stains but he doesn't comment.

"We're leaving the trailer here. That way the white knights will know they're headed in the right direction, and it will be much easier to maneuver *Casita* through the busted gate without the extra length."

I pull *Casita* forward a foot, park, and jump back down. Separating the two parts is not an instant operation. I check that the pin is out, that the dollies are holding the trailer, and jump back into the truck. Seven minutes start to finish.

I text Nick about the trailer. It's an arrow pointing toward the ranch gate. I shove the phone in my back pocket.

"When we bust through the gate, if I remember what Em said, we still have a ways to go before we get to the guts of this horror show," I say as I gradually increase *Casita*'s speed. "After we bust through—I don't want any debris kicking up and flying in—open your window and prepare to make like Bruce Willis. You see anyone that's not our girls, you shoot to incapacitate."

Oakley nods once, and he has such confidence, I think he's going to do okay.

Casita is running at 72. I can see the gate a hundred yards ahead.

"You're going to want to put your seatbelt on and brace for impact. I don't know exactly what will happen since I've never tried to ram through steal gates before." I say with a grin. I start singing, first quietly, then louder and with great enthusiasm, and eventually, Oakley joins me.

Come on and join our convoy, Ain't nothin' gonna get in our way, We gonna roll this truckin' convoy cross the USA!

CHAPTER SIXTY-SIX

Saturday, September 12, 2009, Midday

ANGEL

I push to my feet, ignoring the pain in my hip and my side. I point the revolver at him and try to shoot again, and again, and again, but all I hear is *Click. Click. Click.* I fling the gun away, just in case. I don't want him to be the one who finds the one remaining bullet, if it exists.

As he stumbles around, hands extended in search of something to steady himself, I find the pillowcase. I cast about, searching for the magazine pages. There they are! I grab them. I don't have time to make a pretty cone. There's no time for anything! My hand dips into my jeans pocket, searching for the matches but coming up empty. *Where did it go? Where? He's getting closer!*

I spot the matchbook on the floor and dive for it. I watch him coming toward me as I scramble back onto my feet.

His eyes are filled with blood. He's moving like a blind man. Every few seconds he coughs and sputters. Now that we're close, I can see the damage to his face. There's a large hole where his mouth and cheek join, giving me a nightmarish view of teeth and gums. The eye on that side of his face isn't in good shape, either. Blood must be filling his throat. His arms are flailing as he tries to grab me. He's between the ladder and me, only a couple of feet away!

Oh please, oh please, oh please...

I tuck the magazine cone into my armpit, so I have both hands free to light the match. I rub the tip of the thin cardboard strip across the sandpaper. Nothing. The head of the match changes from red to reddish-gray. Shit! I focus, and this time it catches. I pull the cone from under my arm and hold the burning flame against the torn fringes of paper. At first, nothing happens. Then, finally, just as he's near enough to touch me, I have a good flame.

He's so close! I can't look away. His handsome face is gone. One whole side is obliterated, including a chunk of his nose. There's nothing but flesh and bone. The top front of his skull is exposed where his hairline was shot away. One of his eyes is still intact, but clearly he's not seeing well, if at all. Only shock and adrenalin keep him coming for me.

I have the cone of burning paper in one hand, the weighted feather-filled pillow in the other. I bring the two together, and as soon as the pillow begins to burn, I swing the fiery pillowcase and its hidden Jack Daniels bottle at Jonny Law's head.

He's upright, barely, only a few steps from the place where the ladder reaches the loft. The pillowcase is fully engulfed, but I'm not sure he can see the ball of flame coming at him. The pain of the glass bottle crashing into the raw meat that was his face is another unexpected event. The blaze catches what is left of his hair, and he pats at it like it's a pesky fly.

With an inhuman roar, he gropes forward, desperate to grab me and take me down with him.

No! I raise my foot and kick hard, connecting with his thigh. The kick sends him backward, flying over the edge of the loft, arms thrashing. He's screaming as he falls.

I look for the rifle and realize he must have dropped it over the edge when I shot him. I peer over and see him writhing on a pile of clothes on top of the bales of hay. His features—his hair, his face— are mostly gone. The hay is now a bonfire, the junk and trash and years' worth of crap acting as kindling.

Well, hell. The bottom of the ladder ends right in the center of the inferno.

CHAPTER SIXTY-SEVEN

Saturday, September 12, 2009, Midday

ANGEL

Part of me feels bad. That must be a horrible way to go, missing half your face, and on fire. It's shocking to me that I did that to him. If I'd had any other way, I would have taken it, wouldn't I? I didn't enjoy doing that to him, did I?

Obsess about it later, idiot, Bud orders. *Right now, you need to figure out how the hell you're going to get out of here before the barn burns to the ground.*

Yeah, that's definitely a priority.

Angel, seriously, enough with the wisecracks! Get your ass out of there!

The problem is, I have no idea how to get my ass—which now hurts like a mothereffer—out of here. I look over the edge of the loft one more time to determine exactly how much trouble I'm in. A lot.

Jonny isn't moving. He's more flame than man now. The run of hay bales is completely engulfed and the fire is moving across the barn floor.

There is no other way to get from up here to down there. With each second, the fire spreads and eats up more of the junk and trash, Miss Pacman style.

Just as I think that thought, a banshee scream fills the barn, and a tiny woman with long, thick dark hair rushes in, machete in one hand, ax in the other. This must be the infamous Vero. Veronique.

She's a grim version of CB. The two are very similar in height, body, hair, attitude. Yet one is good, the other evil. And the evil one is pissed with a capital P. "Jonny! Who did this! I will send them to hell!"

With that promise, she looks up and sees me. "Bitch! You will suffer much worse torments than your stupid *puta* friends even can imagine! *te enviaré al infierno.*"

I think that means she's going to send me to hell. She'd have to get up here first. I watch her disappear out of sight into the barn. I panic—maybe I was wrong. Is there another way up here? But no, there are no trap doors that I can see. Other than the ladder, the only exit seems to be a wood-shuttered window I hadn't noticed until now.

I look over the edge of the loft. Vero is back. She's pouring a line of liquid along the floor, across the barn parallel to the loft ledge. Lighter fluid? Or gas? *Oh, shit. Oh, shit.* She's going to make sure I go to hell with him!

That's not all she has planned for me, the killer of her lover. She has retrieved Jonny's bow and arrow, and she stands at the open barn doors and looks up, a broad, insane grin on her beautiful face. Her accent is thick when she says, "Let's go!"

The first arrow misses me by only an inch.

I have to get out before one of those arrows finds me. Through the barn is no longer an option, even if I could somehow get down. It probably never was, with all that crap just waiting to stab me to death.

My only hope is the window behind me. My side and butt are on fire now, and there's a lot more blood. Whereas the flesh wound from the bullet burned, now everything on that side of my body is in pain from the waist down.

Just get out, Angel, Bud warns. *Now.*

Ping! Ping! Two more arrows come much too close, and that gets me moving more quickly toward the door. There's no handle!

I kick and push at it, ignoring the pain ripping through me. It's not budging. I pound against the wood, hoping it's jammed. Still no release.

Ping! Another arrow lands just next to my head. I hear Vero cackling gleefully below. She must be standing in the barn doorway. I feel the heat from the flames coming up under the loft. The barn will be fully aflame any minute now. How the hell am I going to get the door open? I'm screwed.

CHAPTER SIXTY-EIGHT

Saturday, September 12, 2009, Midday

HARPER

Sports were never my thing, but I could walk a mile or two without getting winded. Not anymore. The barn is maybe thirty feet from the kennel, and I'm completely exhausted by the time I reach the back of the building. I had no idea barns could be built into hillsides, like a house with a walk-out basement, but apparently, it's a thing, because from here, it's easy to see the stone foundation. I lean into it. The coolness of the stones feels good against my skin, solid and strong and reassuring.

Smoke, thick and black and acrid, pours from the front of the building. Fire has a sound and it's loud, crackling and clicking. The junk in the barn is collapsing as its support system burns. I hear screaming. It sounds like Vero. Her screams are from anger and frustration, not fear or pain. She's shrieking at someone. I don't know whether she's trapped Angel or Emily, but whoever it is, is in trouble.

I hobble to the single door at the back of the building and try the handle. It doesn't move. Is it stuck or locked? I take a breath to calm my racing heart and try once more. The handle turns. It's not locked, just stuck. It should open inward. I look around, hoping to find something I can push with, but no such luck. The only thing I see is a rope hanging from the handle of a shuttered door above my head. Not useful at all.

I pound lamely on the door, furious and frustrated and desperate and hopeless.

Suddenly I hear pounding above me, and see the door with the dangling rope quiver. Someone is trying to get out! Why can't they open the door? Oh, I see. The rope is attached to a bar that drops into a tab to keep the door shut. If I pull the rope down, the door will open.

Do I want it to open? What if it's Jonny or Vero?

What if it's Emily or Angel?

I stagger to the rope, say a small prayer, and pull.

CHAPTER SIXTY-NINE

Saturday, September 12, 2009, Midday

ANGEL

The door swings open at the same moment I make another half-assed running attempt to push it open, and I fly through, arms pinwheeling in the air, legs kicking. I have just enough time to think to pull my knees toward my chest and prepare to roll when I hit the ground.

Bam! I land hard but manage a sideways roll, right onto my wounded side, of course, because what else? But I'm out of the barn and away from Vero, and I think the woman standing over me is Harper.

"Harper?" I whisper-hiss because damn, I am hurting. I should push myself up off the ground, but I need a minute to catch my breath.

She nods.

"Thank you," I say.

Does she only have one eye? Oh, wait, no, it's there, it's just infected and bloody. The eyelid is cut away. I suck in a deep breath to avoid puking on my rescuer. That would be unforgivably rude.

"I'd offer a hand, except I'm kind of useless," Harper tries to joke. "But you'd better get up." She points. Flames are coming through the roof where I just was standing. The building is going to collapse around us any time now.

Where the hell is Vero? And where is Emily?

I crawl forward and push up on my knees, scowling each time I trigger a new streak of pain in my hip and thigh. Once I'm standing, I wrap an arm around Harper's waist because there's no way can she walk more than a foot without support and we can't stay here. We move together around the back of the barn. I look up to watch for falling debris. Not yet, but soon.

Then we hear it. The banshee is yelling.

We round the corner of the barn, and Vero is there. She must have left the bow and arrow in the barn because she's swinging the machete. She has Em trapped on the front porch of the house.

This nightmare will never end.

CHAPTER SEVENTY

Saturday, September 12, 2009, Midday

C B

My last thought before *Casita* reaches the gate is, "Oh, lord, if I'm going to go, please don't let me catch fire."

Then I'm too busy trying to control *Casita* to think anything. When we hit the gate, the impact is loud and dramatic. The two pieces of fence burst off the track and fly toward the windshield, then crash to the ground. The glass cracks, but holds. *Casita* roars across the destroyed gates, my pink stallion charging into battle. She rocks and quivers but pushes on. She won't be deterred any more than I will. The long drive is dirt and gravel, with steep wooded embankments on either side for the first hundred feet. Then we're in the center of a large, open field, and I can see the house and barn a quarter mile ahead.

I risk a glance at Oakley. He's got his window down, a gladiator ready to fight. He's half squatting on the seat, his left foot braced on the floor, although our speed, and the rough terrain, are making it hard for him to balance.

I start to say, "Do you see anything- " and then I see smoke pouring from the barn. *Tu chingada madre*! "Oakley! Once we stop there's a fire extinguisher under the sink!"

We're close now. We can see what we're headed into. The drive ends in a large dirt parking pad. To the right is a house with a front porch. There are two rocking chairs and a collection of potted flowers. I expect an *abuela* to be sitting in the chair, sewing or shelling beans. The two-story red barn has seen better days. The doors are open, and fire is coming from inside. I don't see anyone at all.

Oakley is practically hanging out the window, looking for a bad guy to shoot. The problem is, there are no bad guys!

As if I've summoned them with my thoughts, two bodies come from the side of the house: a petite woman with dark hair, and Emily—or at least I think it's Emily. Something happened to her hair.

The smaller woman is wearing tight jeans and a long-sleeved shirt that shows off her ridiculous curves. She reminds me of Salma Hayek in *From Dusk Til Dawn*. And like that character, she's the devil! She's got an ax in her right hand, and a machete in the other. She's swinging each of them at Emily, with wide arcing swoops. Emily has backed herself into a corner on the porch of the house.

I don't know if it's the sound of a semi-tractor barreling into the space, or Oakley's roar of rage as he watches the woman he loves being threatened, but both women turn to us. Emily, at least, has an idea who we are, and why we're here, so she has the advantage and reacts quicker. She staggers off the porch and around the side of the house. Mini Salma Hayek isn't ready to quit. She howls a war cry at us, then takes off after Emily.

Oakley is diving to the ground below before I get *Casita* to a full stop.

The barn is now fully engulfed. Where the fuck is Angel? Holy hell, this isn't good.

CHAPTER SEVENTY-ONE

Saturday, September 12, 2009, Midday

CB

I start toward the barn, pleading with God and all that is holy to keep my girl alive. Just as I approach the open doors, there's an explosion, and I'm thrown backward, landing under *Casita's* front grill.

I lose whatever cool I think I have and start screaming, "Angel! Angel!"

There's another explosion from the barn, and flaming debris falls around me. I scrabble deeper under *Casita*, and yes, I know, it might not be good to hide under a vehicle holding 200 gallons of gas when fire bombs are coming your way, but I believe *Casita* will keep me safe.

The yard is littered with burning things. Boards that were parts of walls, clothes, cardboard boxes, pieces of signs. A lawn mower, a bicycle, multiple tires. The smell of burning rubber hits me and triggers a coughing fit.

Where the bloody hell is she?

There! I finally spot her, to the side of the house, with another woman. That must be Harper. Angel gently lays the woman under a large maple tree, waves to me, then races around the house, following Oakley who is chasing after Emily and the bad woman.

I'm torn between going after Angel and checking on the girl. Angel looked healthy-ish, although she was limping. I decide to check on the girl, who is clearly not healthy—"ish" or otherwise. Getting to the tree requires all my focus because I have to avoid stepping in patches of fire.

Harper looks dead. Her pale blonde hair is the only thing about her that isn't destroyed, although it's streaked with dried mud. She's wearing one of Angel's hoodies. I can see her lower legs, and parts of her face. As bad as the visible parts are, I don't need to see the covered parts.

"Harper," I whisper, dropping to the ground beside her. I brush a clump of hair from her face, and gasp when I see one of her eyelids is missing and the eyeball—or what's left of it—is a bloody, goopy mess. She has a pulse, although it's faint. *Jesus.* These people. *Monsters.* They will go to *carajo!*

I realize I have not seen the terrible Jonny. Where is he? Is that where Angel went?

Harper seems to sense my question, because she whispers, so quietly I barely hear her, "He's dead." She smiles, and it's a grotesque thing. Her upper lip is nearly gone, torn off by something. Most of her front teeth are cracked, or missing completely. "I'll be seeing him soon. I'll personally deliver any messages you have to the bastard."

I stretch my legs in front of me and lift her head to rest on my thighs. She's right, she's beyond help I can provide. But she shouldn't die laying on the cold, hard ground. I stroke her hair, and the few spots of undamaged flesh I can see on her face. Her left hand comes up and weakly grasps mine.

"Who are you?" she asks. It clearly takes tremendous effort to get those three words out.

"I'm Concetta Bonaventura." I tell her. I give her the real me, not the costume I wear. "And you're Harper. I'd recognize you anywhere from everything Emily has told us."

"She's a good kid. Make her sing *Top of the World* for you," Harper says, pushing each word out. "Nice to make your acquaintance, CB."

She's heard about me. I force a smile and continue stroking. I can see the fingers are broken on her other hand. "Nice to make your acquaintance, too, Harper. You should know, Oakley came back that same night. Emily is safe."

She looks surprised, but also looks pleased. She needs to know her best friend will be okay.

Is Emily safe, though? Where is she? And Oakley? And Angel? I want to help them, but I can't leave Harper. Where are the damned cavalry?

Harper smiles a gruesome smile.

"What?" I ask, smiling back, continuing to stroke her hair, her skin.

"I thought Angel was my last new friend, but I was wrong." She takes in a deep breath, and squeezes my hand. "It's you."

And then she's gone.

CHAPTER SEVENTY-TWO

Saturday, September 12, 2009, Midday

ANGEL

Once CB spots us, I know she'll go to Harper. Maybe she can use some of her magic, I tell myself, although I know it's too late. Harper's injuries are just too extensive.

I know Harper would want me to save her friend. I can't leave Oakley to try and help Em on his own. As I come around the side of the house, I pull up sharply. Vero has an arm around Em's neck, and is holding the machete with the blade against Emily's belly. The implication is that if Oakley or I make a move, she'll slice Em and my Def Leppard T-shirt in half. Vero's back is against the house's white siding to give her a protected 180 degree view.

Oakley is still as a statue, six feet to my right, ten feet from Vero and Emily. Vero is more than a foot shorter than Oakley, but her aura is twice his size. His tall, thin body seems inadequate for anything more complex than a rousing game of *Call of Duty*. The way he's clutching CB's pink revolver, I don't believe he's ever held an actual gun before. If he pulls the trigger, he's more likely to blow the flower pot off the window ledge than frighten Vero, much less hit her.

Shit.

"Veronique, right? Jonny told me about you." I say in my calmest voice. Her eyes flare when I say his name, and I think for a moment she's going to pull the machete across Emily's gut with the enthusiasm of a violinist playing Vivaldi. "He told me he wants this to be over. He was tired of this life, tired of repeating his father's sins. Jonny said he was going to end it."

Vero snarls. "Yes? This is so? Then why did you kill him? If my Jonny was going to end it, as you say, why you did murder him?" Her imperfect English supports the story CB heard at the diner.

There's only one answer. "He gave me no choice."

"This is true, yes. My Jonny would have destroyed you, just as he destroyed this *cabróna* and her *puta* friend." Vero smiles a smile so deeply evil, it would send her right to the top of the villain category in my diary, if I had one—ahead of Jonny, even ahead of Alfred. Vero is the craziest bitch of them all.

Emily is shaking so hard we can see it from across the lawn. Her hands clutch Vero's arm where it presses against her throat, in an effort to keep the woman from choking her to death, although that's not how Vero's plan to end Em's life. Em's eyes are huge and filled with tears.

"Who hurt you, Veronique?" I ask, my tone curious and a bit snarky.

Her eyes flash and her mouth twists into a sneer. The arm that is around Em's neck tightens, and Emily gasps. I've touched a nerve. I decide to put my finger in and poke around a bit. I'm channeling Olivia.

"Did your mommy not love you enough?" I say in a sickly sweet voice. *Poke. Poke.*

Angry snarl.

"Did your boyfriend cheat on you with someone more beautiful?" I ask in a voice dripping with fake concern.

Hiss.

"Did you want to fuck your daddy?" I make an 'ew, yuck!' face.

That's the one. Vero jerks away from the wall and takes a step toward me, which forces her to loosen the arm around Em's neck.

Oakley raises the revolver, and shoots Vero in the knee, which is the most exposed part of her. It's a perfect shot, and Vero screams in pain and shock. If he'd tried for Vero's head, no matter how good his aim is—and it's astonishingly good—he'd have a 50/50 chance of hitting Emily instead.

Vero screeches, shoving Emily away from her as pain racks through her wounded leg. Emily stumbles to Oakley, who raises the revolver again, ready to take the kill shot. But Em, in her panic, crashes into him, hard, and shifts his arm just as he pulls the trigger. The bullet goes wild. Vero vanishes into the woods.

Honestly, I don't care. We're alive, and that's a lot more than I expected an hour ago.

CHAPTER SEVENTY-THREE

Saturday, September 12, 2009, Afternoon

C B

We are only an hour northeast of Oklahoma City, so the medical examiner arrives quickly. The ranch is swarming with law enforcement of every flavor: sheriffs, police, FBI, fire, and medical crews. The lead detective from the Oklahoma City PD Sex Crimes Unit is a guy named Larry White. So far he seems not terrible.

Angel and Emily are on gurneys, side by side between two ambulances, with Oakley and I guarding them like centurions. Harper has been taken away, a loss none of us will get over quickly.

Vero has not been found. By the time the cavalry arrived, it was too late to set up effective roadblocks. Besides, there's hundreds of acres of ranch land she can cross on foot.

Together, we watch the officers remove the body bag carrying what is left of Sheriff Jonny Johnson.

One of the FBI agents approaches, looking serious but friendly. "Supervisory Special Agent Mike Whitmer. Nick said to tell you he'll be here tonight for that come-to-Jesus he promised. He said you'd know what that means."

Angel and I look at each other, and she says, "There are a lot of those on the calendar."

"Nick did a good job convincing the cavalry that one of their own isn't such a good guy," I concede reluctantly. "He might be okay for a LEO."

SSA Whitmer ignores me and looks at Angel. "Based on what Johnson told you, this has been happening since he was a boy. Is that correct?"

Angel nods. "He said he was twelve when his brother died, and the 'games' had been going on a while before that. It sounded as though John the father was raping and killing women when Sheriff Jonny was a young child, possibly even before he was born."

Whitmer mutters, "Jesus."

"He said there are bones in the creek, in the pool there. Including his mother's. And I think, maybe his father's." One of the EMTs is poking around Angel's hip, and she grimaces and smacks his hand away. "He said there's been at least one victim a year, more since the woman named Veronique joined him."

"Jonny Johnson is in his 40s." Whitmer says with a 'that's absurd' undertone as he does the math in his head.

"Yes." There's the Angel eyebrow. "And it's your job to figure out whether he was telling the truth. I'm just reporting what he said to me."

She looks at all of the men and women in the yard and adds, "He also said his father's friends were involved, but he wasn't sure to what extent."

The SSA's expression doesn't change, but he sighs deeply. "For now, our priority is getting you to the hospital to be checked out and repaired." He smiles wanly at Angel. "You already know there'll be lots of conversations in our future. I'm sorry you have to go through this again."

Angel rewards him with a small smile of her own. "I'm a pro."

Oddly, my head and heart are with Sheriff Johnson's coworkers, and especially his family. They're going to have one hell of a lot to deal with over the coming months, probably years. Whatever his sins, his wife and children should not have to carry them. That's what started this mess in the first place.

I'm reminded of a quote from long ago. *"No man, for any considerable period, can wear one face to himself and another to the multitude without finally getting bewildered as to which may be the true."[1]*

May you finally find peace, Jonny Johnson.

---

1. The Scarlett Letter Nathaniel Hawthorne

CHAPTER SEVENTY-FOUR

Sunday, September 13, 2009

ANGEL

My right side is kind of roughed up. One bullet graze, a dozen cuts from the broken glass, rash from the poison oak, and a serious bruise will make it hard to wear a bikini for a while.

I free my healthy leg from the thin sheet covering me and nudge Nick Winston awake with my foot. My favorite FBI agent nearly jumps out of the chair. I smile. "Why are you always the first thing I see when I wake up in hospitals?"

"You're just lucky, I guess," He says and yawns. "How're you feeling, asshole?"

"Hey, is that how the FBI talks to citizens?" I feign shock.

"Citizens that run into situations they have no business running into—absolutely." He nods. Then he's quiet and just stares at me. No smile. No jokes. "Girl, you scared the holy hell out of me. And you got CB all riled—I was half expecting to see a scene from a Robert Rodriguez movie when I got here."

I pull a guilty face. "I know it wasn't the brightest move. But I couldn't just ignore the situation." Then I catch the last bit and pout. "You and CB met without me, huh? Damn it. I was looking forward to watching that."

"She didn't know I knew about her. Why's that?" Nick asks.

I pluck at the sheet, study the generic pastoral painting on the wall between the doors to the hallway and what I presume is the bathroom. Finally, I shrug. "Because I wanted my life now to be completely scrubbed of the past. She knows about Alfred and everything, but more like an entry in a diary or a book report. Not something that's every day, ya know? If I introduce you officially, that makes a connection I wasn't ready for. I made sure you and Peter knew about her, so you wouldn't worry, but she didn't know that because it didn't really matter."

He looks pissed, and I'm caught off guard. "It didn't really matter? Do you know she's been worried for the last two years that Peter or I would swoop in and haul her off to prison for kidnapping you? Jesus, Angel, sometimes you're a narcissistic jerk."

Oh, God, I didn't realize! I'm mortified. I should have known. I should have thought about her, not just me. He's right. I'm not going to admit it, but he's right.

"Well, you've met now. Who won?" I ask to change the subject.

He looks confused. "Who won what?"

"The big dick contest." I grin.

He sucks his lips into his mouth to hide a grin, then gives up and laughs. "Toss-up."

That sounds right. "Are you besties?"

"Besties? Not sure about that. Once she realized I could haul her to jail if I felt like it, she decided I was part of the general law enforcement category she seems to despise. Do you know why that is?"

It's not my story to tell, but I give him the Cliffs Notes. "Her brother was killed by police as he entered his own home in a white suburb. You'll have to ask her if you want more."

Nick grimaces. "No wonder she looks at us like we're the devil. Useful devils in this case, but damn."

"Damn, what?" CB demands, clicking into the room in floofy feathered slippers with kitten heels. The heels don't really go with her flimsy hospital gown, but whatever. They can't expect her to wear the crappy slippers. I wonder what else she had Oakley bring in from *Casita*.

CB is mostly fine except for some minor burns on her forearms, which is why she is wearing the not-so-sexy cotton gown.

I smile at her, and she perches on the edge of my bed, avoiding all my injured bits. "I told Nick about Alex. Not the details, but enough to know why you're not a fan of law enforcement."

CB makes a face and shrugs. "Clearly, not all LEOs are alike."

Nick nods and stands. "I'll leave you two alone -"

"No, please stay. I need your help." CB says, and it looks like the words might burn coming out of her mouth. She motions for him to sit.

"What?" I ask, completely confused. "What do you mean you need his help?"

CB gives me a look. "The reason I couldn't stay with you and Emily is that I was being blackmailed, or is it extorted? I don't know which is what. Bad people told me if I didn't move something for them, they would release photos of my niece that would destroy her life."

I gasp. "Lexi?"

CB nods.

Nick is frowning. "What did they have you move? Do you know who they are?"

"Never met them. Just got texts. They sent me a couple of pictures to show me they were serious. Then they told me to pick up my load and leave the truck for an hour in a certain spot." CB looks at me. "That's why I had you meet me instead of riding with me from the distribution center."

My mouth is hanging open, I realize. I close it.

"I picked up the load, and everything was going the way it normally does, and then you found Emily," CB explains, and her eyes are squinty. She's pissed, but not at me, I don't think. "You know

I wanted nothing more than to stay with you and figure shit out. But I couldn't let the assholes fuck with Lexi. When I went to the Diner, I learned they were following *Casita*! They texted, asking why we were at a motel."

No wonder she wasn't herself. She must've been scared not just for Lexi but for us, too.

"That's why I had to finish the load and couldn't hand it off. It wasn't even an option. But I couldn't tell you, either. It was a no-win situation." CB sighs.

Nick has been listening quietly. Now he has questions. "So, you got to—where was the load going?"

"San Diego. Automotive parts. That's what I usually carry."

"Did you learn what they put in the truck?"

CB pauses, then nods. "I have a couple of cameras positioned discreetly inside the tractor and the trailer. All the time, not because of this. Actually, because of Angel." She half-smiles at me. "A fat lot of good cameras do when you pick up the trouble in a truck stop bathroom and walk it right into our lives."

Nick makes a face at me. "And did these cameras capture anything interesting?"

"They did. I mean, whatever it was they loaded into the truck is in boxes, but I'm pretty sure, based on the shape and type, I transported weapons of some sort." CB stares straight at Nick. "And I trust that my sharing this with you will be treated as information and not used against me."

He holds up a hand. "Absolutely. I'm on your side. Always have been, truth be told," he winks at her, and CB turns a little bit pink. That makes me snort, and she smacks me. "If you can get me that video, or stills, whatever, I will get someone working on identifying the bad actors and tracing the packages."

"And more importantly, you will help me keep them from blackmailing Lexi?"

Nick nods. "I'll do everything I can. The least I can do to thank you for you taking care of this troublemaker." He tips his head at me.

"Oh, come on. I don't get in trouble often." I object.

CB rolls her eyes. "That's a conversation for later."

"Whatever. Nick, you can help, right?" I demand.

"I just said I would, didn't I?" He looks at CB. "Does Lexi know about this?"

CB shakes her head adamantly. "No. And I don't want her to. I haven't seen her since she was a small kid. I don't want this to be the thing that reconnects us."

Nick sighs. "Well, it would be best to come from you rather than an agent, don't you think?"

"I just said I don't want her to know—"

"Do you really think that's possible? Or fair? If someone has something they can use against her, she should know about it." Nick counters.

I'm enjoying this. It's like watching two bulls bumping up against each other. A cute little bull with feathered kitten heels and long eyelashes versus a big, brawny bull with great eyes and a nice butt. The only kind of bullfight I ever want to see.

They continue arguing. I drift off, feeling safe.

CHAPTER SEVENTY-FIVE

Saturday, October 24, 2009

ANGEL

Because I'm not testifying, I'm allowed to sit in the courtroom. However, the federal attorneys, as well as my own personal 'team'—Nick, CB, Marnie and Peter—have all advised against it. They say Olivia will know I'm in the hallway supporting her and that will be enough. Maybe, but it's not enough for me. I want to see the man who took so much, who changed my life. I'm not afraid of him any longer. I'm not scared of anyone.

The courtroom is packed. There are journalists, and law enforcement folks from all branches, from all over the country. Alfred had victims in at least five states that we know of, and those states have sent representatives. There are at least a few groupies. They hold up signs supporting Alfred every once in a while, although they refer to him as "Edward."

Alfred's legal team is impressive. The Stanhopes were a very wealthy family, and he is the only survivor, so that wealth went to him. According to Peter, some of that money is coming to me, Olivia, and Grace thanks to civil litigation. Right now I don't care.

The federal team is impressive, too. This is one of those 'career maker' cases, I guess. Again, I don't care.

The judge is a no-nonsense Black woman. The jury is five men and nine women, including the two alternates. They're every shade and age and size.

Since I'm determined to sit in the courtroom, everyone else has joined me. All for one and all that jazz. Peter sits on one side of me, CB on the other. Nick and Ben, Olivia's younger brother, are next to CB. Marnie, the mother of Alfred's youngest victim, is sitting beside Peter. I notice their thighs aren't the only thing touching; her hand is wrapped tightly in his. One thing I've always appreciated about Marnie is that her anger is clear, even when she's teary-eyed. She's mad as hell right now.

Olivia gets on the stand, tells her story, tells our story, and addresses questions from both sides. She's calm, cool, and collected. I don't think her fiancé is here. I met him last night. Christopher something. He's nice enough. Good-looking in a California entertainment attorney sort of way, which is what he is. He's ten years older than Olivia. They met because Olivia will soon have her own talk show, on the heels of her successful tell-all book. She's going to be one of the youngest talk show hosts in history.

I don't want to think about any of that right now.

Both sides declare an end to questions, and the Judge puts the court in recess until tomorrow. Our little band shuffles out of the courtroom, security hired by Peter forming a shield around us to take us to hired cars. We're not going to the Baden house because paparazzi are assholes. Instead, we're staying at a generic 3-star chain hotel near LAX. No one would think to look for us there. Peter booked the whole floor.

Everyone retreats to their rooms to wash off the day and rest for dinner, which will be served in Peter's suite. CB and I have adjoining rooms at my request. We haven't opened the connecting door, but I feel better knowing she's nearby.

That's why, when there's a knock at the hallway door, I know it's not CB. I'm pretty sure I know who it is. I open the door and retreat to the bed. Olivia kicks off her shoes and sits next to me, leaning back into the headboard. We don't look at each other. Her hand creeps across the bedspread, and grasps mine. I don't pull away.

The TV is playing, the sound off. The Simpsons are doing things on the screen, and every once in a while, one or both of us will giggle.

"Thanks." She says finally.

I don't respond, just wiggle my fingers in her hand.

"Sounds like you had another big escapade." She says, crossing and uncrossing her ankles. She's wearing shorts and a tank top and I can see some of the scars from the Dollhouse. She doesn't have as many scars as I do, but hers are worse. "Dad says you've been riding around in a semi for the last two years. Craziness. When are you going to settle down? Is that seriously what you're going to do with your life? Be a trucker?"

I take my hand back. "There is nothing wrong with riding around in a truck. I've seen this country, met amazing people, and learned things I would never have learned otherwise. Love and kids and a career were never part of my plan." That's kind of a lie, but it's a lie I tell myself, too, so that makes it almost true.

"I wish you'd at least try to be a little bit careful. Most people never have one traumatic event in their lifetimes, and you've now had two, and the second one you went into with your eyes wide open! No one made you get involved."

And that, right there, is why Olivia and I will never see eye-to-eye. I think she would have found Emily in that bathroom and turned around and walked out. That doesn't make her smarter or me braver; it just makes us very, very different.

"When's the wedding?" I ask to change the subject.

"April. Will you be my maid of honor?"

I make a face. "Come on. You know that's not me."

"Angel Evanston, there's no one in the world I'm closer to. You're my sister in every sense of the word. I cannot get married without you standing beside me."

THE HUNTED: SINS OF THE FATHER

I make a rude sound. "Fine. I'll be in your damned wedding. But I'm not wearing anything girly."

"You'll look beautiful in pink taffeta." She says, and when I turn to her, mouth open in protest, she falls into a fit of giggles.

"So mean." I shake my head. "Seriously, though, I'm really happy for you. You're getting all the things you want, and you deserve them."

"I'm happy. I really am." Olivia's voice is soft and she looks at her hands. "Christopher is great. He's supportive and understanding and loving. He seems to know when to push and when to hold back and that's not easy to do well, as we both know." She sighs. "My wish is for you to find your person."

I'm silent for a while, thinking about it. "I already have my person. Not in the same way, not a romantic relationship. But CB is that person for me. Nick, too, really. I don't feel my life is missing anything. Hell, I'm only seventeen." It strikes me that she's just a year and a bit older. How are we so different? "I have lots of time to figure out who I am and what I want. Or maybe I'll spend the rest of my life exploring all the options. But right now, today, I don't feel like I'm in a hurry to do much of anything except live an interesting life."

Olivia is studying her hands. Maybe she's focused on the giant rock on her engagement finger. I don't know diddly about jewelry, much less carrots—carets?—and all that stuff. But I know money when I see it. She looks at me, finally. "Do you think you'll ever move past it? Losing so much? You carry so many scars—first from Alfred, and now you have a bullet hole to add to the collection."

This one is easy because I've thought about it a lot. "Scars are like tattoos. They tell the story of who you are, where you've been, what's happened in your life. I refuse to let them be rocks I carry as penance. They're just memories engraved in my flesh."

Enough of this. This isn't Dr. Phil and I'm not on her talk show.

I roll off the bed and head to the mini bar. "Thirsty? I could use some liquid refreshment."

Olivia shakes her head no.

There's another knock at the door. This time it's the cutest monster on the planet. She looks just like her parents with wavy blonde hair and huge blue eyes and a contagious smile. Rosie B races to the bed and we pull her up and she nestles between us, the one good thing to come out of our time in the Dollhouse.

CHAPTER SEVENTY-SIX

Thursday, November 5, 2009

ANGEL

The good news is, Alfred's trial is over, the verdict is in, and now we're just waiting for sentencing. Nick is confident he'll get multiple life sentences. There's a vocal group demanding the death penalty, but I'm okay with life sentences. I like the idea of him being completely controlled by other people. I *really* like it.

Last year, after the Texas trial, Marnie finally divorced her dopey husband. It's no secret she and Peter are a couple. Peter sold the Westwood house and bought an estate on the Palos Verdes peninsula at the southern end of LA. It's a sprawling ranch on six acres at the top of a hill with gorgeous ocean views. The views are not the part that appeals to Peter. There's only one way to get to the property, and it's through a guarded gate. No more paparazzi outside the front door at all hours of the day and night. When you're at the Baden estate, you're safe. Really safe.

We are all hanging out while we wait for sentencing. Marnie has announced we're having an early Thanksgiving with our Framily— friends + family—before we all go our separate ways.

Because Peter is Peter, he has given me the small guest house behind the pool, so I can feel part of things, but also have my own space. I've finally accepted he truly does care for me. It may have started as obligation, but now it's real affection. Every night as I lay in bed and listen to the coyotes, I have a conversation with Bud that's part 'dear diary' and part affirmations. I promise I'm going to make an effort to be less standoffish with Peter. Maybe someday I'll find a way to let him know I see everything he does for me. Someday.

Em has been here since we left Oklahoma and I spend a lot of time with her. Mother hen Marnie will not allow her to leave until she's totally healed physically, and feeling strong mentally. A nurse practitioner comes twice a week, and a physical therapist visits daily. Unlike me, she welcomes the psychologist that comes up the hill on Mondays. No one is in a rush to see her go. I'm pretty sure if she wants to, Em can stay forever.

I feel kind of bad for Oakley. He moved to LA to be near her, but Em isn't so sure she wants him. Harper is dead because of his selfishness and stupidity. Of course he would do anything to take it back, but he can't; nothing will bring Harper back. Not everything in life can be undone.

After the sentencing, I'm going back on the road with CB. I have no idea what I want to do with myself, but I have all the time in the world to figure it out. I'm going to start online college courses. Until recently, I hadn't grasped the size of the trust fund that came out of the civil trial against Alfred. Peter says I can use it to go to college, or travel, or whatever I want. He's invested it for me so I'm sure when I figure out what I want, there will be more than enough.

Right now, all I want to do is breathe.

CHAPTER SEVENTY-SEVEN

Saturday, November 7, 2009

ANGEL

Thanksgiving has never been a big deal to me. In the time before the Dollhouse, we'd go to Lynn's diner for Thanksgiving dinner. I don't know what the Badens do normally; I left before Thanksgiving that first year. CB and I usually have a feast, making a turkey big enough for a dozen people, even though it's just us, so we can binge on turkey sandwiches and leftover stuffing for the whole week after. We're just like the rest of America, only we do it on 18 wheels.

The table is round, large enough for all eleven of us. There's an empty seat and I imagine Bud there, sneaking chunks of stuffing from the platter in front of him. We each have a glass of wine, except Grace and Rosie B, who have sparkling grape juice.

Peter stands and raises his glass. "This has been one hell of a year. We lost someone very special." He nods to Emily. "Now we're waiting to learn the fate of a man who brought pain to so many." He looks at me, and Olivia, and the littlest girls.

"Still, I feel nothing but joy today. How can I feel anything else? We are together, we are safe, we are healthy, or we're getting there. I'm grateful for each of you. You are my friends, you are my family. You bring me smiles each day, make me curse on occasion, but always, always make me proud. I love you, whether I've known you forever, or for only a little while. You are my heart, my family. That's what I'm grateful for."

He sits down, looking slightly embarrassed. Good. That was super awkward. I've heard about the "tell everyone what you're thankful for" tradition but I've never experienced it. I wonder if I can sneak away.

Marnie goes next. "Since Peter was babbling, and everyone's starving, I'll just say I'm thankful for having everyone I love, old friends and new, together and safe this year."

"I'm thankful Marnie is here to keep Dad's ego in check. And I'm especially grateful I don't have to wear a monkey suit for five more months." Ben grins.

Christopher, Olivia's fiancé, looks nervous. "I'm thankful I get to marry this beautiful woman," he smiles at Olivia, who smiles back, "and that I will be part of this crazy gang. I just hope I can keep up."

"I'm thankful Peter is going to buy me a pony for Christmas!" Grace says in a hopeful voice, wiggling her eyebrows at him. "Aren't you?"

Marnie protests, and Peter laughs. I will be surprised if there isn't a pony in the stables, which are currently empty, by my next visit.

Instead of declaring gratitude, Rosie B slides out of her chair, comes around the table, and pries my clenched hands from lap. She climbs up and announces, her face so close my eyes cross when I try to look at her, "I'm thanful for my Angel!" She plants a loud, wet kiss on each of my cheeks. Everyone laughs. I turn her around so she's facing the table and let her pull my arms around her middle. Damn it, my eyes are stinging.

Emily goes next. Her voice is still gravelly but there's hope she might be able to sing again someday. "I'm grateful to be alive, and that two strangers—who now feel like family—were willing to put their lives at risk to help me, and someone they never really got to know." I'm sure for her, Harper is sitting in the empty chair with Bud. Ghosts are skinny.

CB says, "I'm just going to share a favorite quote, from the beautiful Maya Angelou: 'We delight in the beauty of the butterfly, but rarely admit the changes it has gone through to achieve that beauty.' When I look around this table all I see is butterflies."

I have a feeling Nick and Peter had a couple of glasses while they were in Peter's study working on the top secret project. Nick stands and winks at me. "I'm thankful for being included at this table full of butterflies, I'm thankful my friend Angel is safe, I'm thankful for CB even though she's kind of a pain in my ass, I'm thankful for excellent scotch—"

Peter shakes his head, laughing. "You're done. Sit." He looks at me, and raises an eyebrow, asking if I want to participate.

"I'm thankful for you people." I mumble it twice but I know they all hear me. I feel my cheeks burning again.

Peter rescues me. "Eat! Eat!"

Chaos ensues. There's laughing and teasing and the occasional squabble over the wishbone or a last olive. Two hours later, we're all full and exhausted.

CB and I start to clear, but he directs us to sit.

"I have one more thing to say." Peter says. "Because of all of you— and I do mean, *all* of you," he looks at Emily and CB and smiles, "Nick and I have started a new project, with Marnie's help. The Foundation has had a website for years. We added a new section. In January, there will be a private area that can only be accessed if you're given the link. Then you have to log in. Once you're inside, you'll have access to lots of resources. There's an area where families can come together to support each other, make connections with professionals, ask advice, reach out for help."

"There's another area where survivors can talk with others who have been through similar situations, find help if they need it, or just know they're not alone."

Huh.

Nick chimes in, and he's got his FBI voice on. He seems to have lost his buzz even though I know he's had plenty of wine. "This will not be publicized. Only a few trusted partners will be aware. There will be strict security and nondisclosures for all participants. Participants will be invited, after being vetted by the Foundation to keep out the media and lowlifes."

Peter makes a face at the suggestion the 'media' and 'lowlifes' are somehow related.

I glance at Olivia to see her response. Did she already know? I don't think so. Her eyes are large and she seems—what. Annoyed? Angry? Christopher covers her hand with his and squeezes.

Emily is silent, but from the look on her face, I can tell this is not a surprise. It makes sense. Who better to ask than someone who is a recent candidate for this tiny club?

I feel Marnie's eyes on me, hot little laser beams of concern. "Angel? What do you think?"

I have no idea what to think yet, so I say the first thing that comes into my head. "It's depressing there are enough of us that we need a clubhouse."

"What will it be called?" Olivia asks.

"Komorebi. It means sunlight filtered through the trees." Marnie says.

In the silence that follows, I sneak another peek at Olivia. Her expression is blank. It's a look I'm all too familiar with. I wonder if she's angry because of the actual idea, or because she wasn't involved in the planning. She's Peter's closest connection to the sorts of people who would need this support. Why wouldn't he talk to her when it's clear he spoke with Emily? Is it because of her new position in the spotlight? Or something else?

There's a rumbling in my gut and it's not from too much stuffing. Something's coming.

CHAPTER SEVENTY-EIGHT

Thursday, November 26, 2009

ANGEL

"You've got mail," CB says and tips her head toward the hall table.

We're taking a little break for the official holiday, staying at the house in North Carolina for a few days. It's hard to make turkey and all the fixings in a tractor cab. Especially when you have a relative coming that you haven't seen in many, many years.

"What time is Lexi getting here?" I rifle through the ads, catalogues, utility bills and credit card statements. The envelope is white, thick, fancy and hand-addressed to Angel Evanston. Only my Framily, as Marnie calls them—the Badens, Nick, Emily—know the Pittsboro address. Maybe it's the formal invitation to Olivia and Christopher's wedding. I slide a finger into the small gap between flap and body and rip it open.

It isn't a wedding invitation. It's a "wish you were here" greeting card with a couple of old ladies on the outside. I open the card, and a photograph falls out, image-side down. My skin instantly twitches and I feel a bit woozy. "CB—" I whisper, and when she doesn't hear me from the kitchen, I say it louder. "CB!"

She hurries into the entry hall, impatient and annoyed that I'm interrupting her cooking, until she sees my face. "What? What's happening?"

I point to the card, which I've let drop to the table, next to the envelope and the photograph. I haven't looked at the photo but I know it's bad.

CB wipes flour on her jeans and picks up the greeting card. "No hand-written note or signature." She looks at the envelope. "From California. That's why I didn't think anything of it. But I don't know everyone's addresses." She pulls the photograph to her before turning it over. When she sees the image, she gasps and growls. "¡*Hijo de tu chingada madre!*"

As much as I don't want to look, I have to look. I hold out my hand for the photo. She shakes her head, no. "It needs to go to Nick."

"Fine, we will send it to Nick. After I see it. Show me." I insist.

Slowly, eyes filled with tears, she turns the photo so I can see the image. It's Harper, bound to the exam table in the rape room at the ranch. She is still whole, and beautiful, not yet destroyed. Hand-printed in red at the top. "Playtime is just beginning."

Did Vero pique your curiosity? Mine, too! That's why she's got her own short story. Send an email to charlie@saraennis.com with "Vero!" in the subject line and you'll get a link to the story!

If you were cheering Angel on in *The Hunted: Sins of the Father*, you don't want to miss the next part of her journey, coming in spring 2022.

Don't miss any part of the Duality Series:

Two Truths & A Lie (free short story prequel)
The Dollhouse (June 2021)
The Hunted: Sins of the Father (December 2021)
The Mercy: Angel of Death (Spring 2022)

Visit saraennis.com and be the first to know when Angel's next story is coming out! You can also sign up for Charlie's newsletter, and enter to win a free books and goodies!

One of the best compliments to an author is to tell people about it. If you enjoyed *The Hunted: Sins of the Father*, please leave a review wherever you bought the book—and thank you!

Let's be friends! I'm on Goodreads, Facebook, and Instagram and would love to connect.

ACKNOWLEDGEMENTS

When I was a little kid (vs now, when I'm a big kid), I decided I wanted to be a writer because writers got to learn about everything and anything, not just one thing like (bleck) math. There was a lot of learning in this one—I've never lived on a ranch, or driven a truck. I am very fortunate to have great friends (looking at you, Brandee and Chad!) who are more than happy to share their knowledge and let me pester them with "What about" questions in exchange for tacos and a margarita or two. I need to thank my team—Alicia Rideout and Mariëtte Whitcomb for applying their critical eye to the earliest draft. And of course, the beta gang—Adrienne, Brandi, Cathy, Cheryl, Diane, Kim, Lois, Mike and Tracy.

ABOUT THE AUTHOR

Sara Ennis has been telling stories since before she could hold a pencil. First she used flash cards, then a typewriter her grandfather gave her for her sixth birthday. When she was seven, she'd write book reports about books that only existed in her mind. In third grade, her class produced a play she'd written. People who know her well think some of the details from her real life would make a fascinating story, but Sara says the stuff she writes is much more believable and a lot less traumatic. She is a fan of good tequila, travel, cooking, and animals, not in that order. Sara was born in Santa Monica, California, but moved on purpose and with intent to Des Moines, Iowa. She lives with her floofy personal assistant Charlie, who edits her newsletter, and camera shy but very bossy feline, Sasha.

Printed in Great Britain
by Amazon

86531262R00154